BLACK
MAIL

BLACK MAIL

BILL DALY

First published in Great Britain in 2014 by Old Street Publishing Ltd
Trebinshun House, Brecon LD3 7PX
www.oldstreetpublishing.co.uk

ISBN 978-1-908699-54-1

10 9 8 7 6 5 4 3 2 1

A CIP catalogue record for this title is available from the British Library.

Printed and bound by CPI Group (UK) Ltd, Croydon, CR0 4YY.

For Jane

PROLOGUE

September 1980

Billy McAteer, a private in the British army, was on his first tour of active duty in Northern Ireland when the bomb exploded in the crowded pub. Off-duty, perched on a high stool and chatting to his mates when the blast erupted from behind the bar's floor-to-ceiling plate glass mirror, his sixteen stones plucked from the stool and flung like a rag doll across the room, pursued by a million shards of mirror.

His body slammed into the far wall, the fragments of lancing glass ripping away his ear, exploding his left eyeball, slicing the flesh from his cheekbone and ripping his nostrils to shreds.

It took several hours on the operating table to rebuild his features, followed by months of plastic surgery to graft skin from his buttocks to his face.

CHAPTER 1

Wednesday 15 December

A stiff northerly, whipping off the Clyde, was swirling the sleet past the shimmering floodlights and driving it down on Ibrox stadium. A mid-week, early evening kick-off to suit the television schedules, but still the ground was heaving.

The biting wind all but drowned out the lone drunken voice emanating from the back of the North Stand, but Billy McAteer mouthed the words along with him, a wry smile on his lips as he recalled the old days when the Copland Road end would lift the roof off the stadium throughout every match as they went through their anti-Papist repertoire.

Pausing for breath, the singer launched himself into:

> *It's old but it is beautiful.*
> *And its colours they are fine*

McAteer grinned. 'The Sash' was his favourite. When he heard reproachful muttering breaking out behind him he scrambled to his feet and spun round. 'Gaun yersel, pal,' he shouted in the general direction of the unknown singer. 'Gie it fuckin' laldy!' He glared along the row of disapproving faces, all of them avoiding eye contact. 'Anybody got a problem wi' the man singin'?' he demanded. The muttering quickly died away.

> *It was worn at Derry, Aughrim,*
> *Eniskillen and the Boyne.*

McAteer joined in, shouting out the words, the left side of his face glowing pink with the blood pulsing through his veins, just beneath the surface of the blotched tissue.

> *My father wore it as a youth,*
> *In bygone days of yore.*

Turning back to the game McAteer raised his face to the black heavens, allowing the stinging sleet whipping under the overhang of the stand roof to pour down his scarred forehead and seep into his vacant eye socket.

> *And on the Twelfth I love to wear*
> *The sash my father wore.*

McAteer stamped his feet in time as a long, shrill blast on the referee's whistle signalled the end of the match, the cue for all the Rangers supporters in the packed stadium to rise to their feet, red white and blue scarves stretched taut above their heads, bodies swaying. McAteer mimed playing the flute as he sneered in the general direction of the despondent Celtic fans trudging towards the exits.

Draping his scarf around his shoulders McAteer stiffened his spine and stood tall, his right arm aloft, the Red Hand of Ulster tattoo on the back of his clenched fist proclaiming its challenge to the world.

'Ten days to go – and would you look at them?' Charlie Anderson rubbed at the grubby storeroom window with the back of his glove, serving only to smear grime around the cracked pane.

'Sir?' Detective Sergeant Tony O'Sullivan glanced up from rummaging in his sports bag.

'I said, would you look at them, Tony? There's nothing in this world worse than frozen toes squelching inside soggy socks.' Twisting his back, Charlie massaged the base of his spine with both hands as he peered down from the fourth-floor window, through a carpet of multi-coloured fairy lights, on the sea of heads bobbing along Argyle Street's pedestrian precinct. 'And these are the lucky ones. I've still got it all to face.'

O'Sullivan stared down on the sodden, weary procession trudging through the early evening gloom; countless numb fingers welded to the stretched handles of over-laden carrier bags. 'It's late-night opening tomorrow,' he offered as he tugged a pair of powerful binoculars from their carrying case and untangled the leather strap.

'You have got to be joking!' Charlie pursed his lips and blew hard into his gloved fists. 'I'm leaving it all till Rainday.' O'Sullivan's pale blue eyes squinted enquiringly in Charlie's direction. 'Family joke, Tony. Last week my grandson's teacher asked his class to come up with words that were more descriptive than those in current use. Jamie suggested changing "Sunday" to "Rainday".'

O'Sullivan's freckled features creased in a smile. 'I like it. Sunday – Rainday! Monday – Sleetday! Tuesday – Snowday! There's a ring to it. It could well catch on.'

Detective Chief Inspector Charlie Anderson pulled a handkerchief from his trouser pocket and used it to wipe the melting sleet from his head. Completely bald, apart from a few white wisps of hair at his temples and some desultory tufts clinging to the nape of his thick neck, he was well over six feet tall, heavily built and round faced – 'ba'-faced' in Glasgow parlance. As he pushed his handkerchief back into his pocket, his prominent stomach strained against his buttoned-up overcoat. 'Have you done your Christmas shopping yet?' Charlie asked.

'No one to buy for, sir.'

Charlie winced. 'Sorry! I forgot that you and Anne had –'

'No problem,' O'Sullivan said. 'I do need to stock up on the booze, though. I was hoping I might get off in time to get to Oddbins tonight,' he added, his raised eyebrows indicating a distinct lack of optimism on that score.

Draping the binoculars around his neck O'Sullivan gripped both handles of the sash window and tugged hard, but it refused to budge. He examined the painted-in frame, then took a long-handled screwdriver from his sports bag and used it to prise the window open, sending a cloud of faded-green paint flakes and splintered wood fluttering down towards the floor. A blast of freezing air invaded the cramped storeroom, along with Noddy Holder's strident voice proclaiming:

> *So here it is*
> *Merry Christmas*
> *Everybody's having fun*

Charlie looked across at the two Salvation Army guitarists on the opposite pavement. A few minutes earlier they had been attempting to tune up but had given up the unequal struggle and they now stood shivering, flexing their fingers and stamping their feet, waiting impatiently for Slade to run their course. As soon as the closing bars started to fade away they strummed a quick intro and launched themselves into a dirge-like rendition of 'Silent Night'.

O'Sullivan dropped down on one knee and balanced the binoculars on the window ledge to trawl the far pavement. Beyond the musicians, a drenched, kilted piper had given up all hope of keeping his instrument dry and was squatting on the kerb, puffing on a hand-rolled cigarette and swigging from a can of lager. A *Big Issue* seller with a weary, fixed smile was trying to drum up business in the middle of the precinct and, behind him, several small children had their noses pressed hard against Marks & Spencer's brightly lit windows. O'Sullivan continued panning left, stopping abruptly when a familiar profile, huddled in Marks & Spencer's doorway, came into view. 'Looks like the tip-off was kosher, sir,' he said, recognising Gerry Fraser's unshaven features. 'Our ageing hippie is propping up the wall.'

Fraser's blue trench coat was belted tightly round his waist, his long, grey hair pulled back into a ponytail and held in position by an elastic band. Through the powerful lenses O'Sullivan could see the folds of flesh hanging loose from Fraser's scrawny neck and he sharpened his focus on the spiky hairs protruding from the mole at the base of his nostrils.

Charlie stepped back from the window and whacked both arms around his shoulders in an attempt to get his circulation moving. 'What's he up to?' he demanded, his breath puffing out in a series of frosty clouds.

O'Sullivan tinkered constantly with the focus ring as he ran the binoculars up and down Fraser's body. 'He has a collection box of some kind.' He zoomed in close. 'Looks like Save the Children.' Easing down the sash window he took the binoculars from around his neck and wedged them between the window frame and the sill. Having checked the binoculars were still trained on Fraser he rammed his hands deep into the pockets of his leather jacket while continuing to stare through the sleet-splattered lenses.

'You wouldn't think it beyond their capabilities to come up with a heated stakeout,' Charlie grumbled.

'It could've been worse. Renton drew the short straw. He's out on the roof of W.H. Smith's.'

Charlie craned his neck to squint in the direction of the figure huddled behind the low parapet on the flat rooftop, two floors lower down and thirty yards further along the precinct. DC Colin Renton was easy to make out; his tartan flat cap never left his bald head in winter. He was crouched on one knee, scanning Argyle Street with his binoculars, but Charlie could see that the angle of Marks & Spencer's doorway was wrong for him. He wouldn't be able to see Fraser from where he was.

'The joys of a Glasgow winter!' Charlie sighed. 'Have you ever noticed how Glaswegians behave in this kind of weather?'

'I believe you might have mentioned it, sir.' O'Sullivan hid his grin behind the binoculars.

'You'd think umbrellas had never been invented.'

'Perhaps the Sally Bash have cornered the market?' O'Sullivan suggested.

> 'Silent night, holy night,
> All is calm , all is bright

Charlie looked in the direction of the music. There were six uniformed figures on the far side of the precinct, the two guitarists having been joined by a trumpet player and three tambourine-waving vocalists, one male, two female, each with a hand-held microphone – their voices trilling from beneath a Heath Robinson structure of interlocked golf umbrellas. Charlie turned and stared in the direction of the Trongate. He shook his head; no one hurrying, no one even trying to huddle close to the buildings for shelter. Confirmation of the resignation bred into the Glaswegian psyche. The Almighty has ordained that they're on this earth to be pissed on, so that's how it has to be, even tilting their heads forward as if offering up their necks to some unseen celestial guillotine.

> *Sleep in heav–enly pe–ace,*
> *Sle–ep in heavenly peace.*

Charlie turned away from the window and strode up and down the cramped storeroom, his black brogues stomping on the cracked linoleum, his arms flailing like a beached walrus in distress. 'What's happening?' he demanded, stopping in his tracks and staring at the back of O'Sullivan's head.

'Not a lot. I've never seen a less enthusiastic flag seller in all my puff. Several people have gone up to him and they've virtually had to force their money into his can. The stingy wee bugger isn't even handing out stickers.'

Charlie took the walkie-talkie from O'Sullivan's sports bag and switched it on. 'Anderson to all units,' he barked. 'Gerry Fraser's been sighted in Marks & Spencer's doorway. Hold position and await further instructions.' Dropping the walkie-talkie back into the bag, Charlie resumed his pacing to the opening bars of 'Good King Wenceslas'. 'Still nothing?'

'No, sir.' Charlie repeated the question every couple of minutes, getting the same answer each time. After the third time of asking O'Sullivan gave up responding.

'Still noth –'

'Hold on a minute!'

'What is it?' Charlie froze in mid-flap, arms fully extended.

'I think it's . . . Yes! It's Tosh McCulloch.'

'Bingo!' Charlie slapped his back hard, flinching as an arthritic spasm shot the length of his spine.

O'Sullivan pulled his hands from his pockets and his frozen fingers gripped the binoculars. As McCulloch approached the flag seller O'Sullivan zoomed in hard on Fraser's face and saw his cracked lips move. He panned out to a full body shot as the two men came together and he watched as McCulloch reached into his inside jacket pocket and produced a wad of banknotes which he started to thumb through under Fraser's nose. Counting off several notes, McCulloch's fist hovered over the extended collection box and then words were exchanged as he stuffed the money into the slot. Fraser peeled several Save the Children stickers from his pad and stuck them onto the collar of McCulloch's faded blue anorak before McCulloch scuttled off.

'What the hell's going on?' Charlie demanded.

O'Sullivan wrenched up the window frame to release the binoculars and scrambled to his feet.

'McCulloch stuffed a wad of notes into the collection box, but there was no handover.'

'Are you sure?'

'Yes.'

'Shit!' Charlie slammed his fist into the palm of his hand. 'What happened then?'

'McCulloch buggered off.'

'In what direction?'

'Towards St Enoch's.'

'Give me those,' Charlie said, snatching the binoculars from O'Sullivan's grasp and lowering himself stiffly into position to train the glasses on Fraser.

'Should we nick them, sir?' O'Sullivan asked.

'On what charge?' Charlie growled. 'Excessive generosity to Save the Children? I doubt if that stingy wee bastard McCulloch has ever donated a penny to a charitable cause in his life. Now, all of a sudden, he's Santa fucking Claus!'

When Charlie stared through the binoculars he saw Fraser raise both arms high above his head. Swivelling the glasses in the direction Fraser was facing he came to a juddering halt when the familiar, liver-spotted features of Johnny Devlin filled the lenses. 'Well, what do you know? If it isn't his drinking pal.' Charlie switched quickly back to Fraser. 'They're using the old tick-tack. Who said spending my youth at Ayr races was a waste of time?' Charlie studied Fraser's flailing arms. 'Four hundred quid on number two, whatever the hell that might mean. He's repeating the same message.' Charlie swung the binoculars back to Devlin who was now tapping on the keypad of his mobile phone.

> *When a poor man came in sight,*
> *Gathering winter fu–el*

'It's a three-way routine.' Charlie had to shout to make himself heard above the screech of the tenor who was attempting the descant to the detriment of the sopranos who could no longer hold the tune. 'A pound to a pinch of shit a handover's being authorised,' Charlie roared as he watched Devlin gabble into the mouthpiece. 'Tell the team to move in now, Tony! I want all three of them – as well as whoever's on the other end of that phone call.'

O'Sullivan grabbed the walkie-talkie from his sports bag and flicked it on as he raced towards the store room door. Taking the steep stairs two at a time, he barked out instructions.

'It's after half-past!' Jude Ramsay stood on the bottom step and shouted up the stairs to the study where her husband was gazing out of the bay window. 'Did you hear what I said?' she yelled in an attempt to make herself heard above the driving beat of the music.

'I heard you!' Simon continued staring out of the window, intrigued by the sight of a large black crow with its beak buried deep in the snow, tugging hard at some unseen morsel. 'More's the fucking pity,' he muttered under his breath.

'It's time you were getting ready.' Jude peered short-sightedly into the hall mirror to massage the excess blusher into her cheeks. Checking her hair, she fussily twisted a sculpted blonde strand into position against her high cheekbone. 'You know what Helen and Bjorn are like. They'll be here on the dot.'

Simon crossed to the desk to tweak down the volume of the CD player in his computer. 'I'm almost through. I just need to check my email.' He coughed harshly – a hacking smoker's cough that brought up a mouthful of phlegm. Fishing in his trouser pocket for a tissue he wiped it across his mouth as he slumped down on the swivel chair and swung round to face the screen. 'As soon as I've done that I'll get changed.'

'Don't take all day about it. And don't forget – it's DJs.'

'What!'

'Bjorn's hired one specially and Mike's coming in his dress kilt.'

'You can't be serious! There's no way Alison will ever get Norman into a monkey suit.'

'They won't be able to make it. Alison's just phoned. They're snowed in.'

'Why the hell do I have to dress up like a bloody penguin?' His words came wheezing out from between clenched teeth.

'Bjorn and Mike are making the effort for your birthday, for God's sake!' Jude shouted, peering into the mirror again and licking her fingertips to smooth down her plucked eyebrows. 'The least you can do is show willing.'

Simon cursed under his breath as he took an envelope from the top drawer of his desk and spilled the white powder onto a CD case. Using a credit card to divide the cocaine into two parallel lines, he took a ten-pound note from his wallet and rolled it into a tooter which he used to snort a line up each nostril. Inhaling deeply, he wiped the back of his hand back and forth across his nose. He licked his index finger and rolled it in the remaining powder dust to rub it hard into his gums. Reaching for the mouse, he clicked on the 'send and receive' icon. 'I don't see why I should have to spend my fortieth with your bloody sisters,' he muttered to himself, 'to say nothing of their mind-bendingly boring appendages. Can't decide what I'm looking forward to more – Bjorn's incomprehensible ramblings or Mike's hoary jokes. And who ever heard of dressing up in dinner suits for eating at home? Load of fucking nonsense!'

When the words 'Receiving message 1 of 6' appeared on the screen he reached down to the bottom drawer of the desk and pulled out a fresh carton of Marlboro. Bursting open the cellophane wrapping he removed a packet and tapped out a cigarette as he prised his cigarette lighter from his jeans' pocket. The first five items of mail arrived quickly but the progress bar showed that the sixth message was downloading slowly. 'What pillock's spamming me now?' he muttered, drumming his nicotine-stained fingers on the mouse pad as he stared impatiently at the flickering screen. Getting to his feet he crossed to the window, but the crow had gone.

The snow, which had started falling before lunchtime in flakes the size of golf balls, had now turned to sleet. From the vantage point of Park Terrace he could see through the leafless branches of the trees on the opposite side of the road and across the deserted, white wasteland of Kelvingrove Park as far as the Glasgow Art Galleries where batteries of concealed floodlights had transformed the Victorian building into an enchanted castle with its phalanx of white turrets stretching up towards the lowering skies. His gaze swung left towards the Scottish Exhibition Centre on the north bank of the river, its striking armadillo profile smoothed away by the drifting snow that had almost filled in its ridges.

Glancing at his watch he strode along the corridor towards the master bedroom, unbuttoning his shirt and unbuckling his belt as he went. He flicked on the top light and stripped to his underwear, discarding his clothes in an untidy heap on the bed. His electric razor was lying on the bedside table, already plugged in. Picking it up he flicked it on and made a token gesture of skimming it over his cheeks and his stubbly chin. He ran his fingers along the row of hangers in the wardrobe until he came to his dinner suit and his dress shirt, still wrapped in the dry-cleaner's polythene bag. He took a long lingering drag on his cigarette, inhaling deeply, before folding the half-smoked cigarette into the ashtray on top of the chest of drawers. Ripping the polythene cover from the hanger he slipped his arms through the shirt sleeves and buttoned the shirt one-handed while rummaging in the dressing table drawer for his clip-on bow tie. When he stepped into his dinner suit trousers he had to suck in his stomach in order to fasten the top button, the cheval mirror at the foot of the bed reflecting the folds of flesh bulging over the taut waistband. 'Flabby before you're even forty!' He sighed and slapped his stomach, then breathed in hard as he yanked up the zip. Selecting a pair of cufflinks from the jewellery tray on the dressing table he fumbled to thread the cufflinks through the awkward double cuffs. He pulled on his dinner jacket and shot the shirt cuffs through the sleeves. Checking his appearance in the mirror, he ran his tongue across his tobacco-stained teeth, then picked up a comb to smooth his thinning hair across the bald patch on the crown. Squinting again in the mirror, he flicked away the spots of dandruff from his shoulders.

'Get a move on, Simon!' Jude's anxious voice came echoing up the staircase. 'Helen and Bjorn will be here any minute.'

'Relax, for God's sake! I'm ready.'

When he returned to his study he saw that all six messages had now been received. He flopped down in front of the screen and scanned them : two copies of the same spam email offering the possibility of a penis enlargement that would change his life for ever; another peddling cut-price Rolex watches; a cancellation of a rendezvous next week from one of his bridge partners; a confirmation from his bank concerning the price of the shares he'd sold that afternoon and a message from someone he didn't recognise – 'liam.black@hotmail.com'.

His brow creased as he read the text:

> I thought you might appreciate a wee preview, Simon. If you'd like to see the whole video I've got the full, two-hour, unexpurgated version. I'll call you on your mobile at ten o'clock tomorrow morning. I'm sure we'll be able to come to an amicable arrangement.

Narrowing his eyes he slid the mouse across to click on the attachment, then his jaw went slack as a photograph gradually filled the screen. He felt his legs go weak and he grabbed hold of the arms of the chair for support. Globules of sweat broke out on his forehead. Spluttering, he reached for the packet of cigarettes on his desk and, as he fumbled to light up, the Westminster chimes rang out downstairs.

CHAPTER 2

Charlie Anderson gave a sharp toot on his horn as he pulled up at the entrance to the underground car park of CID headquarters in Pitt Street. With an acknowledging wave the security guard in the adjacent booth put down his newspaper and raised the barrier, Charlie winding down his window and shouting his thanks as he drove slowly down the steep slope. Twisting round in his seat he reversed carefully into a tight parking space between two wide concrete pillars before levering himself out of the car and hurrying across the courtyard, turning up his coat collar as he went to protect his neck from the biting wind funnelling down the slope.

Charlie plodded up the flight of steps to the main building and kept climbing until he reached the second floor. When he came to the vending machines he rummaged in his pocket for change and dropped the coins into the slot, punching in the code for black coffee with extra sugar. He waited until the last drops of liquid had dribbled out before picking up the plastic cup between thumb and forefinger and heading along the corridor. After a few paces he stopped in his tracks and turned on his heel. 'Second time this month,' he muttered as he made his way back along the corridor. Nudging open the fire door with his knee, he trudged up another flight of steps.

What was it Niggle had said when they'd bumped into each other on the second floor last week? 'Old habits die hard', probably, though to Charlie's ears it had sounded more like: 'Old habits, die-hard!'

Charlie paused in front of his office door to admire the gleaming brass name plate with 'DCI Charles Anderson' etched in black letters. Glancing up and down the corridor he transferred the coffee cup to his left hand and burnished the plate with his coat sleeve. Six months now.

Earlier in the year Charlie had been on the verge of packing in the force due to the cumulative effects of twenty years in the same job, Kay nagging at him to quit, his arthritis giving him gyp, modern technology he didn't understand and a new Welsh boss he didn't get on with. The paperwork for his early retirement had been signed off and a date had been set – the nineteenth of June.

In the last week of May a drunk driver had hit DCI Williams' car head-on in Rutherglen and Williams had lain in a coma for a fortnight before, at his family's request, the life support system had been turned off.

The Assistant Chief Constable had waited until the funeral breakfast in the Marriott was breaking up before taking Charlie to one side for a quiet tête-à-tête. 'Have a think about it,' he'd said, wrapping an avuncular arm around Charlie's shoulders and guiding him towards the bar. 'It would only be for a couple of years,' he'd added, signalling to the barman for two more large Ballantines. 'You'd be doing us all a favour. No one else is ready to step into the breach right now and two years would give me time to groom an internal candidate – a much better arrangement than having to draft in another outsider.' Charlie had agreed wholeheartedly with the latter statement. 'And two years as a DCI would give a nice wee boost to your pension. Like I said, have a think about it over the weekend. Talk it over with Kay and let me know on Monday what you decide.'

When Charlie had got home the discussion had lasted late into the night, Kay doing her best to persuade him to stick to his plans, primarily for the sake of his health. Charlie had realised the arguments weighed heavily in favour of him leaving; after all, hadn't he introduced most of them himself to justify his early retirement? And to complicate matters, if he were to accept the promotion it would mean he would be reporting to Detective Superintendent Nigel Hamilton, someone he disliked even more than Williams. Despite all that, the carrot of attaining the rank of Detective Chief Inspector was dangling before his eyes; his aspiration, his dream these past ten years, his chance to prove to them all that he should have been promoted years ago. How could he adjust to a life of pottering around in his allotment knowing he'd turned the opportunity down? Realising how much the promotion meant to him, Kay had finally opted for the pragmatic approach. She'd go along with his decision as long as he promised to delegate a lot more and cut down on the ridiculous amount of time he spent in the office. Charlie had agreed. His resolution had lasted for the best part of a fortnight before he was sucked back into the quagmire.

Charlie was crumpling the plastic coffee cup in his fist when Tony O'Sullivan appeared in the office doorway. 'Did we manage to nail them?' he demanded.

'We got Fraser and Devlin, sir, but McCulloch did a runner into St Enoch's Centre and we lost him in the crowd.'

'Forget about McCulloch.' Charlie waved his hand

dismissively. 'We can pick him up any time. Where are we holding Tweedledum and Tweedledee?'

'Downstairs, in the interview rooms.'

Charlie heaved himself to his feet and dropped his coffee cup into the waste paper basket. 'You take Devlin. I want a go at Fraser. Especially now I know for sure he's supplying McCulloch,' he added with feeling. 'My daughter saw McCulloch mooching around outside her school again last week – and she didn't get the impression he was trying to sell the kids sweeties.'

Jude Ramsay passed round a silver platter containing blinis smothered in caviar, black olives, cheese fingers and pistachio nuts. 'Simon,' she hissed out of the side of her mouth. 'Would you please pay more attention to our guests!'

'What?'

Jude pointed towards the empty champagne flute standing on the coffee table. 'Helen needs a refill.'

'Oh! Right. Sorry.' Struggling from his armchair he hurried to the kitchen and returned with a chilled bottle of Veuve Clicquot which he uncorked expertly, tilting the bottle at an angle to prevent any spillage. Flicking her long blonde hair away from her eyes, Helen Cuthbertson picked up her glass and stretched out a slim arm. As Simon poured, his eyes were drawn to her shapely legs, displayed to full advantage by a minuscule black dress. She held her champagne flute at an angle until the bubbles died down, then straightened her glass. When Simon topped it up to the brim she fluttered her long eyelashes in appreciation.

'Put on a few pounds since the last time I saw you, little sister?' Jude said, popping an olive into her mouth.

'Miaow!' Helen jabbed out her tongue.

'No!' Jude laughed. 'It was meant as a compliment. You were far too thin. It wasn't healthy.'

'Not a lot I could do about it,' Helen shrugged. 'I had to waste away to almost nothing for a swimsuit catalogue during the summer, but the shoot in Rio last week was more interested in the handbags and the shoes than the models so I could afford to let myself go a bit.'

'And you've definitely decided to pack it in?'

'You'd better believe it! Ten years of that lifestyle is enough for anyone. Besides, Bjorn wants to see me for more than a couple of days a month, which suits me down to the ground. The days of starving myself so I could flounce down a catwalk are behind me for ever.'

'Welcome to the civilised world,' Jude said, offering the platter.

Helen took a cheese finger and raised her glass in front of her eyes. 'Cheers!' She toasted the room. 'Another thing I won't miss about the fashion circuit is being ogled by dirty old men,' she added disdainfully. 'There was one particular pervert who seemed to get a press pass for all the London shows. I never did find out his name. I'm not even sure he was attached to a magazine. He would always turn up early, grab a seat in the front row and sit with his nose stuck in a newspaper until a model appeared in something skimpy, then he'd leer at her through his piggy little eyes. I'm sure that all he lived for was a flash of nipple.'

'There's plenty more where he came from.' Jude curled her lip.

Helen popped the cheese finger into her mouth and washed it down with a long sip of champagne. 'It's a shame Alison and Norman weren't able to make it tonight. It's ages since I've seen either of them.'

'Anyone mad enough to buy a farmhouse in Ballinluig has to live with the consequences.' Jude smoothed down her silk dress. 'Getting snowed in comes with the territory. When I spoke to Alison on the phone she told me they haven't been able to put a foot across the threshold since last Saturday.'

'There's something comforting about that,' Bjorn said. 'Don't you think so, Simon?' Bjorn Svensson's English was fluent, albeit with typically Nordic, stretched-out vowels.

'Comforting about what?'.

'Don't you think there must be something very satisfying about being completely cut off from the rat race?' Bjorn was perched on the edge of a high-backed chair in front of the smokeless fuel fire. His hair was spiked with gel and his long fingers fiddled constantly with his deeply dimpled chin. A hired dinner jacket sat awkwardly on his narrow, sloping shoulders.

'I can see the pros and cons,' Simon said, balancing his buttocks against the arm of the settee while adding a splash of champagne to his already half-full glass. 'However, if I had the choice, I'd rather live within range of civilisation during the week – by which I mean decent pubs and restaurants – as long as I had the option of heading off to the wide open spaces at the weekends when –' His comment was interrupted by the jangle of the Westminster chimes. 'That'll be Laura and Mike – late as always,' he said, placing his glass and the champagne bottle down on the coffee table.

Mike Harrison stomped the snow from his shoes on the doormat as he ushered his wife in ahead of him. 'It'd freeze the goolies off a brass one out there,' he complained, tugging off his scarf and overcoat and shaking out the sleet. 'My knees are red raw. If I'd known it was going to be chucking it down like this I'd have come in salopettes instead of a bloody kilt.'

'Laura! What on earth happened?' Simon stared at her face in astonishment.

Despite her best efforts, Laura Harrison's make-up couldn't disguise her swollen jaw and blackened left eye. 'It looks a lot worse than it is,' she said, slipping her ocelot coat from her shoulders and handing it across.

'Mugged, she was,' Mike said, draping his coat over the hallstand.

'What!' Simon said incredulously. 'When? Where?'

'Monday night,' said Mike. 'The back of eleven, in Renfrew Street, right outside the cinema. I was trying to flag down a cab when two morons on a motorbike mounted the pavement and tried to snatch Laura's handbag.'

'Good God!'

'I managed to hang on to my bag,' Laura said, delicately fingering her bruised cheek. 'But I got a punch in the face for my trouble.'

'Did you get a good look at them?'

'Sure!' Mike snorted. 'Two thugs, dressed in black leather gear, wearing crash helmets, on a bike with no licence plates. As much chance of identifying them as flying to the fucking moon.'

'Come on in here, you lot!' Jude's voice came echoing out from the lounge. 'I don't want to miss anything!'

Tracey Reid came to a tittupping halt outside the cashpoint booth and stared through the slush-splattered glass door. Relieved to see there was only one person inside she swiped her cashpoint card through the reader and pushed open the door.

The elderly woman, huddled over the screen, snatched an anxious glance over her shoulder when the blast of cold air hit her in the small of the back. She eyed the shivering young girl up and down, frowning disapprovingly at the diamond stud piercing Tracey's shiny nose and the rows of pewter rings lining both her ears. Hunching her shoulders she turned her attention back to the screen, peering myopically over the top of her spectacles at the faint instructions. The cubicle door swung closed and the traffic noise was once again muted.

'It's, like, starting to freeze out there,' Tracey said, forcing a cheerfulness she didn't feel, not quite sure whether she was trying to reassure the woman or herself. There was a grunt of a response, more in annoyance that her concentration had been broken than in acknowledgment of the comment. Tracey stood near the door, twiddling her cashpoint card in one hand while flicking at her braided hair with the other, trying to dislodge the melting sleet. The woman pulled her headscarf tightly underneath her chin and moved her face as close to the screen as possible to block it from prying eyes. Tracey idly wondered why she needed to withdraw cash so late at night, but to ask would have been an invasion of privacy too far.

Tracey was annoyed with herself. She'd meant to come to the cashpoint earlier in the day but it had slipped her mind. She hated the silence and claustrophobia of this place. She wouldn't normally come here this late at night but she couldn't go clubbing with the two pounds fifty she had in her handbag and she wasn't prepared to tramp through the snow in her high heels to a busier cashpoint. She'd thought about giving the Arches a miss – she was shattered – but it was the last chance she'd get to see Linda before Christmas and exchange presents.

It seemed to take an age before the woman finally withdrew her card and tucked the single banknote that emerged inside her woollen glove. Avoiding eye contact with Tracey she depressed the button to open the cubicle door.

Tracey slid her card into the slot and was entering her PIN when she saw his reflection in the screen. He'd caught the door with his foot before it could close. She felt her heartbeat quicken as he shuffled to a halt behind her. No reason to panic, she told herself. She'd intended to withdraw a hundred so she could give Stevie the money she owed him but she decided to ask for twenty instead – just in case. Stevie had already waited a month for his money – another couple of days wouldn't be a problem. She kept her eyes glued to the screen, not wanting to give this guy any pretext to start up a conversation. Snatching out her card as soon as it reappeared she shoved it into her coat pocket, the pounding of her heart against her ribcage seeming louder than the mechanical shuffling of the notes about to be disgorged. She could hear his quick, shallow breathing and she sensed he was standing very close to her. His cold breath came wafting over her shoulder and she felt something brush against her earlobe. Instinctively she lifted her hand to flick it away, then there was a sudden, violent, searing pain in her left ear as she was yanked across the confined space, her ankle twisting beneath her as she toppled over on her high heels and thumped down painfully on the tiled floor, skinning both knees. Her handbag fell from her grasp.

He was standing with his back against the cubicle door, staring at her through pinpricks of dark eyes sunk into deep red sockets. In his late teens, thin as a rake, his hair was close shaved, almost skinhead, his forehead acne-pitted. He was wearing white tracksuit trousers, pinched at the ankles, above a pair of white trainers. His light blue jacket was unzipped, the sleeves rammed above his elbows exposing his skinny forearms, blotch-marked from the cold.

Tracey saw him move his hands slowly back and forward in front of his face and she realised he was holding something. When she tried to scramble to her feet he yanked his hands backwards, sending her pitching forward onto the floor. She screamed in agony as the pain shot from her ear to her brain and when she jerked her hand to the side of her head she felt the piece of string he'd looped through the pewter rings in her left ear.

'On your feet,' he panted, tugging on both ends of the string and forcing her to her knees. When she grabbed at the string again he pulled on it hard, bringing her crashing down. 'Try that again,' he snarled, 'an' your fuckin' ear's comin' aff.'

Tears of pain and terror were bubbling from Tracey's eyes, rivulets of mascara oozing down both cheeks. 'What do you want with me?' she whimpered. 'Why are you doing this?'

Gripping her by her braided hair he dragged her to her feet. He snatched the money from the cashpoint machine, glaring at her when he saw the two ten-pound notes. 'Twenty measly fuckin' quid!' He stuffed the money into his hip pocket. 'That's sod all use! I need more than that.'

'It's all I've got.'

'I'm warnin' you.' He gripped her arm painfully. 'Don't mess me about.'

Tracey looked in desperation over his shoulder at the cars queuing up at the traffic lights; a line of bored drivers, staring straight ahead. When she saw two youths hurrying past on foot she let out a scream, but neither head turned, then she screamed even louder when he yanked her across the booth by the string in her earrings and slammed her face into the cashpoint machine, splitting open her bottom lip. Spinning her round he pressed his body hard against hers, pinning her to the wall, their faces inches apart.

Tracey screwed her eyes shut. 'That wisny very clever,' he panted. His breathing was coming in short gasps. She could feel his spittle in her face. Her whole body went rigid.

'Look at me when I'm talkin' to you,' he commanded. Tracey sank her teeth into her bottom lip, tasting her own blood, but kept her eyes squeezed shut. Taking a step back he launched a sickening punch at the pit of her stomach. 'I telt you to fuckin'-well look at me, you stupid wee bitch!'

Tracey folded at the waist, clutching at her stomach. He grabbed her by the hair and forced her to straighten up. 'Did you hear what I fuckin'-well said?' he screamed in her face. Wheezing for breath, she slowly opened her eyes. Tears were coursing down her swollen cheeks.

'I need more money,' he panted. 'My dealer won't give me anythin' until I settle up.'

'I've only got a couple of quid. Look for yourself,' she whimpered, pointing at her handbag lying on the ground.

'You can get more out the machine.'

'Twenty's all it would give me – and you've got that,' she sobbed, raising both arms above her head and flailing at his chest. 'So take it and leave me alone!'

Her assailant grabbed Tracey by the wrists and pinned her against the cubicle wall, holding her in that position until all the energy had seeped from her body. 'Show me,' he said, releasing her wrists.

'Show you what?' she sobbed.

'Put your card back in the machine an' try again.'

'I've already told you! It won't give me any more!'

'I'd try awfy hard if I was you, because if you don't give me two hundred quid, I've got somethin' I'm goany give you.' He reached into his jacket pocket and producing a syringe. 'Two hundred quid or AIDS.' He held the point of the needle against her throat. 'Your call.'

'Oh, no! Not that! Jesus Christ!' Tracey flattened her back against the wall and screamed at the top of her voice. 'Take that fucking thing away from me! For God's sake! I'll get you the fucking money!'

As Tracey fumbled in her coat pocket for her cashpoint card she saw the headlights of a car arc up and down as its wheels bumped onto the kerb outside the booth. Her fingers felt the plastic card but she continued to fumble to hold his attention while the driver got out of his car. The cubicle door was pushed open and a slim, middle-aged man in a three-piece suit stepped inside. When he heard the door opening, Tracey's attacker spun round and launched himself at the man, stabbing the syringe into the side of his neck . Without a backward glance he hurdled the collapsed, screaming figure and sprinted off down the road.

CHAPTER 3

As Bjorn Svensson was coming back down the stairs from the toilet the conversation around the dining table died away. He sensed the air of expectancy and he felt all the eyes following him as he made his way back to his seat. 'What's up?' His cheeks flushed and his hands dropped instinctively to his crotch. 'Forgot to do up my flies, or something?'

'Helen's been hinting that you've been up to something rather clever, you sly old bugger.' Mike Harrison's chubby features, florid from the effects of the wine, creased in a mischievous grin. 'It's always the quiet ones, isn't it?' he said, plucking his gold toothpick from his sporran and using it to prise out a piece of steak lodged between his closely-spaced front teeth. 'It's time to reveal all, my lad.'

Bjorn's fair complexion reddened even more. Tugging off his rimless spectacles he polished them furiously on the handkerchief he'd yanked from his trouser pocket. 'Helen!' he hissed across the table. 'I thought we'd agreed?'

'Oh, come on, Bjorn! Don't be such a spoilsport.' She giggled tipsily. 'We're among family. Anyway, I think it's *so* clever,' she added, slurping down a mouthful of wine.

Bjorn replaced his glasses and his disconcerted gaze travelled slowly round the table. Jude Ramsay was gnawing on a stick of celery, looking mildly amused. Mike Harrison's bulky, kilted frame was wedged between the constricting arms of a carver chair, his jabot long since discarded, his top shirt button undone, the remaining buttons straining across his broad chest. He was grinning like a Cheshire cat as he twiddled with the white rabbits' feet on his sporran. Laura Harrison's hazel eyes were fixed on him, a smile playing at the corners of her wide mouth. Helen was running her tongue back and forth along her slightly parted lips. She had a startled, confused expression, as if she thought she'd done something rather daring but wasn't quite sure of the consequences. Simon Ramsay was the only one avoiding eye contact. He had the same distracted air he'd had all evening, gazing towards the high, corniced ceiling.

'You'll have to spill the beans now, Bjorn, otherwise we'll all assume the worst,' Mike said, leaning across the table and prodding Simon in the arm. 'Isn't that right, Simon?'

'Eh? Sure.' Simon blinked and stretched for the wine bottle to top up his glass.

'I don't know about this.' Bjorn cast his eyes down while he folded his handkerchief and put it back into his pocket. He looked up quickly. 'It goes without saying that this mustn't go beyond these four walls.'

'Don't tell me you've finally got round to robbing the bank?' Laura said with a smile.

'Close!' Helen squealed and let out a shriek of laughter, suddenly truncated as she clapped both hands across her mouth.

'Fascinating stuff!' Mike stifled a burp. 'Come on, Bjorn, my boy.' He gave an exaggerated, knowing wink. 'Let's be having you.'

Bjorn ran his fingers through his spiky hair. 'The idea came to me back in 1999 when I was updating the bank's computer programs to handle the change of millennium,' he began. 'Do you have any idea how many accounts the bank handles?'

'Not a clue,' said Jude.

'We've got over four hundred thousand customers. When you include the deposit accounts and the various savings schemes there are more than a million active accounts, the majority of which attract interest payments in some shape or form every month. The bank's computers are programmed to round interest to the nearest penny. If, for example, the calculation says you're due two pounds fifty three point two pence, you get two pounds fifty three, but if it comes to two pounds fifty three point seven, you get two pounds fifty four. It's swings and roundabouts for the bank. Statistically, it breaks even.' There was an intrigued silence while Bjorn broke off to sip his wine. 'So, I thought to myself, who would ever notice if I changed the logic to always round down? I mean, who's going to question an interest payment of two pounds fifty three instead of two pounds fifty four?'

'Who, indeed?' Laura dabbed at the corners of her mouth with her linen napkin.

'If you do the arithmetic you'll find that skimming, on average, half a penny from a million accounts comes to five thousand pounds a month.'

'A nice wee earner.' Mike nodded approvingly. 'And tax free, to boot.'

'The only problem was that tampering with the interest calculation logic at the time of the millennium changes wasn't on. Everyone and his wife was checking and rechecking those modules.'

'So?' Jude asked.

'So I introduced a bug into a different part of the program – in fact, the routine that handles standing orders. When the change of century fuss had died away customer complaints started filtering through about standing orders being unexpectedly terminated and I was asked to check the program logic. While I was fixing it I slipped in my 'rounding down' routine, at the same time setting up a complex series of fund transfers for the surplus cash which eventually ends up in an account in Helen's name in the Cayman Islands.'

'Bravo!' Mike Harrison started applauding loudly.

'Did the banking crisis not put a bit of a damper on your scheme?' Jude asked. 'God knows, it's almost impossible to get an account that pays any worthwhile interest these days.'

'To some extent, in that the current accounts stopped earning interest. But as for the rest, whether I'm skimming a half penny off a ten-pound interest payment or a one-pound interest payment, it's all the same to me.'

'Been running for about ten years now,' Helen said. 'So far – touch wood,' she said, slipping her hand underneath the lace tablecloth and tapping a fingernail on the mahogany surface. 'No one's twigged.'

'The really clever part,' Bjorn continued with a self-satisfied air, 'is that I've set it up as a separate load module which is invoked on a date-controlled basis. Without wanting to blind you with science, that means I can switch the routine off when I go on holiday so if anyone has a reason to look at the program logic during my absence they won't stumble across my personalised code.'

'Tell them about the promotion, Bjorn,' Helen giggled.

Bjorn's grin broadened. 'Last month I was offered a job in head office. Step up on the career ladder and all that jazz. My boss couldn't understand why I was turning down a promotion and a five thousand pounds a year salary increase. Difficult to explain to him that I saw it as a fifty-five thousand pounds a year salary cut.'

Everyone joined in the laughter.

'What do you think of that, Simon?' Mike said. 'Impressed by Stockholm's answer to Bernie Madoff?'

'I only wish the stockbroking business offered such creative possibilities,' Simon grumbled. 'At this rate, Bjorn, you'll be stashing away your first million before Mike.'

'Don't give me your worries.' Mike's mood changed suddenly. 'I'm on my bloody uppers.'

'Pull the other one.'

'I kid thee not, Simon.' He drew his bushy eyebrows together. 'I've never known a month like it. You have to have turnover to survive in the bookmaking business. Do you know how many days' racing we've had so far this month?' Simon shook his head. 'Two. And to top it all, Kempton was the only meeting to survive the frost last Saturday and the first five fucking favourites trotted in. I lost a bloody fortune!'

'Stop it, Mike!' Jude smiled expansively as she got to her feet. 'You'll have us all in tears.'

'It's no laughing matter, Jude,' he protested. 'It's not as if the overheads and the wage bills go away when there's no racing. I'm telling you, I'm seriously having to consider giving up the Cathcart shop to cut back on expenses.'

'And how many would that leave you with?' Jude asked as she walked round the table to collect in the cheese plates. 'Six? Or would it just be five?' She stopped to tickle Mike under the chin. 'What you need is some of my home-made tiramisu to help keep body and soul together.'

*

'Let's go over it one more time.' Charlie Anderson picked up the Save the Children collection box from the desk and balanced it in the palm of his hand.

'Oh, for fuck's sake!' Gerry Fraser leaned forward on the chair on the opposite side of the desk in the sparsely furnished interview room, elbows on knees, stubbled chin resting on clasped hands. 'I've already telt you everythin',' he protested. 'Twice.'

Charlie rocked back in his seat and swung his legs stiffly up on to the desk. 'Third time lucky, then.'

'Oh, gie us a fuckin' break!'

Opening his notebook, Charlie thumbed through the pages. 'Ready when you are. Let's take it from eleven o'clock this morning in The Three Judges.'

'Goany no' let me smoke?' Fraser whined.

Charlie smiled coldly and jabbed an arthritic finger in the direction of the NO SMOKING sign attached to the far wall, high above the head of a young plain-clothes officer who was sitting by the door, flicking through a newspaper. Charlie looked quizzical when they made eye contact, mildly surprised that he didn't recognise him. 'I don't make the rules around here,' he said, turning his attention back to Fraser, 'but I sure as hell enforce them.'

Fraser ferreted in his trouser pocket and produced a grubby stick of gum. 'I suppose there'll be a law against chewin' as well?'

'Be my guest – as long as you're not thinking of sticking it to the bottom of the chair.' Tugging his half-moon reading glasses from the breast pocket of his shirt, Charlie slipped them on. 'Let me make sure I've got this right,' he said, referring to his shorthand notes. 'You told me you borrowed the Save the

Children collection box from The Three Judges this morning because you were struck by a sudden burst of altruism.'

'What the fuck does that mean?'

'"Sudden" – or "burst"?'

'Piss off!'

'You reckoned you'd be able to do well collecting from the Christmas shoppers in Argyle Street,' Charlie continued, 'but you didn't mention to the barman that you wanted to borrow the collection box because he was busy.'

Fraser shrugged. 'That's about the size of it,' he said, unwrapping the stick of gum and stuffing it into his mouth.

Charlie examined the collection box minutely. 'Why did you go to the trouble of widening the slot?' Fraser glared at him sullenly. 'Expecting some large donations?' Fraser chomped noisily on his gum. 'Always the optimist, eh?' Charlie weighed the box in one hand, then flipped it over and started to prise open the seal with the blunt end of his pencil.

'You're no' supposed to do that,' Fraser protested, chewing open-mouthed.

'I just want to see how well you did,' Charlie said, rattling the box and tipping the contents out onto the desk. He let out a long, low whistle as several bundles of notes came tumbling out. 'Come over here, son,' he called out, waving the young officer across. 'What's your name?' he asked.

'Freer, sir. Tom Freer.' Freer was tall, slim and clean-shaven.

'Don't think our paths have crossed?'

'This is my first week. I've just transferred up from the Met.'

'Welcome to the frozen north. Glaswegians have a reputation for donating generously to worthy causes, Freer, as you can see.' Charlie pointed to the wads of notes. 'Save the Children are going to be chuffed to buggery with this lot.' He slid the banknotes across the desk. 'Count it for us, would you?'

Fraser's darting eyes never left the money as Freer licked his fingers and thumbed through the notes.

'I make it one thousand six hundred quid, sir, plus the small change.'

'You'll be able to sponsor a lot of children with that, Fraser.' Charlie interlocked his fingers and cracked his knuckles. 'The generosity of the Glasgow public never ceases to amaze me. This time next year Africa will be awash with wee black Gerry Frasers – bless their cotton socks.'

Fraser spat his chewing gum out onto the floor.

Charlie unlocked his fingers and slowly clenched and unclenched his right fist. 'You were just about to pick that up?'

Fraser held eye contact. 'You wouldny dare, Anderson,' he sneered. 'No' in here.'

Charlie turned to Freer. 'Take that money over to main reception and ask the duty sergeant to lock it in the safe until someone from Save the Children can come across to collect it. Stop off for a coffee on the way back, son. No hurry.'

Freer scooped up the money and moved towards the door. Fraser made eye contact with Charlie, then bent down and snatched up the chewing gum. He rammed it back into his mouth.

Jude Ramsay caught her husband's eye across the dining table as he was pushing tiramisu around his plate. 'What's the matter with the birthday boy?' She didn't try to hide her annoyance. 'You've hardly eaten a thing tonight, Simon. Something wrong with my cooking?'

'Sorry, Jude,' Simon said, reaching for the wine bottle and refilling his glass. 'Bit of an upset stomach. That's all.'

Jude rolled her eyes. 'It doesn't seem to be having too much effect on your drinking.'

Mike Harrison pushed his chair back from the table and patted his bulging stomach. 'Brilliant meal, Jude. As always.'

'It's a pleasure to cook for someone who appreciates it, Mike. How about some more dessert?'

'You know me, Jude. I can never say no.' As Jude stretched across the table for his plate Mike took a grip of her hand and made a production of kissing each finger in turn. 'Just a spoonful now, Jude. And I mean that.' He patted his paunch. 'I'm in serious danger of exploding.'

As soon as Jude had disappeared into the kitchen, Laura leaned across to whisper in Simon's ear. 'What's the matter with you tonight?'

He gulped at his wine. 'It's not been a good day,' he mumbled.

'Being the first of the crowd to turn forty can't be all *that* traumatic. It'll happen to the rest of us soon enough.'

'It's serious, Laura,' he said quietly.

'Anything I should know about?' she whispered, furrowing her brow and glancing across towards her husband who was engrossed in telling Bjorn and Helen his latest crude joke.

Simon's bloodshot eyes stared at her bruised face. 'It's nothing I can't handle,' he said unconvincingly. Reaching for the wine bottle he cursed when he saw there were only dregs remaining. He dragged himself to his feet and made his way unsteadily to the drinks cabinet, returning with a decanter of port, a bottle of malt whisky and a bottle of Armagnac balanced on a tray.

'What's your poison, ladies?' he asked.

'Do you have any Drambuie?' Helen asked.

'One Drambuie coming up.' Swaying his way to the drinks cabinet he came back with a liqueur glass filled to the brim. 'How about you, Laura?'

'I'd like a port, please.'

Tawny port splashed onto the lace tablecloth as Simon poured from the decanter. 'Let me make a wild guess, Mike. I'm prepared to bet you'll be having an Armagnac.'

'How does the man do it?' Mike unclipped his silver belt and loosened the side buckles of his kilt. 'It must be some kind of paranormal gift,' he said, tugging the straining folds of material away from his stomach. 'Thank Christ I wasn't laying odds!'

'How about you, Bjorn?'

'I'd prefer to stick to wine, if there is any?'

'There's gallons of the stuff in the kitchen.' Simon glanced in the direction of the closed kitchen door. 'Do me a favour, Bjorn. Nip through and grab a couple of bottles. The wine rack's just behind the door. I don't want to go in there and have to face old misery guts whining on about –'

Simon broke off as Jude reappeared in the doorway carrying a plate stacked high with tiramisu.

Charlie Anderson glanced up at the clock on the interview room wall and saw it was almost midnight. 'Let me try this one on for size.'

'Oh, for God's sake, Anderson! When are you goany let up?' Gerry Fraser slumped forward in his chair and massaged his temples with his fingertips. 'I've already telt you everythin'.'

'How about this for a scenario?' Charlie said. 'A punter tells you what he wants to buy and he sticks his money in the collection box. You tick-tack the order to Devlin who then gets on the blower to someone else further down the precinct, telling him to hand the stuff over to the guy plastered in Save the Children stickers.' He stood up to stretch his aching back. 'How am I doing?'

'You're fuckin' doolally.'

'That way, you've got nothing on you apart from the collection box, Devlin doesn't have anything more incriminating than a mobile phone, and neither of you is in the vicinity when the stuff's handed over.'

'You'll be able to prove all that in court?'

Charlie stretched across the desk and grabbed hold of Fraser's shirt collar, twisting on it hard until his pallid features turned red. 'Tosh McCulloch's been supplying kids,' Charlie hissed in his face. 'Primary school kids. A ten-year-old boy in my daughter's school died from an overdose last month. Did you fucking-well know that?' Tom Freer, sitting by the door, glanced up from his newspaper and then quickly cast his eyes back down. 'You really don't give a shit! Do you?' Charlie roared in Fraser's face.

When Fraser started to splutter and choke, Charlie relaxed his grip and sank back onto his chair.

'I know my rights,' Fraser whined. 'I want a lawyer.'

Charlie glared at him across the desk. 'On your bike,' he snapped, jerking his thumb in the direction of the door. Fraser looked perplexed. 'Thought I was going to book you? No such luck.' Charlie stared ostentatiously at his watch. 'I've still got plenty of time to make sure the story breaks in the morning papers. "A man who was suspected of using a Save the Children collection box as a front for selling drugs in Argyle Street last night managed to evade arrest by mingling with the Christmas shopping crowds." Someone will be mighty relieved to know his one thousand six hundred quid is safe.'

Fraser shifted uncomfortably on his seat. 'You wouldny do that?'

'Try me. Unless, of course, you've got something you want to get off your chest?'

Fraser's tongue flicked across his cracked lips. 'Such as?'

'Such as who you're working for. If I happen to believe you I might just see my way to locking you up for the night.'

'I don't know what you're on about.'

'Fine. Have it your own way.' Grabbing the edges of the desk Charlie pulled himself to his feet. 'See this chancer off the premises, officer, then get the night editor of the *Record* on the blower for me.'

Striding out of the room Charlie walked down the corridor and into the adjacent interview room where Tony O'Sullivan was sitting opposite Johnny Devlin. Devlin's skinny frame was propped on the edge of an upright chair, his faded denim jacket draped around his hunched shoulders, his lank hair tumbling over his slow, cloudy eyes.

Charlie exchanged a nod with the craggy-faced officer leaning against the far wall. DC Colin Renton was the only person in Pitt Street with a longer service record than Charlie, most of it in the uniformed division. With Charlie's encouragement, Renton had transferred to the CID late in his career.

Devlin twisted round in his seat when he heard Charlie enter. 'How much longer do I have to put up with this crap?' he demanded.

Charlie ignored him. 'A word, Tony,' he said, inclining his head towards the door. 'Are you getting anywhere with him?' he asked quietly in the corridor.

'He's sticking to his story. Says he wasn't in contact with Fraser. Claims to have no knowledge of tick-tack. Says he was phoning a pal to find out what he wanted for Christmas.'

'Any grounds for holding him?'

O'Sullivan shrugged. 'He had a couple of sticks of cannabis on him – nothing to get excited about. Claims it was for personal use.'

'Unlucky for him that this happens to be zero tolerance week.' Charlie winked. 'Book him for possession, confiscate his mobile and have him locked up for the night. When you've done that, come up to my office.'

Tom Freer was waiting for Charlie at the far end of the corridor. 'Did you really want me to put a call through to the night editor of the *Record*, sir?'

'Don't bother, son. I was just putting the wind up him.'

When he got back to his office Charlie found an even bigger stack of paper than usual in his in-basket. On top of the pile was a note from his secretary. He skimmed her scrawly handwriting:

The first draft of your year-end report is due to be submitted to Superintendent Hamilton on Monday. I've consolidated the spreadsheets on the statistics (there are copies of all the graphs in your mail). The bottom line is a 4.3% year-on-year increase in reported crime up to end-November, however, the overall figure for violent crime is up by 9.6% and, within that, knife crime is up by 15%. The ratio of solved to unsolved crimes is 7% worse than last year. The Super. has seen the preliminary figures and he sent you an email this morning asking for your comments and an explanation for the adverse trends.

Heaving a weary sigh Charlie flicked through the rest of his correspondence, starting with the printouts of his emails. Anticipating his early retirement he had sat through the computer literacy seminar back in April without taking anything in, spending the time day-dreaming about how he was going to lay out his allotment. Now his lack of attention had come home to roost. His boss was not only computer literate, he was wildly enthusiastic – there was a rumour going around that Niggle was more proficient on an Xbox than his nine year-old son – and he used emails incessantly to issue directives and demand information. Charlie, who had barely mastered how to log on, had come to an arrangement with Pauline whereby she printed out his emails and he hand-wrote his replies, which she then transmitted from his account the following day.

Charlie was wading through his mail, scribbling his responses in the margin, when O'Sullivan walked in.

'Devlin's been booked for possession,' he stated.

'Fine. Get in touch with his mobile phone company first thing in the morning and find out whose number he was calling at whatever time it was,' he said, raising the back of his hand to his mouth to stifle a yawn. 'I don't know about you but I'm whacked.'

'Anything else need doing tonight?'

Charlie shook his head. 'It's high time both of us were out of here. Grab some kip and we'll pick up the threads in the morning,' he said, interlocking his fingers and stretching both arms high above his head. 'Tony,' he said as O'Sullivan was heading towards the door. 'Have you got anything planned for Friday night?'

O'Sullivan turned back. 'If you're thinking about another stakeout, I can feel a sick granny coming on.'

Charlie smiled. 'I was thinking more about a steak-in. How about coming round to our place for dinner? Nothing fancy, mind. Just a bite to eat and a few beers.'

'That's a nice idea, sir. Thanks.'

After O'Sullivan had left, Charlie spent another half hour ploughing through his emails and jotting down replies, then he sorted through the memos, shuffling the priority items to the top of the pile. Lifting the heavy stack of paper he dropped it into the bottom drawer of his desk and turned the key in the lock.

There was little traffic about and the lights were in his favour as Charlie took his usual route home – along Pitt Street, down the steep slope of West George Street, left into Holland Street and past the row of concrete and glass buildings before turning into Waterloo Street and joining the Clydeside Expressway. He couldn't stop yawning. There were still a few flakes of snow gusting in the light wind but the roads had been well gritted. He had once worked out how many times he'd driven home from Pitt Street, but he couldn't remember the number. He tried to do the calculation again in his head to keep himself awake; twenty years, times forty-seven weeks, times, on average, six days a week. His tired brain soon gave up the struggle. He flicked on the car radio, permanently tuned to Radio Scotland. Frank Sinatra was crooning 'Strangers in the Night'. Turning up the volume he joined in, straining unsuccessfully to hit the high notes.

Charlie merged with the light traffic on the M8 and after a few miles he filtered off the motorway at the Renfrew exit to head along Paisley Road. When he turned into Wright Street, a row of neat, 1940s, semi-detached houses, he found himself driving on hard-packed snow. He pulled up at the kerb outside his gate, deciding against trying to negotiate the short, steep

drive alongside his pebble-dashed house. Last week's attempt at
that manoeuvre had resulted in a dented bumper and a couple of
bricks dislodged from the wall – another repair job added to the
ever-expanding list of 'things to do when I retire'.

Picking his steps carefully up the snow-covered drive, he
glanced up at the front bedroom window and saw the light was
on. He turned his key in the lock and called upstairs. 'Just me,
love.'

'Everything all right?' Kay's voice came drifting down the
staircase.

'Fine,' he said, tugging off his overcoat and hanging it on the
hallstand. 'I'll be up in a wee while. I could fair use a nightcap.'

The central heating had long since cut out. Charlie went to the
kitchen and poured himself a generous measure of Springbank,
adding a splash of water from the tap. He wandered into the
lounge and switched on both bars of the electric fire before
pulling his favourite armchair close to the source of heat and
slumping down on the seat.

Blakey stood up in his basket, stretched his long legs and
arched his back. Padding purposefully across the room, he leapt
straight up onto Charlie's lap and turned twice in a full circle
before settling down with his head nuzzled between Charlie's
knees. Charlie took a long, slow swallow of whisky as he rubbed
the cat's jet-black fur up the wrong way. He picked up the
Evening Times from the coffee table and flicked through the
sports pages. After a few minutes he could feel himself nodding
off due to the combined effects of the alcohol and the heat from
the fire. Finishing off his whisky, he lifted the limp cat in both
arms and struggled to his feet to carry him across the room and
place him gently back in his basket. Having switched off the fire

he trudged up the narrow staircase and when he went into the bedroom he found Kay sitting up in bed reading a paperback, a white cardigan wrapped around her shoulders. Her close-cropped black hair was sticking out like an urchin's where she'd towel-dried it before going to bed.

'How did it go tonight?' Kay asked, placing a bookmark in her page and closing the book.

Charlie tugged at his tie knot. 'Not wonderful. We managed to nick a couple of small fry but we didn't nail anyone who really matters. By the way, Sue was right – Tosh McCulloch is involved.'

'She was sure it was him.' Kay gave a quick shake of the head.

'We might be able to make some progress tomorrow,' Charlie said, draping his jacket over the back of the chair at the foot of the bed. 'How was your day?'

'Pretty uneventful.' Kay stretched across to switch off her bedside lamp. 'I went across to see Sue this afternoon,' she said, slipping off her cardigan and plumping up her pillow before settling down on her back. 'I was there when Jamie got home from school and, of course, he was desperate to know when his grandad would be coming over to play football with him. It's his birthday on Sunday – or 'Rainday', as he now insists on calling it. I'm going over in the afternoon to help Sue prepare the food for his party and I promised him you'd drop by on Sunday morning. Was that okay? Sue's getting him a new football and I told him you'd go across and try it out with him.'

Charlie's face lit up. 'Wild horses couldn't keep me away,' he said, stripping off his clothes and pulling on his pyjamas. 'By the way I've invited Tony O'Sullivan over for dinner on Friday night,' he added casually.

Kay opened her eyes wide and propped herself up on both elbows. 'You've done what?'

'I've invited Tony over for dinner. Is that a problem?'

Kay looked puzzled. 'Not a problem. Just a bit of a surprise. I can't remember the last time you invited a work colleague home for dinner.'

'Och, I was feeling sorry for the lad. It's Christmas, his family are all down in Ayrshire, he's been working his arse off for the past few months and, to top it all, his fiancée gave him the old heave-ho last week. I thought it wouldn't do any harm to socialise a bit. He's not the type to take advantage. Is that okay?'

'Fine by me,' Kay said as Charlie ambled along the corridor in the direction of the bathroom. 'Charlie!' she called out after him. 'You do know Sue's coming over here on Friday night?'

Charlie appeared in the bedroom doorway with his toothbrush rammed into the side of his mouth. 'Is she?' he mumbled. 'I'd forgotten.' He headed back towards the bathroom. 'No matter.'

'Forgotten?' Kay muttered under her breath. 'That would be a first.' She switched her bedside light back on. 'Charlie Anderson!' She had to shout to make herself heard above the noise of the running tap. 'I hope you're not matchmaking?'

'She could do a lot worse,' was interspersed with the sounds of coughing and spitting.

'The *last* thing this family needs is another copper!'

'I've invited him round for dinner, for God's sake,' he spluttered, wiping his mouth on a hand towel as he came back into the bedroom. 'I suppose he might bring a bottle of wine or a bunch of flowers, but I'm not expecting him to turn up with an engagement ring!'

'You are impossible!' Switching off her light Kay rolled onto her side to face the wall.

'It's time we were making a move, Bjorn,' Helen said, glancing at her watch. 'It's after one o'clock.'

'Got to rush home and count all your money, I suppose?' Mike Harrison slurred his words as he sat slumped on the settee.

'I'd rather you didn't go on about that,' Bjorn said.

'Oh you would, would you?' Mike reached for the Armagnac bottle and topped up his glass. 'It's okay for you, poncing around in your flash pad with money coming out your ears. You don't give a bugger that some of us are struggling to get by.'

'Back off, Mike,' Laura said. 'You're drunk.'

'I'm fucking-well not drunk!' Mike yelled, slamming the Armagnac bottle back down on the coffee table. 'That smug, self-satisfied Swedish prick gets on my tits. Who the hell does he think he is, lording it over us and boasting about what a smart arse he is?' Mike glared at Bjorn. 'How about spreading some of the largesse around in the family, Bjorn? That way, I might not need to have a chat with the police.'

'Give it rest, Mike,' Simon said. 'You're hardly in a position to threaten anyone with going to the police.'

'Listen to Mr holier-than-thou,' Mike sneered. 'Are you trying to tell me you've never tried your hand at a bit of insider dealing?'

'At least I've never been responsible for putting anyone in hospital.'

'What are you driving at?'

'You know fine well what I'm driving at. You've never earned an honest penny in your life.'

'Who the fuck do you think you're talking to? Mike said, struggling to get to his feet. He started peeling off his jacket. 'Come outside and say that!'

'Grow up, all of you!' Jude screamed. 'This is supposed to be a fucking party!'

Thursday 16 December

Gerry Fraser was chilled to the marrow and his feet were killing him as he hobbled down the Broomielaw in the direction of Glasgow Green. He'd been wandering around the city centre all night, too frightened to go back to his flat. It wasn't yet daylight as he trudged the length of Clyde Street, yanking up his jacket collar and bending low into the stinging wind whipping off the river. The only consolation was that it had stopped snowing. When he turned into the Saltmarket he managed to get some shelter from the buildings as he headed towards Glasgow Cross. As he approached the Gallowgate he looked at his watch and quickened his pace. He knew Shuggie opened up at six.

Fraser had a stream of unanswered questions churning in his head. He'd tried phoning Johnny Devlin several times during the night but there had been no reply – neither from his flat nor his mobile. Why not? Had the cops locked him up for the night? If so, why Devlin and not him? Were they trying to keep them apart? Trying to prevent them getting their act together?

The blackboard in the steamed-up window of Shuggie's café advertised an all-day breakfast at £5.99: sausage, bacon, egg, black pudding, tomato, fried potato scone and baked beans, with tea or coffee and toast. Three regulars were already installed, sitting side by side on a wooden bench with their backs to the door, their fingerless mittens wrapped around steaming mugs of milky tea. All the heads turned round when Fraser walked in. He nodded a curt greeting.

'The usual, Gerry?' The question had come from the squat figure perched on a high stool behind the counter.

'Bung on double sausage an' an extra egg, Shuggie. I'm starvin'. I didny get anythin' to eat last night.'

Shuggie Morrison wiped his hands on his grubby apron and rammed his shirt sleeves above the elbows, revealing thick, tattooed forearms. He got the fry-up going, regularly flipping the sausages and bacon, then took two eggs from the fridge and juggled with them expertly before cracking them into a smoking pan.

Fraser sat on the wooden bench by the window from where he could see along the road in both directions. While waiting for his breakfast his red-rimmed eyes flicked constantly up and down the street, deserted apart from the first stirrings of the city's cardboard kingdom in the shop doorways. When Shuggie brought across a heaped plate and a mug of black coffee Fraser sprayed the food liberally with salt and thin brown sauce from a plastic bottle before diving in. He kept one eye on the street while he munched.

The phone behind the counter rang. 'Aye, as a matter of fact he is,' Fraser heard Shuggie say. This was followed by a pause. 'About ten minutes ago.' Shuggie had lowered his voice and Fraser strained to follow the conversation. Another pause. 'Fine. I'll let him know.'

Shuggie came out from behind the counter and sat down on the bench next to Fraser. 'That was Billy McAteer on the blower,' he said quietly.

Fraser's jaw froze in mid-chew. 'What was he wantin'?'

Shuggie craned across to whisper in his ear. 'He wanted to know if you were here.'

Fraser gulped down his food. 'What did you tell him?'

Shuggie shrugged. 'I don't mess about wi' the likes of McAteer, Gerry.'

'Did he say anythin' else?'

'He told me to tell you to wait for him here. He'll be over in five minutes.'

Fraser stuffed a slice of toast into his mouth and washed it down a slurp of coffee. He scrambled to his feet. 'How much?' he demanded, pointing at his plate.

'Six seventy-five, wi' the extras.' Shuggie placed a restraining hand on Fraser's arm. 'You'd be better off waitin' for him, Gerry,' he whispered forcibly. 'You'll only make things worse for yourself if you try to do a runner.'

Fraser pushed Shuggie's hand aside and dropped seven pounds onto the plastic tablecloth. As he bustled towards the door Shuggie's voice was ringing in his ears. 'What the fuck am I supposed to say to McAteer?'

Fraser trotted along the Gallowgate, glancing over his shoulder every time he heard an engine, hoping it would be a bus. He was breathing hard by the time he reached St Mungo's Academy, and he clung to the iron railings beside the football field as he struggled to get his breath back. He cursed aloud when he saw a bus approaching. 'Too fuckin' late, you useless bastard!' Cutting across the road he headed up Whitevale Street, past the bricked-up swimming baths, his wheezing lungs on fire. He looked over his shoulder to make sure he wasn't being followed before ducking into his close. 'Grab a few things an' head up to Oban,' he panted to himself as he plodded up the worn stone steps. 'Lie low at Andy's place till the heat dies down.'

When he reached the second-floor landing he leaned with his back against the door of his flat as he scrabbled in his coat pocket for his keys, then he suddenly stumbled backwards as the door swung open on its hinges. He stared in terror as his eyes were drawn to the jemmied lock.

'Is that you, Gerry?' He recognised the voice floating out from the kitchen. 'Come on in. I made myself at home. Hope that was all right?'

Fraser heard the slow, rhythmic ring of footsteps coming up the staircase behind him. The hairs on the back of his neck started to crawl and when he spun round he found himself confronted with Billy McAteer's deformed features.

'You're awfy predictable, Fraser.' McAteer's scarred face was leering at him. 'If I'd left a message for you to go home straight away I bet you'd have stayed on at Shuggie's place.' Fraser's eyes darted all around, desperately looking for any way to escape, but before he could make a move McAteer dropped the holdall he was carrying and lunged forward, his fists locking around Fraser's throat and lifting him clean off his feet. He was held dangling at arms' length as his face turned blue, his feet flailing. 'The boss wants a wee word with you.' McAteer laughed in his face. 'Lucky for you that he needs you to be able to talk, otherwise I'd be squeezin' a lot harder than this.' McAteer smiled as he drove his powerful thumbs into Fraser's windpipe, causing him to black out.

Gerry Fraser blinked slowly as he regained consciousness. He recognised his own living room but when he tried to move he found he was bound hand and foot to an upright wooden chair. When he raised his head and blinked again, Billy McAteer's profile came into focus, lying stretched out on the settee in the middle of the room, reading a newspaper and picking his nose. As Fraser stared at the recumbent figure through petrified eyes, he felt his bowels slacken involuntarily.

McAteer scrambled to his feet when he saw Fraser stir. 'He's comin' round, boss!' he called out. Fraser's eyes swivelled towards the living room door when he heard the sound of footsteps approaching from the kitchen.

'You were supposed to deliver the money last night, Fraser,' Mike Harrison snarled. 'Billy waited for you in The Three Judges until closing time. Why didn't you show up?'

'We got nicked in Argyle Street, Mr Harrison,' he whimpered.

'Don't give me that crap! Where's my money?' Harrison towered over the cringing figure, his fist hovering inches from Fraser's jaw.

'I huvny got it, Mr Harrison!'

'Oh, for fuck's sake!' Harrison backed off, wafting his hand underneath his nose. 'What a fucking pong! Have you been shitting your breeks, you dirty wee midden?' Producing a set of knuckle-dusters from his jacket pocket, Harrison slipped them over his fist. 'I'm warning you. This is your one and only chance. What have you done with my money?'

'I huvny got it,' Fraser wailed. 'I'm tellin' you the God's honest truth, Mr Harrison! Devlin and me got nicked in Argyle Street. The cops hung on to the collection box.'

Harrison slammed the knuckle-dusters into Fraser's nose, stepping back quickly to avoid the jet of blood that spurted from the gaping wound. 'You don't expect me to swallow that load of crap!' he yelled in his face. 'Where have you stashed my money, you snivelling wee bastard?'

'I huvny got it! Honest!'

Harrison lashed out again, splitting open both of Fraser's lips. 'Where's Devlin?'

'I don't know,' he whimpered.

'You and Devlin are in this together, aren't you?' Harrison growled. 'You're trying to play me for a mug.'

'No!'

Harrison stood over Fraser with the knuckle-dusters poised. 'Billy phoned me at midnight to tell me you'd done a no-show. He had to interrupt me at a dinner party. I didn't get to my pit until after two o'clock and I've got a very sore heid – and I don't take kindly to having to get up at five in the morning to go chasing after a miserable wee nyaff like you! So, I'm warning you, Fraser. This is your last fucking chance.' Placing the knuckle-dusters under Fraser's chin, Harrison used them to lever up his head. 'Either you tell me right now where my money is or one thing's for sure – your heid's goany be an awful lot sorer than mine.'

'I'm tellin' you the God's honest truth, Mr Harrison.' Fraser spluttered, choking on the blood swilling around in his mouth. 'The cops hung on to the money.'

On Harrison's curt signal, McAteer took a faded yellow duster from his holdall and stuffed it into Fraser's bloodied mouth. Tugging off his jacket, McAteer rolled his shirt sleeves above the elbow, then wrapped Fraser's ponytail tightly around his fist. His whole body tensed as he strained to lift man and chair into the air. The veins on the side of Fraser's neck turned purple and his eyes bulged in their sockets as he swung back and forth, inches off the ground, trying desperately to take in oxygen through his blood-caked nostrils. Rummaging in McAteer's holdall, Harrison produced a large pair of scissors which he used to cut through Fraser's hair at the point where his ponytail joined his scalp, snipping away until only a few strands of hair remained. McAteer's biceps bulged and the tattoo of the Red Hand of Ulster on the back of his fist started throbbing. His whole body was quivering with the effort of supporting Fraser's weight. Beads of sweat glistened on his forehead.

'You can do it, Billy!' Harrison shouted in encouragement, nudging his knee into Fraser's dangling body and causing him to spin round slowly. 'Hang in there! He's going to go any minute!'

There was a manic sparkle of triumph in McAteer's eye as the last remaining strands of Fraser's hair tore out by the roots and his body crashed to the floor, the wooden chair splintering on impact.

'You know the score.' Harrison spat on the moaning figure. 'You're responsible!' he shouted, launching a swinging boot and catching Fraser full in the testicles. 'Make sure he's not holding out on us, Billy.'

As Harrison turned and strode from the room, McAteer pulled a pair of pliers from his holdall.

CHAPTER 4

Niggle was on the phone when Charlie arrived to brief him. Superintendent Nigel Hamilton had acquired his nickname when he was a detective sergeant and it had stuck with him throughout his career. As far as Charlie was concerned, he embodied the worst possible combination – an inferiority complex along with a rank that allowed him to throw his weight around. Charlie had long since concluded that nothing he did would ever please Hamilton, with his round, unsmiling face, his sallow complexion and his narrowly-spaced eyes. Niggle had the irritating habit of continually sucking on his teeth, causing his thin lips to be permanently pursed and contributing to his pedantic manner of speaking – a slow delivery that made Charlie want to finish his sentences for him.

'What was the result of last night's operation, Anderson?' Hamilton demanded as he replaced the receiver.

'The tip-off was good. We arrested a couple of small-time dealers in Argyle Street and we confiscated their money but we didn't lay our hands on any drugs.'

'The object of the exercise was to find the source of the supply. Did you manage to achieve that?'

'We gave the dealers a grilling but they're not talking.'

'So that's a "no"?'

Charlie's eyes narrowed. 'If that's the way you want to look at it.'

'What I want to look at is results!'

Charlie bit into his bottom lip. 'I'll keep you posted, sir.' Spitting out the last word, he strode out of the office.

Simon Ramsay drove down the steep ramps beneath his city-centre office block until he reached the lowest level, where there were only a few vehicles parked. Manoeuvring his Jaguar head-on to the concrete wall he switched off the engine, his eyes glued to the digital clock. He drew hard on his umpteenth cigarette of the morning as he peered through the gloom at the luminous display, swallowing hard as it flicked over to ten o'clock. Snapping open his briefcase he fumbled for his mobile phone and gripped it tightly in his fist as he shivered in the unnerving silence, his gaze continually flitting between the clock and the phone.

It was a further twenty minutes and two more cigarettes before he felt the phone start to vibrate in his palm. On the first trill of the bell he depressed the button to make the connection.

'You got my message?' The voice sounded mechanical, as if disembodied.

'Who the hell is this?'

'If you got my email, you know who it is – Liam Black.'

'How the fuck did you get your hands on that photograph?'

There was a low chuckle. 'That's hardly relevant. As I said in my note, that was just a sample. I've got the full, two-hour, uncensored video.'

The phone was twitching in Simon's trembling fingers. 'What do you want?'

'That's more like it. I'm not an unreasonable man,' the deep, metallic voice intoned. 'I'll settle for fifty grand.'

'You're off your fucking head!' He screamed into the mouthpiece. 'I can't lay my hands on that kind of money!'

'Come on now! Flash pad in Park Terrace, top of the range Jag, round the world cruises, winter skiing in St Moritz.' He chuckled coldly. 'It might take a wee effort, *Simon*.' His name was dragged out. 'But it'll be well worth it.'

'Don't you fucking-well "Simon" me!'

Black's tone changed abruptly. 'You're not calling the shots around here. What do you think your wife'll call you if she sees that photo? It sure as hell won't be "Simon". Probably "Pervert". That suits you right down to the ground. I can see it now – "Pervert Ramsay" – splashed across the front page of the Sunday papers.'

Simon stubbed his cigarette into the already overflowing ashtray and lit up again immediately. 'Nobody would publish it,' he croaked.

'That particular photograph? Probably not. A bit on the crude side for a family newspaper, don't you think? But the tabloids would fall over themselves to get their hands on the story. How much do think I'd get for an exclusive? 'Son-in-law of leading Glasgow stockbroker caught in flagrante'. I reckon that would be worth fifty grand of anybody's money. So you see, I'm not being unreasonable, *Simon* – just asking the market rate.'

'I need time . . . I need time to think,' he blurted out, grabbing a tissue from the packet in his briefcase and using it to dab away the perspiration from his brow.

'It's a bit late in the day for that, Pervert. The time to do your thinking was before you dropped your breeks. Now's the time to focus on how you're going to raise the cash. I want it in used notes – fives, tens and twenties, nothing bigger. You've got forty-eight hours to get the money together. I'll call you at the same time tomorrow and give you instructions for handing it over.'

'You're crazy! I'm telling you I can't lay my hands on that kind of money!'

'Forty-eight hours, Pervert.'The staccato words reverberated in his ear. 'If you don't come up with the cash by Saturday morning the story will break in the Sunday papers. It's up to you. By the way, that's a nasty-looking big plook you've got on your bum. If I were you I'd get that seen to.'The connection was broken.

Simon threw the phone into his briefcase and rammed his cigarette into the ashtray. He started coughing uncontrollably. His whole body was shaking. All the colour had drained from his face and his forehead felt as if it was burning. Firing the ignition, he hammered the gear lever into reverse to pull out of the parking bay, then slalomed up the ramps to street level, tyres squealing. He sped across the city centre as far as Charing Cross but when he reached the bottom of Lynedoch Street he had to slow to a crawl to negotiate the treacherous conditions as he climbed towards Park Terrace. Pulling up outside his house he grabbed his briefcase and took the stone steps two at a time.

Jude was in the kitchen, drinking coffee and flicking through *The Herald*, when she heard the front door being thrown open. She hurried out to the hall. 'What on earth are you doing home at this time?'

'I forgot to print off a report I need for a meeting this afternoon,' Simon said as he head towards the staircase.

'Are you feeling all right?'

'What are you talking about?'

'You look as if you've seen a ghost.'

'A bit hungover, that's all.'

'Do you have time for a coffee?'

'No. Can't stop.' Dropping his briefcase onto the chair in the hall he loped up the stairs. He closed his study door, turned the key in the lock and switched on his computer. Paging quickly through his files until he found the photo he was looking for he hit the print key. He studied the image carefully, then folded the sheet of paper twice and slipped it into the zip-up section at the back of his wallet before reaching for the phone and tapping in a number.

It was answered on the second ring. 'Hello, Laura Harrison speaking.'

'Laura, it's me.' He spoke in a hoarse whisper, his hand covering the mouthpiece.

There was a stunned silence. 'Oh, it's you, Alison. For a minute there I didn't recognise your voice. Shame you couldn't make it to Jude's last night. You missed a good evening.'

'Shit! Is Mike there?'

'That's right.'

'I have to see you!'

'When do they reckon the snow will clear?'

'I have to see you straight away. It's an emergency. Meet me in Rogano's in half an hour.' He hung up without waiting for her response.

'I'm glad you're able to get out and about now.' Laura spoke to the dialling tone. 'Give me a call the next time you're in town and we'll meet up for lunch. Give Norman my love. Bye.' She replaced the receiver slowly.

Simon unlocked the study door and crept down the staircase, taking care to avoid the squeaky step. Opening the front door as quietly as he could he stepped outside and tugged the door shut behind him. When Jude heard the tell-tale click of the Yale lock she went out to the hall. 'In one of our more sociable moods, I see,' she muttered in the general direction of the front door. As she turned back towards the kitchen her eye caught the briefcase lying on the chair. Snatching it up she wrenched the front door open, just in time to see Simon accelerating away from the kerb. She stood on tiptoe and waved the briefcase in the air and she kept on waving until the Jaguar had turned the corner into Park Gate. With a shake of the head she went back to the kitchen and dropped the case on the table. She picked up the phone and dialled Simon's mobile number, spinning around with a start when she heard the ring tone coming from inside the briefcase.

'Brilliant!' She cut the connection and dialled his office number.

'I'd like to leave a message for Simon Ramsay, please.'

'I'm sorry, he won't be in the office today.'

'Really? Are you sure about that?'

'He's taken a few days off. Can anyone else help?'

'No, thanks.'

'Do you still want to leave a message?'

'No message,' Jude said, replacing the receiver.

Laura Harrison slid onto the bench seat in the booth opposite Simon. Rogano's was still quiet, the staff preparing for the imminent lunchtime rush.

'What do you want to drink?' he asked, nodding towards the half-full whisky tumbler clenched in his fist.

'I don't want anything to drink,' she fumed. 'What I want is a bloody explanation! And it had better be good. I've told you a hundred times *never* to call me at home.'

Simon reached into his jacket pocket for his wallet, his eyes darting round the room to make sure no one was observing them. Opening the zipped compartment he produced the sheet of paper which he unfolded and slid across the table.

Every vestige of colour seeped from Laura's bruised face. The photograph had been taken looking down on the bed from above and most of her body was hidden by the naked torso lying on top of her. Her legs, bent at the knees, were splayed on either side of his buttocks and her arms were wrapped around his back, fingernails clawing at his shoulder blades. Her head was lolling on the pillow, her eyes shut, her tongue protruding slightly from parted lips. Simon's face was buried in her neck, his hair falling forward and revealing the bald patch on the crown of his head.

'Where in the name of God did this come from?' she croaked.

'A blackmailer,' he mouthed.

'Jesus wept!' Laura grabbed the whisky tumbler from Simon's hand and poured the contents straight down her throat. 'How the hell did he manage to get hold of this?' she spluttered.

'God only knows!' He spoke in a strangulated whisper. 'It must've been taken in the Hilton. Where else?'

'What can I get you?' The smiling waitress had appeared from nowhere.

Laura quickly placed her handbag on top of the photograph. 'Gin and tonic, please. Make it a large one.'

'Ice and lemon?'

'Yes.'

'Anything else for you, sir?'

'Same again. Glenmorangie. Large,' he said, sliding his empty tumbler across the polished surface.

Laura waited until the waitress had moved out of earshot. 'How did the blackmailer contact you?'

'He sent me that photograph yesterday, attached to an email, then he phoned me this morning.'

'So that's why you were uptight last night?' Simon nodded. 'Why didn't you say anything?'

'Not the easiest thing to slip it into the dinner conversation. Laura, he says . . .' Simon was stammering over his words. 'He says this is only a sample. He claims to have a two-hour video.'

Sliding the sheet of paper from underneath her handbag Laura crumpled it in both hands while staring unseeingly across the room.

'I've had a good look at it,' Simon said. 'From the angle of the shot I reckon there must've been a camera concealed on top of the wardrobe in the hotel room. Someone must have found out about us – where we go and when – and set us up. He must have found some way to install a video camera pointed at the bed and leave it running.'

'What does he want?' Apart from the angry bruising around her eye Laura's features were chalk white.

'Fifty thousand pounds.'

'Or else?'

'He's threatening to sell the story to the tabloids.'

Feeling her stomach starting to heave she dropped the crumpled sheet of paper onto the table and clasped both hands across her mouth to prevent herself from retching as she rocked back and forward on the bench seat. It was a full minute before she tentatively withdrew her hands. 'We'll have to –' She broke off as the waitress arrived with their drinks and placed them on the table in front of them.

'Would you like to see the lunch menu?'

'No!' Simon snapped, waving her away.

'We'll have to pay him off,' Laura whispered. 'I don't see that we have any other option.' Her fingers drifted towards her bruised face. 'You realise that if Mike ever sees that photograph we are both as good as dead?' She spoke in a dispassionate tone. 'You heard his cock and bull story last night about the yobs on the motorbike?'

'What are you talking about?'

She continued to finger her bruised eye. 'Mike did this.'

'What!'

'We were at a friend's housewarming party on Monday night and he got it into his head that I was flirting with someone. I'd been chatting to a bloke for about ten minutes – having a bit of a giggle – nothing more. Mike was pissed out of his brains and when we got back to the car he started ranting and raving about me trying to get off with the guy. When I told him he was talking rubbish he punched me in the face.'

'Jesus!'

'He made me go along with the handbag snatch story to avoid embarrassing questions.'

'Is this the first time he's hit you?'

Laura paused while she poured tonic into her gin. 'To borrow a well-worn cliché – the first time where it shows.'

Simon cupped his whisky glass in both hands. 'Why don't you walk out on him?'

'Oh for God's sake, Simon! Spare me the B-movie routine. I stay with Mike for exactly the same reason you hang in there with Jude. I need someone to pay the bills. But I'm not exaggerating. If he ever gets wind of this . . .' She broke off and tapped the crumpled paper lying on the table. 'If he ever sees that photograph – he'll have no compunction about killing both of us.'

Simon took a deep breath. 'If I'm going to pay the blackmailer off I'll need your help. I can't lay my hands on that kind of money. Jude controls everything. You know that.'

'We're not exactly what you would call flush right now. You heard Mike wittering on about his cash-flow problems last night?' Simon nodded. 'That's not the half of it. The Inland Revenue are conducting an investigation into his affairs and he's about to get landed with a huge bill for back taxes, to say nothing of a hefty fine. A prison sentence isn't out of the question.'

'What in the name of God are we going to do?' Simon downed a stiff swig of whisky.

Tears started forming at the corners of Laura's eyes as she gazed at her drink, her focus locked on the melting ice cubes clinking gently against the sides of the glass. 'Do you not have any idea who's behind this?'

'Not a fucking clue! He said his name was Liam Black.'

Laura forced a mirthless smile. 'Not the most subtle anagram of all time. You didn't recognise his voice?'

'He was using some sort of gadget to distort his speech – made him sound like a Dalek.'

'Which increases the probability that it's someone you know.'

'He certainly knows enough about me. He knows my email address and my mobile number – God only knows how he got hold of that. He knows where I live, what kind of car I drive and even where I go on holiday.'

Laura's fingers strayed back to her swollen cheek. 'How long do we have?'

'Forty-eight hours.' He glanced at his watch. 'Forty-six. He wants the money on Saturday morning.' Simon paused. 'Laura, this isn't the answer. Let's say, for the sake of argument, that we did manage to scrape the money together. What guarantee would we have that that would be the end of it? Even if he gave us the video, how could we be sure he hadn't made a copy? We know for a fact that he's downloaded one image onto a computer. For all we know he might've downloaded the whole video. Paying him off isn't the solution.' Simon swilled down the rest of his whisky. 'This bastard has to be stopped – once and for all.'

'*Stopped? Once and for all?*' Laura stared at him uncomprehendingly. 'Does that mean what I think it means?' she gasped. Simon nodded quickly. 'The very idea is preposterous, Simon. It's totally insane!'

'We have to stop him publishing that photo, Laura.'

'My God!' Laura gulped at her drink. 'This is B-movies gone mad. We can't get involved in anything like that.'

'You said yourself Mike would kill us both if he saw that photo – and I believe you. There's only one way we can make sure that doesn't happen.'

'Stop talking like that! It's utter madness!'

'Do you have any other solution?'

'Can't you stall him? Tell him you'll give him what he's asking for but it'll take you some time to raise the money?'

'He wasn't negotiating. It was pay up on Saturday or the Sunday papers will have the story. Even if I did manage to buy a few more days – and even if we did manage to scrape the money together – what good would that do us? He'll never be satisfied.

As long as he has that video in his possession he has us over a barrel. We have to find a way to deal with him, otherwise Mike is going to see that photo in the Sunday papers.'

Laura clasped both hands to her mouth. There was a long pause before she spoke. 'How on earth do you propose we go about doing it?' she whispered through her fingers, her whole body visibly trembling.

'Jesus Christ! I don't know!' Simon caught the waitress's eye and waved his empty glass in her direction. 'Mike has people like that working for him, doesn't he? Couldn't you get one of them to help us out?' Laura stared at him in disbelief. 'What's the alternative?' he insisted.

'You want *me* to get one of Mike's heavies to commit a murder? Are you out of your fucking mind?'

'I'm thinking of you, Laura. You're the one who'll be in the firing line when Mike sees the Sunday papers. You're the one who'll get the full brunt of his wrath – and you don't need me to tell you what that'll be like.'

'There must be some other solution.'

'I'd love to hear it.'

'I need to think this through,' Laura said, regaining some composure. 'What's the next step?'

'He's going to phone me at ten o'clock tomorrow morning to tell me where and when he wants the money handed over.'

'Give me your lighter,' she said, finishing off her drink. Setting fire to the crumpled sheet of paper, she held it by one corner until the flames had taken hold, then dropped it into her empty glass, watching as it blackened and curled at the edges. 'Play along with him when he calls tomorrow,' she said calmly. 'Tell him you're prepared to pay up.' She tucked her handbag underneath her arm. 'Don't phone me again. I'll get in touch with you tomorrow, sometime after ten.' Angling her legs, she slid out of the booth as the waitress arrived with another large Glenmorangie on a tray.

'I have to see Sergeant O'Sullivan.'

PC Lillian McArthur eyed the slight, nervous figure in the faded denim jacket who had sidled up to the main reception desk in Pitt Street. 'I don't know if he's in the office this morning, sir,' she said.

'I've got to talk to him, hen.' He gripped the edge of the desk and leaned across to whisper in her ear. 'It's awfy important.'

'I'll try his number for you. Who will I say wants to see him?'

'Devlin. Johnny Devlin.'

'Can I tell him what it's about?' she asked as O'Sullivan's extension was ringing out.

'He'll know.'

'Lillian McArthur here, Sergeant. Someone by the name of Johnny Devlin is at main reception. He says he needs to talk to you urgently. Says you'll know what it's about.'

'I'm tied up in a meeting, Lillian. Wheel him along to an interview room and leave him there to sweat it out. Tell him I'll be down in half an hour.'

When O'Sullivan walked into the interview room forty minutes later Devlin was standing by the window, gazing at the traffic struggling to negotiate the icy slope of West Regent Street. He spun round when he heard the door open. His liver-spotted features were ashen.

'What's the panic?' O'Sullivan asked.

'They got Fraser.'

'Who *got* Fraser?'

Devlin's tongue flicked across his cracked lips. 'I need protection.'

'Let's take things one step at a time.' O'Sullivan sat down and took out his notebook, motioning towards the seat on the opposite side of the desk. Devlin walked slowly across the room and slumped down.

'What's this all about?'

'As soon as I was let out this mornin' I tried phonin' Gerry but there was no reply, so I went round to his flat. When I got there I found his front door had been busted open. The place looked like a bomb had hit it.' Devlin's hand twitched back and forward across his mouth as he spoke. 'An' I found Gerry.'

'Found him?'

'Lyin' unconscious on the floor. A chair had been smashed to smithereens an' there was blood everywhere. His face was a fuckin' mess. There were teeth lyin' on the carpet.' Devlin's whole body shuddered. 'I tried to wake him up, but I couldny.'

'What did you do?'

'I phoned 999 for an ambulance and then I fucked off.'

'Why did you leave him?'

'I was scared they might be back.'

'Scared who might be back?'

Naked fear was showing in Devlin's cloudy eyes. He half rose from his chair and leaned across the desk. 'Goany gie us a break, Mr O'Sullivan,' he pleaded. 'I need protection. You've got to tell the papers that the polis got the collection box or else I'll be next. When they didny find the money at Fraser's place they'll think I've got it.'

'First, I'll need a full statement about what you and Fraser were up to in Argyle Street last night, then we'll get round to discussing what protection might be appropriate – and what information we might release to the papers.'

'Jesus Christ!' Devlin sank back down on the chair.

O'Sullivan produced a tape recorder from the top drawer of the desk and having checked the cassette was fully rewound he depressed the 'record' button. 'Thursday the sixteenth of December,' he said into the microphone. He glanced at his watch. 'Two fifteen p.m. This is a recording of an interview between Detective Sergeant Anthony O'Sullivan and Johnny Devlin.' Swinging the microphone round to face Devlin he pointed to the recorder. 'On you go.'

Devlin coughed into his fist and his agitated fingers twitched around his stubbled chin. 'Gerry Fraser an' me were workin' Argyle Street last night,' he mumbled.

'Doing what?'

'Floggin' stuff.'

'What kind of stuff?'

Devlin caught O'Sullivan's eye. 'What do you think?' he mouthed.

'I'm not paid to think.' O'Sullivan pointed towards the tape recorder. 'Answer the question.'

Devlin cast his eyes down to the floor. 'Sherbet,' he said quietly.

'What flavour?'

He shrugged. 'Bit of this – bit of that.'

'How were you selling it?'

'We've got a system. Fraser hangs about outside Marks & Spencer's with a collection box an' the punters give him their orders an' hand over their cash. Fraser gives them a code word an' tells them where to pick the stuff up. Last night, it was from Ted Wilson at a sandwich bar in St Enoch's. Fraser tick-tacks the order to me an' I get on the blower to Wilson an' tell him to get a package ready to hand over when someone with Save the Children stickers stuck to his jacket gives him the code word.'

'Who's Ted Wilson?'

'Fraser's cousin.'

'Where does he live?'

Devlin stared across the desk and shrugged. 'I'm no' sure. Elderslie, I think. Or it might be Johnstone. Somewhere over there.'

'How much did you sell last night?'

Devlin stopped to think. 'There were three big orders and a few footery ones.'

'Who was buying big?' Devlin screwed up his face. 'And what were they buying?'

'Oh for fuck's sake!' he mouthed. O'Sullivan jabbed his finger at the microphone. Devlin rubbed hard at his chin. 'Dan Atherton paid five hundred for half an ounce of China white,' he said. 'Tosh McCulloch picked up a load of crack – canny remember how much he paid – an' someone I've never seen before got three hundred quid's worth of heroin.'

'Who were you selling for?'

Devlin was sweating profusely. 'I have to have protection,' he whined.

O'Sullivan leaned forward and depressed the pause button. 'I said a *full* statement, Devlin. If I'm happy with what I hear, then I'll consider protection.' He released the pause button. 'Who were you selling for?' he repeated.

Devlin moved to the edge of his seat and stared wide-eyed at the revolving cassette. He opened his mouth as if to speak, then shook his head and collapsed back into his chair.

CHAPTER 5

Charlie Anderson depressed the buzzer on his desk intercom. 'Pauline, try to find Tony O'Sullivan and ask him to come to my office.'

Charlie was standing by the window, gazing out at the drifting snow and lost in his thoughts when O'Sullivan's discreet cough jerked him out of his reverie.

Charlie turned round with a start. 'Sorry, Tony, I was miles away.'

'Pauline said you wanted to see me.'

Charlie indicated the seat opposite. 'Got a bit of a sensitive one here. He slid a manila folder across the desk. 'I'd like you to handle it. It appears that the bloke who got stabbed with a syringe at a cashpoint last night was Councillor Frank Mullen.'

'You don't say!' O'Sullivan exhaled noisily.

'Not my favourite person, as you well know, but you still have to feel sorry for the miserable wee sod.'

'Was the needle dirty?'

'They're checking that out.'

O'Sullivan pursed his lips. 'He'll be demanding we bring back the death penalty for this.'

'Absolutely! Nothing less than hanging will do.'

'What do we have to go on?'

'The attacker was a white, male teenager. He assaulted a

young girl at the cashpoint and tried to force her to give him two hundred quid. He told her he needed the money to pay off his dealer. She got a good look at him so she should be able to ID him without any problem. She's downstairs right now giving her statement to Lillian McArthur. The cashpoint should've been covered by CCTV. Have a word with the bank and see what they can come up with.'

DC Colin Renton made a call from his mobile. 'Is that you, Bert?'

'What can I do you for, Mr Renton?'

'Gerry Fraser had a nasty accident this morning. I was wondering if you might know anything about it?'

'This morning, you say?'

'Yes.'

'You know Shuggie Morrison's café in the Gallowgate?'

'Sure.'

'That's one of Fraser's regular hang-outs. He went there this morning for his breakfast.'

'And?'

The voice hesitated. 'Not on the phone. Can you meet me?'

'Where?'

'How about Shuggie's place?'

'What time?'

'Would half-past three be okay?'

'Fine.'

When Renton walked into the café he was eyed up and down by both the owner and the solitary customer. Producing his warrant card he waved it in under Morrison's nose.

'Would you like the all-day breakfast, officer?' Morrison asked, wiping his greasy fingers down his apron front.

'No, thanks. I've already eaten.'

'Cup of tea?'

'Nothing, thanks.'

'What can I do for you then?'

'I believe Gerry Fraser is one of your regulars,' he said, taking out his notebook and pen.

Shuggie hesitated. 'He drops in from time to time.'

'Have you seen him recently?'

Another pause as Morrison exchanged a quick glance with the customer. 'He was in this mornin'.'

'Anybody with him?'

Shuggie shook his head. 'On his tod. He had the full monty,' he added.

'With extras.' The comment had come from the sallow-faced customer sitting on the bench seat by the window, nursing a mug of tea.

'What did you say?' Renton turned to face him.

'Gerry had extra sausage an' an extra egg this mornin', didn't he no', Shuggie?' Bert Tollin tilted back his head and swilled down his tea. 'Said he was starvin'. Said he hadn't eaten anythin' last night.'

'Did he say anything else?'

'No' to me,' Tollin said, getting to his feet and winking at Renton on Morrison's blind side. 'Time I was makin' tracks,' he said, glancing at his watch. 'I've got a cert for the four o'clock at Market Rasen. Do you want a piece of the action, Shuggie?'

'I think I'll take a chance an' pass up the opportunity of a lifetime, if it's all the same to you, Bert.'

'Suit yourself.' Tollin gave a dismissive shrug. 'It's your funeral.'
He shuffled towards the door. 'See you tomorrow, Shuggie.'

'See you, Bert.'

Thanking Morrison, Renton put away his notebook and
stepped outside. He strode along the Gallowgate, catching up
with Tollin opposite the Meat Market. As he drew alongside he
slowed to match Tollin's pace.

'Good information about the drug dealing in Argyle Street
last night, Bert. Inspector Anderson told me to let you know he
appreciated the tip-off.' Tollin nodded without turning to look at
Renton. 'You said on the phone that you might know something
about what happened to Gerry Fraser?'

'Someone phoned the café this mornin', Mr Renton. Shuggie
took the call, then he went over an' whispered somethin' in
Fraser's ear. Gerry looked like he'd seen a ghost. Took off like a
bat out of hell. Didny even finish his breakfast.'

'Do you know who was on the phone?'

Tollin shrugged. 'Might have a wee idea.' Renton fished a
twenty-pound note out of his wallet and slipped it into Tollin's
waiting fist. 'Shuggie shouted after Fraser as he was runnin' out
the door. "What the fuck am I supposed to say to McAteer?"'

Renton caught his breath. 'That wouldn't happen to be Billy
McAteer by any chance?'

'If I was a bettin' man, Mr Renton, I'd be prepared to risk a few
quid on that one.'

'That would explain a lot. You wouldn't happen to know where
Fraser lives?'

'It's not far from here. I don't know the address but I could
show you where his flat is.'

'Thanks.'

'Follow me – but not too close, mind. I've got my reputation to think of.'

Renton gave Tollin a fifty-yard start before following him along the Gallowgate and into Whitevale Road. Turning into Fraser's close, Tollin waited for Renton to catch up before leading the way up the staircase to the second floor.

'It looks like McAteer might've caught up with him already,' Tollin said, pointing towards the splintered door lock. 'I'll leave you to it,' he added, turning round and plodding back down the staircase.

Renton nudged the front door open with his toe cap. When he stepped into the hall he was greeted by a strong smell of dampness and stale tobacco. He eased open the door off the hall and saw the splintered chair and bloodstained linoleum. The stench of excrement permeated the room. Whipping out his handkerchief he used it to cover his nose and mouth. His eyes caught sight of four tobacco-stained teeth, their bloody roots still attached, neatly arranged on the threadbare carpet. Feeling his stomach starting to heave he turned around quickly and ran out of the door and down the stone staircase, gulping for air.

Tony O'Sullivan showed his warrant card to the security guard at the entrance to the St Enoch's Shopping Centre. 'How many sandwich bars are there in there?' he asked.

'Sandwich bars?' The guard looked perplexed. 'Christ, let me think.' Easing back his peaked cap, he scratched at his forehead. 'Just two, as far as I know. Both on the ground floor. One half-way along,' he said, pointing. 'And the other one down the far end.'

'Thanks.'

O'Sullivan walked past the first sandwich bar which was

staffed by three young girls. The small, grey-bearded man behind the counter at the second one was looking harassed. O'Sullivan waited until he'd finished serving his customer before flashing his ID. 'I'm looking for Ted Wilson,' he said.

'You and me both, pal,' he growled.

'Meaning what?'

'You try to give these people a break – and this is the thanks you get,' he complained. 'I got the old sob story from the probation services lassie last week. The guy's just out of jail. He's done his time, paid his debt to society. All the usual guff. I normally tell them to get stuffed – I've got enough misfits in my own family without taking on the rest of the world's. But it's Christmas, I could use an assistant, so I agreed to take Wilson on part time. I do the morning shift, eight to two – and he's supposed to do two to eight. What time is it? Half-past fucking five,' he said, answering his own question, 'and no fucking sign of him. I tried calling his mobile but he's not answering and when I phoned his digs his landlady told me he'd done a runner last night without paying the rent. I'm knackered. I've been on my feet since half-past seven this morning. Where am I going to find someone else in the week before Christmas? The next time I see that wee lassie from the probation I'm going to tell her to go and take a running jump.'

Having asked for Wilson's address and phone number, O'Sullivan extracted himself from the conversation as quickly as he could.

Friday 17 December

Simon Ramsay scraped the last piece of boiled egg from its shell and opened up *The Herald* at the sports pages.

'Busy day in prospect?' Jude asked casually as she stretched across the kitchen table for the coffee pot to refill her cup.

'Looks like it might be a bit of a bugger.' He spoke from behind the newspaper. 'I'll probably be late home tonight.'

'Not too late. Don't forget we're going to the opera.'

'Oh shit!' He crumpled the newspaper in his fists and quickly got to his feet. 'Look – why don't you get someone else to go with you? I can't be sure of getting away from the office in time and it would be a shame to waste the ticket.' Jude didn't respond. 'What do you think?' he insisted.

'Makes sense, I suppose,' she said slowly. She stopped spreading marmalade on her toast and looked him straight in the eye. 'I'll give Laura a call. She'll jump at the chance. Mike was supposed to get them tickets but he conveniently managed to forget because the date happened to clash with one of his poker nights. By the time Laura found out he hadn't booked anything it was sold out. She was spitting blood at the time.'

Simon lifted his jacket from the back of the chair and slipped it over his shoulders. 'That's a good idea. Go with Laura.' He looked at his watch. 'Must run.' He bit the end off a slice of toast and picked up his briefcase. 'If I'm not home before you go out,' he called from the hall, 'have a good time.'

Simon drove across town to the car park beneath his office block and again parked at the lowest level. Glancing at the car clock he saw it was half-past nine. He took out his diary to check a phone number and tapped it into his mobile.

'Could you put me through to Bjorn Svensson, please? He works in the computing department.'

The line clicked and an extension rang. 'Bjorn? It's Simon Ramsay. Sorry to bother you at work.'

'No problem. What can I do for you?'

'I'm looking for a bit of technical advice.'

'Fire away.'

'Someone's trying to wind me up by sending me an email under a false name. I was wondering if there's any way I could find out who actually sent it?'

'Who's his service provider?'

'All I've got is a phoney ID, followed by "hotmail.com".'

'It all depends how much trouble he's gone to.'

'How's that?'

'If he used his own name and address when he set up the ID then Hotmail will have a record of it, but I doubt if they'd give that information out. On the other hand if he used a false name when he established the account I don't think there's any way they would know. It's a free service and a user ID can be set up online without an identity check.'

'I was afraid you'd say something like that.'

'If you're really serious about finding out who sent it, an email can usually be traced back to the originating computer, but if someone wanted to cover their tracks they wouldn't use their own PC. They'd go to an internet café and send it from there. If they did that the most you'd ever be able to find out is what café the message was sent from. I suppose, if the sender paid for his computer time with a credit card, that could be traced, but if he paid in cash you'd be none the wiser. Tell you what, I'll drop round to your place this evening on my way home from work and have a look at the email on your machine. If I play around with it there might be something I can do to trace the source.'

'No thanks. Don't bother.'

'It wouldn't be any trouble.'

'I said – no thanks!' He cut the call quickly.

Simon was still huddled and shivering in his car when his mobile rang on the stroke of ten o'clock. He felt his skin creep as he snapped the phone to his ear.

'Liam Black here,' the disembodied voice intoned. 'Have you got the money?'

'I'll have it by tomorrow.'

'Excellent! I knew you'd see sense, *Simon*. Listen carefully to these instructions. Put the money into a briefcase and drive, on your own, to Kelvin Way tomorrow morning. At eight o'clock precisely, leave your car and take the first entrance to Kelvingrove Park. Follow the path down to the river and cross the footbridge at the bottom of the slope. Just beyond the wrought iron decoration on the right hand parapet of the bridge, drop the case over the side onto the embankment. When you've done that go straight back to your car. Have you got all that?'

'What about the video?'

'When I have the money, you'll get the video.'

'No way! I want the recording in my hands before I hand over any cash.'

'This is not a negotiation, *Simon*.' Again, his name was stretched out. 'You have to trust me on this.' A metallic chuckle echoed down the line. 'Don't get your knickers in a twist. As soon as I have the money your precious video will be in the post. And don't even *think* about getting up to any smart-arsed tricks,' he added. 'If you deviate from these instructions in any way whatsoever the photo will be in the hands of the tabloids in time for a big splash on Sunday.'

The line went dead. Simon sat hunched in his seat, chain-smoking and gnawing at his fingernails, until his phone rang fifteen minutes later.

'It's me.' Laura's voice was calm. 'Did he call?'

'Right on time.' She listened attentively while Simon repeated the instructions for the handover. 'Where the hell do we go from here?' he demanded.

'There's someone I need to talk to. I'll call you back later.'

Laura's phone rang as soon as she'd disconnected. 'Laura, it's me.' She recognised Jude's voice. 'Great news. I've got a ticket for you for the opera tonight.'

'That's very good of you, sis, but I'm really not in the mood.'

'What do you mean, you're not in the mood? You went ballistic when Mike didn't get tickets because it clashed with his poxy poker school!'

'I know. But I've got a stinking headache and I'm absolutely stuffed with the cold. I'm going to have an early night.'

'The hell you are! You'll never get another chance to see this production of *La Traviata*. If you don't feel like driving I'll come over and pick you up.'

'That's very kind of you, Jude, but I really don't think I could face it.'

'I'm not taking no for an answer. Besides, there's something I need to talk to you about.'

'What's that?'

'I'll tell you tonight.'

'But –'

'No buts. I'll pick you up at seven.'

*

Charlie Anderson arrived at the primary school in Dennistoun just before ten-thirty. He introduced himself to the secretary and showed her his warrant card.

'Good morning, Inspector. Miss Appleton told me she was expecting you. I'll show you to her classroom.'

'Thanks.'

Charlie followed the secretary along the wide corridor, the click of her heels echoing noisily off the tiled floor. When they reached the classroom she knocked sharply on the door and waved through the glass panel to Miss Appleton. 'I'll leave you to it, Inspector,' she said, turning away as the door was opened by a sturdy, matronly figure dressed in a brown tweed suit.

Walking into a primary school classroom for the first time in fifty years, Charlie was greeted by the animated chatter of ten-year-olds in groups of three or four, poring over large maps of the world spread out over their desks – a far cry, he thought, from the silence and regimented rows of his youth. Clare Appleton smiled warmly as she shook his hand.

'Thanks for agreeing to let me talk to them,' Charlie said.

'Not at all, Inspector. Dreadful business about John.' Charlie saw the emotion welling up in her eyes, but she composed herself quickly. 'All I've told them is that a senior policeman would be coming to talk to them this morning,' she explained. 'They do know it's about John,' she added in a hushed tone. She lowered her voice even further. 'John's best friends were Tommy McPhee, red pullover, second from the front, by the window and Lachlan Brown, striped jumper, sitting behind Tommy.'

'Thanks,' Charlie nodded. 'This'll only take a couple of minutes.'

'Boys and girls.' Clare Appleton clapped her hands to get their attention. 'This is the policeman I told you about. His name is

Detective Chief Inspector Anderson and he works for the Glasgow Police.' The buzz of conversation died away and all the curious eyes turned towards Charlie. 'He's come to ask you for your help so please give him your full attention.'

'Thank you, Miss Appleton.' Charlie turned to the class. 'You all know that John O'Hara died last month,' he stated. 'And you know his death was caused by taking drugs.' A murmur ran round the room. 'I'm not here this morning to tell you about the dangers of getting involved with drugs. You know all about that already. What I'm trying to do is find out who sold John the drugs and for that I need your help. What I want to know is if any of you saw John talking to a stranger near the school.' Charlie's gaze travelled slowly round the silent room, his stare settling on Tommy McPhee and Lachlan Brown. McPhee was making full eye contact and shaking his head from side to side, but Brown had looked away and was staring out of the window.

Charlie turned back to the rows of blank faces. 'You might not be able to recall anything straight away but if you remember anything after I've gone, please tell Miss Appleton and she'll pass the information on to me,' he said with a reassuring smile as the bell for the morning break clanged loudly down the corridor.

'Is that everything, Inspector?' Miss Appleton asked. Charlie nodded. 'All right, children. You can go out now. Now remember – no running in the corridors!' she said sharply as they filed quickly out towards the playground.

'Sorry, Inspector. Not much help, I'm afraid.'

'I wasn't expecting anything straight away – but someone might remember something later.'

'Do you want to see your daughter while you're here?' she asked. 'She's in classroom 5.'

'No, thanks. I won't disturb her – but if it's possible I would like to have a couple of minutes with Lachlan Brown after the interval.'

'Do you think he might know something?'

'I'm not sure – just a gut feeling.'

'The staff room will be free after the break . I'll show you where it is and I'll send Lachlan along.'

Lachlan Brown knocked timidly on the staff room door and entered on Charlie's call. Charlie was seated at the far end of the large, rectangular table. 'Sit down, son.' Lachlan looked all around the room, as if afraid to take a seat. 'It's okay, Lachlan. There's nothing to worry about. I just want to talk to you about John.' Apprehensively, Lachlan took the seat next to Charlie. 'I'm told you and John were best friends?' Lachlan nodded, tugging a lock of curly brown hair back from his forehead. 'Did you ever see John talking to a stranger near the school?' Lachlan shook his head quickly. 'Has anyone ever tried to sell you drugs, Lachlan?' His muttered 'no' was barely audible. 'I know how these guys operate, son. They tell you drugs are great, exciting – real grown up stuff. They give you some to try and then when you want more they demand money – a lot of money. They tell you to steal the money from your parents, or from anyone else, and they warn you they'll beat you up if you mention anything about this to your parents or your teacher – and if you shop them to the police they threaten to mark you for life.' Lachlan's fingers were twitching on his knees as he gazed down at the floor. 'I wouldn't ask anybody to risk that, son, but you remember what happened to John?' A whimper escaped from Lachlan's clenched teeth.

'You wouldn't want that to happen to anybody else, would you?' Lachlan shook his head slowly from side to side as he fought to hold back the tears. 'However, if you don't know anything, then you won't be able to help me,' Charlie said. 'I understand that.'

Getting to his feet, Charlie took a batch of photographs from his jacket pocket and let them spill onto the floor. 'Damn! My photos are all mixed up now,' he said. 'Do me a favour, Lachlan. I need to go to the bathroom. While I'm away could you pick up my photos and try to sort them into order for me? When you've done that just leave them on the table and go back to your classroom.' Lachlan held full eye contact, nodding slowly. 'That would be very helpful, son.'

A few minutes later Charlie returned to the staff room and picked up his photos from the desk. He studied the one on top of the pile and nodded in grim satisfaction. 'Thanks, Lachlan,' he muttered.

'Last bed on the left, Sergeant.'

Putting away his warrant card and thanking the nurse, Tony O'Sullivan walked the length of the ward until he came to the bed where Gerry Fraser was sitting up, his back propped against two pillows. Fraser was dressed in a hospital bed gown and a hypodermic needle, attached to a drip feed, was bandaged into his left forearm. His face was a mass of black and blue, his nose twisted, his lips swollen and lacerated.

O'Sullivan pulled out the bedside chair which bounced and squeaked gratingly on its rubber castors. He sat down and took out his notebook. 'The doctor tells me you had a bad fall, Fraser.'

Fraser's neck craned in O'Sullivan's direction. He inclined his head slightly in recognition. 'Like I said to the doc, I was tryin'' to change a light bulb,' he mumbled. O'Sullivan winced when he saw the stitches protruding from Fraser's swollen gums. 'An' the fuckin' chair I was standin' on gave way.'

'You fell on your face?' Fraser nodded slowly. 'And you tore out four teeth?'

'So it seems.'

'By the roots?' Fraser shrugged. 'And I suppose your ponytail broke off as well?'

'Thought I'd go for a change of style this Christmas. I hear ponytails are right out of fashion.'

'Who did this to you?' Fraser gazed back in silence through sad, red-rimmed eyes. 'What are you trying to prove?' O'Sullivan insisted. Fraser's eyelids drooped. Getting to his feet, O'Sullivan flicked his notebook closed and slipped it back into his pocket. He leaned across the bed to look Fraser straight in the eye. 'Don't you want them put away?'

Fraser's eyelids flickered as he turned his head and stared vacantly across the ward at the empty bed opposite. With a shake of the head O'Sullivan spun on his heel and cursed softly as he strode back down the ward.

The mid-afternoon traffic was light as Laura Harrison drew up outside the Rosevale Tavern in Dumbarton Road and signalled to the figure huddled in the pub doorway, sheltering from the sleet. When Billy McAteer saw the Rover pull up he folded his *Sporting Life* and balanced it on top of his head as he lumbered towards the vehicle.

Laura looked anxiously up and down the street. 'Get in. Quickly!' she snapped, throwing open the passenger door. McAteer stooped to lever his frame into the car and had hardly

time to yank the door closed before the car revved away from
the kerb. Running an amber traffic light, they turned into Crow
Road.

'What's the panic?' McAteer asked, clipping on his seat belt
as they accelerated hard past Sainsbury's towards the top of the
hill.

'I need you to deal with someone for me,' Laura said, checking
in her rear-view mirror to make sure they weren't being followed.

McAteer gnawed at the torn quick of his thumbnail as he
gazed across at her. 'What, exactly, do you mean by "deal with"?'

'I don't care how you do it.' Laura was struggling to control the
tremble in her voice. 'In fact, I really don't want to know anything
about it. The only thing is . . .' Her knuckles were white as she
gripped hard on the steering wheel. 'It has to be permanent.'

'*Permanent*, is it?' McAteer whistled softly and turned square
on in his seat to study her tense profile. '*Permanent* doesn't come
cheap.'

'How much?'

McAteer stroked his chin reflectively as if he'd never considered
that question before in his entire life. 'You'd be looking at ten
grand.'

Checking her rear-view mirror again Laura filtered left into
Broomhill Drive. 'Okay. Ten thousand it is. But it might take me
a week or two to raise the money.'

McAteer furrowed his scarred forehead. 'I don't work for tick,
Mrs Harrison.'

'Ten thousand's a lot to come up with. I assume you'll be
wanting it in cash?' she added.

He continued to study her tight-lipped profile. 'Like I said, I
don't do tick.'

'I'll need to take out a loan to raise the money,' Laura said, pulling out to overtake a slow-moving lorry. 'In itself, that won't be a problem. However, I don't want to do it through the bank, so it might take me a few days to get it organised.'

'In which case I'll deal with your problem when you've got the money.'

'It has to be tomorrow, Billy.'

'Tomorrow!' McAteer sat back in his seat, mulling this over and chewing hard on his thumbnail as they looped back down the hill. 'Okay,' he nodded as they were about to rejoin Dumbarton Road. 'I suppose your credit's good. But just a few days, mind. One week – that's the limit.'

Laura stopped at a red traffic light and turned to face him. 'This has to remain strictly between us.' Her face was flushed. 'Mike must never get wind of this.'

McAteer chortled. 'I didn't think you were giein' me a hurl in your new motor to impress me wi' your drivin'.' Laura spun back round to face the road. 'What's the score?' he asked.

'What do you mean?'

'I mean, who has to be "dealt with"?'

'A blackmailer.'

'You're being blackmailed?'

'Not me – a friend.'

'Does your friend have a name?'

'Does he have to?'

McAteer shrugged and grinned. 'I suppose not.'

As they crawled along Dumbarton Road, hopping from one red light to the next, Laura explained the handover instructions.

'Following the blackmailer after the pick-up won't be easy,' McAteer mused. 'Likely as not he'll have transport lined up. And he'll be on the lookout for anyone tryin' to tail him. He's picked a good spot.' He nodded his approval. 'Kelvingrove Park's got a lot of wide open spaces.'

'Can you handle it?'

'Yes,' he stated confidently. 'Tell your friend to follow the instructions and drop an empty briefcase over the side of the bridge. Leave the rest to me.'

As they were approaching the Rosevale Tavern from the opposite direction McAteer unclipped his seat belt and gripped the door handle.

Darkness was starting to fall as Simon Ramsay shivered alongside three other smokers at a wooden trestle table outside The Rock in Hyndland Road, a bottle of Budweiser in one hand and a half-smoked cigarette in the other. When his mobile started to ring he got to his feet and distanced himself from the other smokers before taking the call.

'It's Laura. Everything's taken care of.' Her voice was trembling.

'What does that mean?'

'All you have to do is follow the instructions and drop an empty briefcase over the side of the bridge.'

'What'll happen then?'

'The blackmailer will be taken care of.'

'Who by?'

'A guy called McAteer. He works for Mike.'

'What's this McAteer character going to do?' Simon demanded.

'I have no idea!' Laura's voice was on the point of cracking. 'And I don't fucking-well care!' He could hear her fighting to hold back the tears.

'Okay, Laura. Try to stay calm. Sorry! I didn't mean to snap. I'm on edge, too. Is McAteer going to get the video for us?'

'He doesn't know anything about a video.'

'What are we going to do about that?'

'That question has been uppermost in my mind all day – believe you me!' Her words were coming in bursts between gulps for breath. 'We'll have to worry about that later. When the police find the body, presumably they'll be able to identify him. Once we know his name and address we'll have to break into his house and recover the recording – or . . . or . . . something . . .' Heavy sobs came pulsing down the line. 'Oh, for Christ's sake, Simon! I don't know!'

'It's okay, Laura,' he said soothingly. 'Take it easy. You've done brilliantly. Once the blackmailer's out of the way we'll find a way to get the video. Don't worry. I'll follow the instructions to the letter.'

It was Laura who broke the connection.

'We've got it all on film, sir.' Tony O'Sullivan walked into Charlie Anderson's office and placed a report on his desk. 'Good clear footage from the bank's CCTV cameras. Especially of Councillor Mullen copping his lot,' he added.

'What's the latest on him?' Charlie asked.

'Nasty stab wound in the side of his neck, but it looks like his pride will be the biggest casualty. It appears that the needle was clean.'

'Thank Christ for that!'

'Of course that hasn't stopped him blowing his proverbial top. All the usual guff. No policemen in the vicinity when they're needed. Any law-abiding citizen walking the streets of Glasgow after dark does so in fear of his life, etc, etc. He's called a press conference for eight o'clock tonight to give vent to his spleen.'

'I've got a lot more important things to worry about than Frank Mullen's temper tantrums. How's the lassie who was assaulted making out?'

'She's quite badly traumatised. Her ear's lacerated and she got two skint knees and a split lip for her trouble, but it doesn't look like there will be any permanent injury. She's given us a statement and a counsellor's talking to her.'

'Have we managed to identify who did it?'

O'Sullivan patted the report on the desk. 'It's all in there. His name's Tommy Hemphill, nineteen years old, never been employed, lives with his parents in Ferguslie Park.'

'Ferguslie Park! Why does that not surprise me?'

'He's got three previous convictions for substance abuse,' O'Sullivan continued. 'His mother claims she hasn't seen him at all in the past couple of months. According to her he went down to London in October to look for a job and she hasn't seen hide nor hair of him since. We're keeping the house under observation.'

'Okay, keep me posted. No doubt I'll get a call from Mullen before the day is out demanding to know if we've made an arrest yet'.

'Anything else, sir?'

'No, I think that's it. Still all right for tonight?'

'Sure. What time do you want me round?'

'I think Kay's planning on eating about eight. Tell you what, why don't you leave your car here and come with me? That'll give you the chance to unwind and have a few bevvies.'

'I was planning to go home first and get changed.'

'On your way, then. I've got a couple of things to finish off here. I'll pick you up at the bottom of Wilton Street at seven.'

Tony hesitated. 'Will I be able to get transport back into Glasgow?'

'Sue'll give you a lift. She has to go across town on her way home.'

'Sue?'

'My daughter.' Charlie picked up a silver-framed photograph from his desk and handed it across. 'She's coming round tonight as well. Did I not mention that?'

'Don't think so, sir.'

O'Sullivan studied the picture of a tall girl in her late twenties with shoulder-length, straight black hair tumbling down over one eye. Her broad nose was slightly crooked and she had an engaging smile. She was wearing fell boots, figure-hugging red jeans and an open-necked jacket. Beside her stood a tousle-haired boy wearing a faded goalkeeper's jersey several sizes too big for him, his arms crossed in front of his chest, his foot balanced on a football.'

'I took that one a couple of years back in Braemar,' Charlie said. 'Jamie will be seven on Sunday. He takes after me, you know,' Charlie stated proudly. 'He wants to be a goalkeeper, like his grandfather. In my youth, I used to play in goal. I wasn't too bad, even if I say so myself – only junior level, mind. I had a couple of senior trials but they never came to anything. Despite the arthritis I can still give the ball a fair whack as long as I don't have to go running around after it. There's nothing Jamie likes better than his grandfather firing shots at him for hours on end.'

'What does your daughter do?' Tony asked.

'She's a primary school teacher in Dennistoun. That's where she met her husband. He taught there as well. Once a month

Paul's parents take Jamie off Sue's hands for the weekend and she usually comes over to our place on the Friday night.'

'Won't Sue be wanting to unwind as well?' Tony asked, handing back the photo.

'She's teetotal. She used to enjoy the odd glass of wine but ever since Paul was –' Charlie broke off and studied the photograph. 'Ever since Paul was killed,' he said with a sigh, 'she hasn't touched a drop – whether she's driving or not. Paul was stone cold sober that night but the other driver was three times over the limit.

'It's bizarre the effect drunk drivers have had on my life.' Charlie took care to replace the photograph in exactly the same position on his desk. 'If it hadn't been for the idiot that ran into DCI Williams' car I'd be happily retired now, tending cabbages in my allotment. And if it hadn't been for the moron that crashed into Paul's car,' he added with a shake of the head, 'my grandson would still have a father.'

Jude Ramsay went up to the bar to collect the interval drinks, then carried the tray across to the table in the corner where Laura was waiting.

'Your cold doesn't seem to have come to much,' Jude said, handing Laura her gin and tonic.

'It seems to have dried up but my head's still throbbing like hell.'

'What did you think of the first half?'

'Very good.'

'Glad I dragged you out?'

Laura smiled sheepishly and nodded as she started to pour the tonic into her gin. 'You said on the phone there was something you wanted to talk to me about?'

Jude lowered her voice. 'Simon's screwing around.'

'What!' Laura froze in mid-pour.

'He's got something going on the side.'

'What makes you think that?' Laura asked hesitantly.

'For the past few months the poor little darling has been too exhausted to do anything in the sack.'

Laura continued pouring her tonic slowly. 'Mike's gone through phases like that. It doesn't necessarily mean he's screwing around.'

'He was supposed to be at work yesterday but when I phoned his office I was told he'd taken time off.'

'There might be some innocent explanation.'

'Come on, Laura! You don't have to stick up for him.'

Laura sipped at her drink. 'Have you confronted him with this?'

'Not yet. I'm biding my time.'

Laura hesitated. 'Any idea who it might be?'

'I'm pretty sure it's his assistant, Maureen. The randy little slut could hardly keep her hands off him at last year's office party.'

CHAPTER 6

'Your steak pie was every bit as good as my mother's, Mrs Anderson.'

'There is no higher praise, Tony,' Kay said. 'What do you think, Sue?' Kay turned to her daughter who was pouring coffee and handing round the cups. 'This must be one for the *Guinness Book of Records*. I do believe it's the first time in his life that your father has gone through a whole meal without once talking shop.' She ignored Charlie's pained expression. 'Then again, it's not every day he has someone who'll discuss football with him all night.'

'Sugar, Tony?' Sue asked.

'Please. Two lumps.'

A click and a loud bang came echoing from the kitchen, followed by a high-pitched plaintive wail. Tony stopped in mid-stir. 'A cat flap, I presume?' His question was answered by a bedraggled jet-black shape appearing in the doorway, its long hair glistening with moisture, its spindly tail erect.

Blakey froze for a moment, surveying the room, before padding over to Sue and rubbing his back up and down against her leg. Putting down the coffee pot Sue took a tissue from her handbag to dry his fur, then lifted the cat gently and draped him over her shoulder. 'This was my fifteenth birthday present, Tony,' she said, scratching gently at the top of Blakey's head as he hung languidly on her shoulder, pink tongue protruding slightly, purring softly.

'You didn't take him with you when you moved out?'

'It wouldn't have been fair on him. When I was at university I shared a flat with three other girls and by that time he was used to a house and a garden. Not that I'd have had much chance of dragging him away from Dad, even if I'd wanted to,' she added.

'Too bloody right!' Charlie snorted and leaned across to chuck Blakey under the chin. 'Many's the time you and I have put the world to rights over a few glasses of malt, haven't we, old boy?'

'I'm back in a house now and I've got a garden,' Sue said, 'but I can't imagine for one minute that Blakey would want to swap his life of luxury here for Jamie trying to tear lumps out of his fur. Would you, my big, spoiled lump?' she said, rubbing harder at Blakey's head, the volume of the purring rising in a crescendo. Levering the cat from her shoulder, Sue untangled his extended claws from her sweater and placed him gently down on the carpet.

'By the way, he was there again this afternoon, Dad,' Sue said, catching a strand of loose hair as she straightened up and hooking it firmly behind her ear. 'I'm talking about Tosh McCulloch, Tony,' she explained. 'He's well known in this family. He and I were in the same class in primary school. His parents still live round the corner in Marjory Road. When I come out of school at four o'clock I often see him hanging around the playground gates. I'm sure he's trying to sell the kids drugs.'

'A ten-year-old boy in Sue's school died last month.' Charlie's eyes were harder than Tony had ever seen them. 'Cocaine overdose. I know in my guts that McCulloch was the supplier and if I ever manage to prove it I'll strangle him with my bare hands, so help me God!'

'Don't let him get to you, Dad,' Sue said. 'He's not worth a heart attack.'

'According to Johnny Devlin,' Tony said, 'McCulloch was buying crack on Wednesday night.'

'And selling it on to primary school kids!' Sue said, tossing back her hair. 'What chance do the poor wee beggars have?'

'I'm going to have that bastard,' Charlie growled, the colour flaring up in his cheeks and his knuckles turning white as he gripped hard on the sides of his chair.

'You're getting yourself worked up, Charlie,' Kay said. 'Let's change the subject. Sue, what do you have planned for the weekend?'

'A few of us from school are going skiing in Aviemore. We're setting out at the crack of dawn tomorrow. Most of the crowd are staying over but I'm coming back tomorrow night to pick up Jamie because I've got a houseful coming round for his birthday party on Sunday.'

'Don't you mean *Rainday*?' Tony suggested.

'You've heard?' Sue laughed. 'I hope you haven't forgotten, Dad? Jamie's expecting you across on *Rainday* morning to play football with him.'

'Don't worry your pretty little head about that, my girl! I'll be there come hell or high water,' he said, getting up from the table to stretch his spine. 'I'll come over early, love – round about half-past eight. Don't bother getting up. You could probably use a lie-in after the skiing.'

Sue took a sip of coffee and glanced at her watch. 'Hey! Is that the time? Sorry to break up the party, Tony, but I really ought to be making tracks. I'm setting off at six-thirty in the morning.'

'Fine by me. It's been a long, hard week.' Quickly finishing his lukewarm coffee, Tony got to his feet. 'Mrs Anderson, thank you again for an excellent meal.'

'Thank *you* for the flowers, Tony.'

Standing on the doorstep, Tony took Charlie's hand in a firm grip. 'Great evening, sir. I really enjoyed myself.'

'I still insist Davie McParland was every bit as good as Jimmy Johnstone.'

'You cannot be serious! No one could destroy a full back like Jinky.'

'How would you know? You're too young ever to have seen him play.'

'I've seen more newsreels and television clips of Jinky than I've had hot dinners. Rain, hail or snow, my father travels up from Saltcoats for every Celtic home game. Other kids might've got bedtime stories, but my abiding childhood memory is of my father sitting on the edge of my bed describing in painstaking detail every run Jinky ever made. Anytime you'd like the full ninety-minute commentary on the 1967 European Cup final, I'm your man.'

'I'd rather hear about the 1971 League Cup final when Partick Thistle stuffed Celtic 4–1. What a match that was! Alan Rough played an absolute blinder.'

'1971! Is that the last time Thistle won anything? My God, that's before I was born.'

'Which doesn't seem to impair your ability to recite chapter and verse about what happened in 1967 when it happens to suit you!'

'Worse than a pair of old fishwives,' Sue said, buttoning up her coat and dangling her car keys in front of Tony's nose. 'If you've both quite finished bickering?'

'I was just getting warmed up,' Charlie complained. 'Are you working this weekend?' he asked, turning back to Tony.

'I've booked time off. Anne was supposed to be coming up for a few days.' His freckles flushed. 'Are you on duty?'

'Not officially, but I'll have to drop into the office for a few hours over the weekend to clear some of the paperwork. I've got a backlog that would choke a horse.'

'Where exactly do you live?' Sue asked as they were merging with the light traffic on the M8.

'Wilton Street. Do you know it?'

'Sure. What's the best way from here?'

'Clyde Tunnel, up Balshagray Avenue, Crow Road and along Great Western Road.'

'Then cut up Queen Margaret Drive?'

'That's it. My flat's behind the old BBC buildings.'

'You must be the blue-eyed boy,' Sue said with an impish grin as she pulled out to overtake an articulated lorry.

'What do you mean?'

'It's only once in a blue moon that Dad invites a work colleague home for dinner.'

'I reckon he was feeling sorry for me. I've just split up with my fiancée.'

'So Mum told me. Sorry to hear that.' Cutting back in from the middle lane, Sue indicated left for the slip road to the Clyde Tunnel. 'Was the break-up on account of the job?'

Tony shrugged. 'Part of the reason, I suppose. Anne and I had been going out together for a long time – ever since fifth year in school. She's a nurse down in Kilmarnock and for the last six months it seemed that every time she was off duty I was working – and vice versa.' He paused. 'But I reckon pressure of work was a convenient rationalisation for both of us. We'd been drifting apart for some time. But look on the bright side,' he added cheerfully. 'At least we managed to bail out before we got hitched.'

'There's nothing puts more strain on a relationship than being married to a copper,' Sue stated emphatically.

'Was your husband not a teacher?'

'I wasn't referring to Paul. I meant Dad. I've lived through it with Mum for years. She worries herself sick in case he gets caught up in the violence. Do you know that in more than thirty years of marriage she's never once gone to sleep before he's come home? He doesn't even realise it. Most of the time she lies awake in bed in the dark until she hears his car, then she pretends to be asleep when he comes upstairs.'

'Doesn't he call and let her know when he's going to be late?'

'Hey! Don't run away with the wrong impression. He's very good about phoning – a lot better than most. But often it's not practical. I don't have to tell you that. Especially in the pre-mobile days – not that Dad has got the hang of those, of course!' Tony smiled. 'It's ironic. Mum worries herself sick about Dad and, touch wood,' Sue said, flicking her fingertips off her forehead, 'the worst that's ever happened to him was a dislocated shoulder when he tried to rugby tackle an intruder. On the other hand I never had a day's worry about Paul and he got himself killed on the way home from a Thursday evening PTA.'

They drove the length of Moss Road in silence.

'Do you know you get a wish if you can hold your breath all the way through the Clyde Tunnel?' Tony said.

'I didn't know that!' Sue's eyes lit up. 'I can never resist a challenge.'

The northbound tunnel was closed for maintenance work and they were diverted towards the southbound where one lane was open in each direction. Taking a deep breath as she approached the tunnel entrance Sue dropped down a gear and slammed her foot to the floor, Tony gripping the edge of his seat and sucking as much air as he could into his lungs as they accelerated down the slope. When they reached the low point in the tunnel they glanced across at each other's bulging cheeks, trying desperately not to laugh. Half-way up the incline they closed in on a refuse disposal vehicle and Sue had to stand on the brakes. They slowed to a crawl. Tony was the first to crack, the breath exploding from his body as he convulsed in laughter, Sue lasting a few seconds longer.

'I was doing fine until you started to laugh,' Sue spluttered as they reached the tunnel exit. Flicking her indicator, she slewed off to the left.

'Wrong way,' Tony said, looking back over his shoulder and pointing. 'It was straight on there,' he said. 'Up Balshagray Avenue.' Sue said nothing as she looped over the intersection and rejoined the tunnel slip road in the opposite direction. 'Where are we going?'

'No stinking rubbish lorry's going to do me out of getting my wish. Hold on tight!' Sucking in her breath Sue hammered the car into third gear. Her lungs were on fire by the time they hit the bottom of the dip and her cheeks swelled up like balloons as they sped up the incline. 'Made it!' she gasped in triumph as they roared out of the tunnel. 'Did you?'

'Just about,' Tony panted, his chest heaving as he spluttered for air. 'But I think I left my stomach somewhere underneath the river.'

'Don't worry. We can pick it up on the way back.'

They had to travel half a mile along Moss Road, as far as the Shieldhall roundabout, before they could execute a U-turn,

Tony chortling all the way, Sue with tears of laughter streaming down her cheeks.

'No fun this time,' Sue said with mock petulance as they re-entered the tunnel behind a line of slow-moving vehicles. 'Still, mustn't be greedy,' she said, dragging her hair behind her ear and brushing the tears of laughter from her eyes with the back of her hand. 'At least we both got one wish.'

'What did you wish for?'

'You mustn't ask. If you tell anyone what you wished for it doesn't come true.'

The main roads were clear of snow but there was a fair amount of slush in Wilton Street when Sue pulled up outside Tony's tenement block.

'Isn't this where I'm supposed to invite you up for coffee?' he asked.

'Can I take a rain check?' Sue smiled disarmingly. 'I really am whacked. And I do have a very early start.'

'Of course. Do you do a lot of skiing?'

'Not really. In my case it's more a matter of slithering down the slopes on my backside. That's how I got this,' she said, tapping the side of her nose. 'A couple of years ago at Aviemore I aquaplaned for twenty yards on my bum before slamming head first into a tree. When they reset my nose they didn't quite manage to get it straight.'

'If you don't enjoy it, why do you keep going back?'

'I don't really know. Because I enjoy the company, I suppose. I much prefer hillwalking, but it's hardly the weather for that.'

'I know.' Sue looked at him quizzically. 'I saw a photo of you in your walking gear,' he explained. 'Your father has it in pride of place on his desk.'

'He hasn't still got that old photo in the office?' Sue shook her head. 'I must have given him at least three more recent ones. I'm telling you, he doesn't hang on to that photo because of me. It's Jamie in a goalkeeper's jersey that turns him on. I'm sure he has secret fantasies about Jamie playing for Partick Thistle and Scotland.'

'Alan Rough reincarnate.' Tony nodded sagely. 'Now that would be something.'

'You're every bit as bad as he is! Be off with you!'

Tony hesitated as he gripped the door handle. 'Sue, if this is out of order, just say.'

'What?'

'I've got a couple of tickets for the Radiohead concert next week. To be frank, I got them as a surprise present for Anne. I was wondering . . . If you happen to be free?'

'I love Radiohead.'

'Have you ever seen them live?'

'I went to the Glastonbury gig a few years back. They were incredible. However, before we take this any further, I have to nail my colours to the mast. I can't stand "Creep".'

'That's all right, neither can they. What do you think of *Kid A*?'

'Not their best.'

'Oh, come on! "Idioteque" is the best thing they've ever done.'

'Not a patch on "Fake Plastic Trees".'

'There's no accounting for taste.'

'We may not be able to resolve this tonight,' Sue said. 'When are they on?'

'Monday night.'

'Is that the twentieth?'

'I think so.'

'Shit! That's the night of the school nativity play. I can't opt out of that. I'm everything from director and producer to set designer and costume maker, to say nothing of joint script writer with Matthew.'

'Is he a teacher?'

'An apostle. He has all the grandiose lines like: 'Unto us, this day, a child is born' and I get to customise them by adding "in Dennistoun".'

'What happened to Bethlehem?'

'Unfortunately, Bethlehem no longer conjures up the magic of Christmas. If six-year-olds these days know anything about Bethlehem it's a place where Arabs get murdered by Jews, or vice versa. Anyway, basing it in Dennistoun gives the story more relevance for the kids.'

'Must make it tricky finding three Wise Men.'

'The Wise Men don't come from Dennistoun,' she pouted. 'They come from the East.'

'Riddrie's not necessarily an improvement.' Sue laughed out loud. 'In any event,' Tony added, 'I recommend you switch the action to Paisley.'

'Why Paisley?'

'According to last month's social work reports, Paisley's got the highest incidence of pregnant virgins in Scotland.'

'I'll bear that in mind for next year.'

'I didn't think it was politically correct to put on nativity plays these days. Doesn't that offend the Sikh and Muslim communities?'

'Give me a break! We're talking about a Catholic primary school in Dennistoun, for goodness sake! Sikhs and Muslims are welcome – as long as they can recite all five decades of the rosary.

That's a joke, by the way,' she added quickly. 'I thought I'd better point that out before you send the PC storm troopers crashing down on us. We actually cater for all religions – except Proddies, of course,' she said with a mischievous grin. 'Getting back to Monday night, what time does the gig start?'

'I'm pretty sure it's eight o'clock.'

'The nativity play will be over by seven. I should be able to find a babysitter without any problem and if I can sweet-talk someone on the skiing trip into staying behind and locking up the school hall I might be able to get away in time. Where are they playing?'

'Glasgow Green.'

Sue reached over to the back seat for her handbag and dug out a notepad and pen. 'Take this,' she said, scribbling down her phone number and ripping out the page. 'If you can give me a call on Sunday afternoon I'll be able to let you know if I've managed to sort something out.'

'Fine.'

Tony's fingers stayed in contact with Sue's hand for a few seconds longer than necessary as he took the slip of paper.

'Thanks for the lift,' he said.

'Thank *you* for the chocolates.'

Tony's freckles flared up as he pushed open the car door and stepped out onto the pavement, taking care to avoid the large puddle of slush.

'A very nice young man,' Kay said, slipping off her dressing gown and sliding under the duvet next to Charlie. 'Very well mannered.'

Putting down the *Evening Times*, Charlie peered over the top of his reading glasses.

'That wasn't the first time you've spoken to him.'

'We've talked on the phone a couple of times, but never what you'd call social chit-chat. He only ever calls here when there's a panic on.'

'He seemed to enjoy himself.'

'That was a lovely bunch of flowers he brought me. And very thoughtful of him to get Sue a box of chocolates.'

Slipping off his spectacles, Charlie leaned across to switch off his bedside lamp. 'Kay Anderson – I hope you're not matchmaking?'

Charlie folded his arms over his head to protect himself from the flailing pillow.

Saturday 18 December

It was almost three o'clock in the morning when Billy McAteer turned off Argyle Street into Haugh Road and pulled up by the kerb. Switching off the Volvo's headlights he got out of the car and, having checked there was no one in sight, he opened the boot, kicked off his trainers, took out his Wellington boots and tugged them on over his black, shell suit trousers. Large snowflakes, caught in an up-draught, were swirling and billowing around the yellow street lamps high above his head. He stretched to the back of the boot for his holdall and rummaged in it for a torch which he clipped onto his belt. Turning up the collar of his camouflage jacket he threw his trainers into the boot and slung his holdall over his shoulder before slamming the boot shut.

McAteer didn't encounter anyone as he headed back towards Argyle Street, his footsteps thudding dully on the compacted snow. Crossing Sauchiehall Street he walked along Kelvin Way, past the tennis courts and bowling greens. Another careful check to make sure he wasn't being observed, then he threw his holdall over the head-high iron railings and clambered over after it into Kelvingrove Park.

On the other side of the fence the snow was powdery and deep. McAteer edged his way down the slope to the river and stepped into the icy water, half a mile downstream from the bridge where the handover was to take place. Unclipping his torch he directed the narrow beam of light onto the slow-running water as he waded through the shallows, the only sound being the breaking of thin ice as he inched towards the bridge, testing each footstep in turn before committing his full weight to make sure the freezing water wouldn't flow over the top of his Wellingtons. It took him half an hour to reach the shelter of the footbridge by which time snow was falling steadily. He stepped up onto the shingly bank beneath the arch and lay down on his back, stretching out full length on the cold, clammy pebbles. He dozed intermittently.

'Thanks for coming round to look after Billy, Harry. It's Molly's birthday and she could do with a break. I'm going to take her down the pub for a few drinks, then we'll go for a quick Chinese. We should be back by eleven.'

'Take as long as you like, Stan.'

'I want to go with you and Mummy!' A child's anxious, whispered voice. 'I don't want to stay with Uncle Harry.'

The sound of male laughter. 'Billy's got you sussed all right, Harry. Just turned six and he's got your card marked already!' More hearty laughter.

'Have a good time, Stan.'

McAteer's body quivered and twitched convulsively on the wet stones.

'I don't want to play the game we played last time, Uncle Harry.'

'You want the big red train set for your birthday, don't you?'

'Yes. But I don't want to play that game again. It hurts!'

'Don't be silly. It's the game all the big boys play. I thought you were a big boy, Billy?'

Laboured breathing, coming in short, sharp bursts.

'Just lie down, Billy, and face the wall. And keep still. It doesn't take long. Think about the big red train set.'

Grunting; pushing; cursing; squeezing. Breathing getting faster and faster . . . then slowing down again . . .

'There now, that didn't hurt, did it?'

Gurgling, gulping sounds.

'Mind now, not a word about this to your dad, Billy. He'll belt the living daylights out of you if he finds out you've been playing big boys' games.'

McAteer jerked back to consciousness with a start. Breathing heavily, he closed his eye for a few moments to try to slow his heart rate, then he sat up straight and took a long swig of whisky from his hip flask. It had stopped snowing. Depressing the button on the side of his watch to illuminate the face, he saw it was ten to six. He rubbed the sleep from his eye and peered in satisfaction through the gloom at the blanket of virgin snow covering the river banks in both directions as far as the eye could see, the white expanse lit up by the glow of the street lamps filtering down from Kelvin Way. Unzipping his holdall he laid the contents out carefully on the pebbles. He timed himself. Butt locked onto stock, slide the barrel home, clip on the magazine, position the telescopic sights, spin on the silencer. Twenty-five seconds. Not bad, considering he was out of practice. He'd been able to assemble the assault rifle in half that time in his army days.

Taking a black woollen balaclava from his holdall he rolled it down over his head, twisting it to line up the slits for his right eye and his mouth. He pulled on a pair of tight-fitting leather gloves and stretched out, face down on the gravel, rifle ranged by his side, then he inched forward in the shadow of the bridge until the drop-off spot on the far bank of the river was within his line of vision.

He took off his wristwatch and placed it on a rock where he could see the watch face without moving his head. He lay prone and flexed the fingers of his right hand, no other part of his body moving. He could feel the cold rising from the dank ground and penetrating his shell suit and his camouflage jacket.

Simon Ramsay slipped out from underneath the duvet and crept round the bottom of the bed. When he eased open the bedroom door the hinges groaned slightly. He glanced anxiously back over his shoulder at Jude's sleeping profile. He froze, gripping the door handle tightly, as she rolled over onto her back and gulped a little for air before her steady, rhythmic breathing resumed. Not wanting to risk the hinges squeaking again, he left the door ajar and padded along the carpeted corridor to the study where he'd left his clothes. Dressing quickly he picked up his shoes and tiptoed down the staircase, taking care to avoid the squeaky step. He used the downstairs toilet without flushing it. Slipping his feet into his shoes he picked up a bunch of keys from the hall table and opened the front door as quietly as he could, turning the key in the Yale lock from the outside to avoid the tell-tale click when he pulled it closed behind him. Every nerve in his body was jangling as he negotiated the icy steps and made his way along the terrace and round the corner into Park Circus where he'd left his car.

Despite spraying the windows with de-icer it took several minutes with the engine running and the heater going at full blast before the windscreen had defrosted sufficiently to allow him to drive. There was little traffic about as he crawled down the hill and along Woodlands Road, his breath freezing on impact on the inside of the windscreen. It wasn't until he'd reached the traffic lights at the top of Gibson Street that the screen had cleared completely. He drove past the University Union where, out of the corner of his eye, he saw a tattered poster, attached to the front door, advertising 'Daft Friday' the previous evening – the formal, all-night ball that marked the end of the first university term.

Random memories of that arcane rite of passage came flooding into Ramsay's hyperactive brain; queuing for hours along with dozens of other hopeful freshers to get a ticket because the popular belief was that going to Daft Friday was synonymous with getting laid; stumbling across Sam Davis, supplier of drugs to half the science faculty, wanking off into a condom in the toilets at four o'clock in the morning so he would have a trophy he could show off to his mates; lying, ashen-faced on top of a snooker table in the billiards room and puking all over his hired dinner suit; staggering down to the refectory at six o'clock in the morning and trying to force down a few sips of black coffee while fighting back the urge to throw up again as the smell of greasy cooked breakfasts came wafting out from the kitchen.

These jumbled, disjointed images dissipated as quickly as they'd appeared and when he reached the bottom of Kelvin Way he pulled into the side of the road, switched off his lights and cut the engine. He checked the time on the car's clock. Quarter to eight. Fifteen minutes to wait.

Through the closed car windows Ramsay heard muffled shouts that seemed to be coming from behind and when he glanced into the rear-view mirror he saw two girls, one blonde, one redhead, at the top of the University Union steps. Both were wearing knee-length coats over ankle-length ball gowns. The blonde had a medical faculty scarf wrapped around her neck. She was pointing in his direction and jumping up and down, waving her arms above her head, shouting and seemingly trying to attract his attention. She looked to be very drunk. Ramsay slouched as low as he could in his seat while angling the rear-view mirror so he could still observe the girls. Giggling hysterically, the blonde grabbed her friend's arm and was trying to pull her down the steps but the redhead was resisting and struggling to hold her back. A taxi came down University Avenue and when the redhead succeeded in flagging it down both girls staggered down the stone steps and piled into the back seat.

Ramsay could feel his heart hammering against his ribcage as his befuddled brain struggled to figure out who the drunken girl might have been. Perhaps the daughter of a friend or a work colleague? Surely there was no way she could have recognised him from that distance? Maybe she'd recognised his car? As the minutes ticked by he failed to come up with any coherent explanation.

Pulling his briefcase over from the back seat he tipped the contents out onto the passenger seat, then closed the case and locked it. His eyes were glued to the time and on the stroke of eight o'clock he snatched up the case and got out of the car.

Yanking open the boot he took out his Barbour jacket and pulled it on, zipping it up to his chin.

From the bottom of University Avenue he could see the full length of Kelvin Way, as far as Sauchiehall Street. Two people in the far distance were walking their dogs. A young couple, who appeared to be refugees from Daft Friday, were sitting on the grass on the opposite side of the road, gazing soulfully into each other's eyes – the boy wearing a crumpled dinner suit, the girl in a red satin dress, a black anorak pulled tightly round her shoulders.

Closing the boot, Ramsay hurried towards the park entrance and as he made his way down the steep, snow-covered incline towards the river it was all he could do to prevent himself from breaking into an involuntary run as his toes pitched forward painfully inside his shoes. His leather soles suddenly hit a hidden patch of black ice and his arms flailed in the air as he struggled to retain his balance, the briefcase slipping from his grasp and skating to the bottom of the slope before slithering to a halt near the plinth of a statue. Ramsay's imagination went into overdrive as he glanced anxiously around the deserted park. Was the blackmailer watching him? Had the briefcase given the game away? Was it obviously too light – bouncing too high from the ridges of ice? He thanked his lucky stars it hadn't burst open. Edging towards the side of the path where the snow was softer and deeper, he shuffled to the bottom of the incline to recover the case.

The plinth at the base of the statue was overgrown with twisted vegetation. As he stooped to pick up the case the inscription in the white stone informed him that it was a memorial to Thomas Carlyle. Dusting the snow from the dented briefcase he turned to face the bridge, furtively scanning the rising ground on the other side of the river, the wide-open, snow-covered parkland stretching as far as the eye could see. All the paths leading to the bridge were deserted, as were the towpaths running alongside the river. There was nowhere for anyone to hide, except, perhaps, behind the statue of a mounted Highland Light Infantry officer on the opposite bank. As he walked towards the bridge the icy air caught him in the back of his throat, causing him to wheeze and splutter. Hacking up a mouthful of phlegm he spat it into the snow.

Billy McAteer's body tensed when he heard the coughing and the muffled footsteps on the bridge above his head. He lay completely still. The twittering of the dawn chorus had just broken out and the first rays of daylight were appearing low in the sky. His watch showed four minutes past eight. He glanced upwards when a cloud of snow billowed from the parapet of the bridge, disturbed by the briefcase being slid across, then he saw the case arc down silently and almost disappear from view in a puff of powdery snow. McAteer heard the pad of rapidly retreating footsteps, interspersed with coughing, as he eased his rifle into position, the sights trained on the spot where the case had landed. It was the first time he'd squinted down rifle sights since he'd lost his left eye. It was a strange sensation not having to wink.

Within moments he heard the laboured breathing of someone sliding down the far bank while holding onto the bushes growing out of the steep embankment to prevent himself slithering all the way down to the river. He stopped when he reached the briefcase. McAteer's view was restricted by the arc of the bridge and he could see only the back of a pair of jeans as far as the top of the thighs. Training the cross wires on the left knee, he wrapped his fingers around the pistol grip and squeezed the trigger. There was an agonised curse as the figure slumped down on to his knees in a cloud of soft snow, bringing his back into the line of sight. McAteer's second shot was aimed between the shoulder blades, slightly off centre, going for the heart. The victim's arms jerked backwards in spasm, clawing at the point of impact as his body started to pitch forward, slowly at first, then accelerating rapidly when the next bullet slammed into the nape of his neck.

McAteer got to his feet and quickly massaged some life back into his frozen legs. Draining his hip flask he slipped his watch onto his wrist, slung the rifle over his shoulder and picked up his holdall. He scrambled up the near bank and checked to make sure the coast was clear before crossing the bridge and slithering down the opposite bank. Blood was oozing from the motionless figure, crimson at the point of contact with the snow, diffusing to a soft pink as it seeped away from the body. Placing the tip of the short rifle barrel against the back of the half-buried head he pumped three rounds into the skull. He dismantled his rifle quickly and stowed the parts in his holdall before picking up the briefcase and clambering back up the steep embankment.

As he headed along the towpath in the direction of his car he tugged off his balaclava and stuffed it into the pocket of his camouflage jacket.

Charlie Anderson was sitting in his office, trying to interpret the crime statistics, when his phone rang just before nine o'clock. Swearing at the unwelcome interruption he snatched up the handset. 'Anderson,' he barked.

'Good morning, sir.' He recognised Colin Renton's voice. 'I realise you're not on duty today but there's news coming in of a homicide. I thought you'd want to know.'

Dropping his pen onto the desk, Charlie's fist gripped the handset tightly. 'Where?'

'Kelvingrove Park.'

'What do we have?'

'It's all rather sketchy at the moment. It seems a girl was walking her dog in the park this morning when she came across a body half-buried in the snow, down by the river. The initial report from the uniformed boys is that half the victim's head was blown away. I'm going across there now with the scene-of-crime officers and the forensic team.'

'Keep me posted, Colin.' Charlie replaced the receiver and tried to pick up the threads of his analysis, but he found it impossible to concentrate.

Colin Renton was updating Charlie when Tony O'Sullivan ambled into the office just after ten o'clock. Charlie raised an open palm to acknowledge his presence.

'Thanks for the alarm call,' O'Sullivan yawned.

'Thought you might appreciate a bit of overtime on the run-up to Christmas.'

'Nice of you to think of me.' O'Sullivan stifled another yawn. 'I was getting bored. I must've been in bed for almost six hours.'

'Not every day we get a high-profile murder on our patch,' Charlie said.

'Anyone we know?'

'Assuming he was carrying his own driving licence,' Renton chipped in, 'we've got Mike Harrison's corpse on our hands.'

CHAPTER 7

'Mike Harrison!' O'Sullivan let out a long, low whistle. 'A gangland hit?'

'A fair assumption,' Charlie stated.

'A professional job, for sure,' Renton said. 'Three shots from behind – one in the knee, one in the back and one in the neck, following which his skull was reduced to bone chippings from close range.'

'Barely enough of his ugly mug left to give us a positive ID,' Charlie said grimly. 'But Bobby Ralph over at the mortuary knew Harrison well and he's in no doubt that it's him.'

'Where did this happen?' O'Sullivan asked.

'Kelvingrove Park, down by the river,' Renton said. 'Sometime earlier this morning.'

'Does earlier than this actually exist?' O'Sullivan said, stifling a yawn.

'As soon as you've had your fix of caffeine, Tony, I want you to go over to Bearsden and break the news to the widow. Here's the address.' Charlie tore a slip of paper from the pad on his desk and handed it across. 'Her name's Laura Harrison. We'll need her to go to the mortuary to formally identify the body. Lillian McArthur's been called out. She'll go with you. Colin, I want you go through the files and dig out everything we've got on Harrison – his associates as well as his known enemies.' Charlie's fingers travelled over his bald skull. 'We never did manage to make anything stick but Harrison had his fingers in a lot of dodgy pies. He's dabbled in just about everything in his time – from porn and pimping to protection rackets and drugs. Half of Glasgow had a motive for seeing the back of him, so work on the assumption that you're both going to be busy little beavers for the next few days.'

'Glad I had the foresight to book time off,' O'Sullivan said, raising his eyes to the ceiling. Committing the Harrisons' address to memory, he tucked the slip of paper into his notebook.

Tony O'Sullivan turned off Great Western Road at Anniesland Cross and took the Switchback in the direction of Bearsden. He glanced across at Lillian McArthur sitting in the passenger seat, humming quietly to herself as she filed away at a chipped fingernail with an emery board. He'd never been able to figure out what age Lillian was. Her greying hair gave the appearance of being in her fifties but the smooth tone of her skin suggested she might be quite a lot younger.

'Did you have anything exciting lined up for this morning, Lillian?'

'Nothing in particular, Sarge.' She stopped filing her nails. 'Smoked salmon and fresh strawberries for breakfast, probably washed down with a couple of glasses of bubbly, then a bit more rumpy-pumpy with Mel Gibson.'

'With or without the woad?'

'Without, of course!' She blew on her fingertips and buffed her nails on the lapel of her jacket. 'You men don't realise what a mess that stuff makes on the sheets.'

O'Sullivan pulled up outside a large detached house in Canniesburn Road and checked the number on the gate post against the address he'd been given. 'This is it, Lillian.'

Getting out of the car they walked up the driveway, their feet scrunching noisily in the frosted gravel. O'Sullivan pressed the bell push and the door was opened before the echo of the ring had died away.

'Laura Harrison?' he asked.

'What can I do for you?' Laura was dressed in a white open-necked blouse and a knee-length, black and white striped skirt. Despite her make-up, the angry bruising around her left eye was clearly visible.

'Detective Sergeant O'Sullivan and Police Constable McArthur,' Tony announced as they both produced their warrant cards. 'Could we please come in for a minute?'

'It's concerning your husband,' Lillian stated.

'Mike's not at home. He plays poker at Ronnie McGavigan's place every other Friday,' she said by way of explanation. 'He always stays over.'

'It's you we'd like to talk to,' Tony said.

Laura furrowed her forehead. 'What about?'

'Could we come inside, please?'

Reluctantly Laura took a step back, allowing them to cross the threshold, then she led the way along the hall towards the lounge, their footsteps making no sound on the plush, thick-pile carpet. 'What's this all about?' she asked, motioning towards the settee while propping herself against the edge of a chair.

O'Sullivan and McArthur remained standing. 'Mrs Harrison,' Lillian began, 'there was a tragic incident in Kelvingrove Park earlier this morning. A man has been killed.'

Laura's body visibly stiffened. 'What does that have to do with me?' she stammered.

'We have reason to believe that the victim was your husband.'

Laura's fingernails dug into the chair. 'That's not possible!'

Taking Laura by the elbow, Lillian guided her down onto the settee. 'The person who was killed was carrying your husband's driving licence, Mrs Harrison.'

'A police officer who knew your husband well has confirmed that he was the victim,' Tony added quietly.

Laura sat in silence, fingering her swollen face and staring unblinkingly at the far wall.

'Would you like me to make you a cup of tea?' Lillian offered. Laura shook her head. 'When you feel up to it,' Lillian said, 'I'm afraid we're going to have to ask you to come down to the mortuary and make a formal identification.'

Laura grasped the arm of the settee and gripped it tightly. She sat rigid for a few moments before pulling herself to her feet. 'I'm ready.'

'It doesn't have to be straight away,' Tony said quickly. 'We could leave it until later in the day.'

'I'd rather get it over with, Sergeant,' she said, picking up her handbag from the coffee table and draping the strap over her shoulder.

'You can come in our car,' Lillian said. 'We'll drop you back home.'

'I'd rather drive.'

'I'm not sure that's such a good idea, Mrs Harrison,' Lillian said. 'You're still in shock.'

'I'm all right,' Laura nodded, taking her car keys from her handbag. 'You lead the way, I'll follow.'

*

'I've dug out all we have on Harrison and his associates, sir,' Renton announced as he walked into Charlie's office carrying a thick sheaf of paper.

'O'Sullivan called in a couple of minutes ago,' Charlie said. 'He's on his way back from Bearsden. We might as well wait till he arrives, then you can brief both of us at the same time.' Renton dumped his papers down on Charlie's desk. 'Tell me something,' Charlie said, indicating to Renton to take a seat. 'I've been trying to make sense of the crime stats this morning. Is this city getting worse or is it just me getting old?'

'Sir?'

Charlie swung his feet up onto his desk. 'My first posting in the uniformed division was in Ferguslie Park. The station sergeant there was a sadist. I was barely eighteen at the time and he started me off on the night shift. It was the worst housing scheme in Scotland by a long chalk – all because some pillock of a town planner had come up with the brilliant idea of moving every reprobate, hooligan and rent defaulter in the west of Scotland there.'

'If I remember correctly,' Renton said, 'the harebrained theory was that if all the trouble-makers were concentrated in one place it would make it easier to keep an eye on them, while at the same time we'd be cleaning up the other estates.'

Charlie nodded. 'Talk about creating a ghetto. It was the nearest thing to a no-go area we've ever had in Scotland. But despite that, the crime stats were never as bad as they are today.'

'There was probably as much in the way of violence, protection rackets and pimping as there is today,' Renton said, 'but most of the aggro was among the gangs themselves – turf wars – and the violence didn't get reported. Nowadays it seems like we're the prime target – like that incident in Barmulloch last week when two officers were dragged from their patrol car in broad daylight and had the shit beaten out of them.'

'And, of course, no witnesses,' Charlie growled. 'Nobody ever sees a bloody thing!' He shook his head. 'I'm no sociologist, but when I see these gangs of louts on the rampage – some of them barely out of short trousers – it makes me want to throw up.'

'It's the casual use of knives that gets to me,' Renton said. 'You just have to look at these kids the wrong way and the blades are out.'

'Is it really all down to drugs?'

'Drugs? Drink? Unemployment? Boredom? Who knows?'

'My son-in-law used to lay the blame at Thatcher's door, but that's too glib. We were already up to our necks in shit before she shoved us under.'

'Politicians are all the same,' Renton said. 'I mean – take New Labour. What's that all about? Who asked for a new Labour? Did you? Did anyone in Scotland? The Labour Party that was good enough for Keir Hardie and Jimmy Maxton was good enough for me.'

'Fair comment.'

'I can't remember the last time there was a socialist politician in charge of the Labour Party.'

'Harold Wilson wasn't bad,' Charlie suggested.

'Wilson was okay, but he was a lot more politician than socialist. What about Kinnock?'

'Welsh – need I say more?'

Renton guffawed. 'How about John Smith?'

'Now you're talking,' Charlie nodded respectfully. 'He would've been one of the great socialist prime ministers if he'd lived.'

'But instead, we got Blair!'

'He did give us our own parliament.'

'What the hell's that all about?' Renton snorted. 'Millions of pounds of taxpayers' money pissed away on a new parliament building so yet another bunch of tossers can sit on their arses all day and contemplate their navels. What's that got to do with the price of mince?'

'I heard a good one down the pub a while back,' Charlie said. 'Round about the time there was a panic on about the possibility of the state opening of the new parliament building having to be delayed. Do you know that: 'Months late – at this price!' is an anagram of 'The Scottish parliament'?'

Renton chortled. 'Right on the nail!'

'If you're not a Blair fan, what did you make of Irn Broon?' Charlie asked.

'At least Gordon was Scottish.'

'So was Blair.'

'Your arse in parsley! He was as Scottish as . . . as the bloody Duke of Edinburgh!'

Tony O'Sullivan nudged the office door open with one knee. He was carrying three plastic cups of coffee and several packets of shortbread biscuits balanced on a tray. 'Breakfast's up!' he announced.

'Just in time,' Charlie said with a grin. 'Colin was flirting dangerously close to high treason.' Taking his coffee, Charlie rummaged around in the top drawer of his desk for a pencil to stir in the sugar. 'When you're ready, Colin, give us the low-down on Harrison.'

Renton lifted his sheaf of paper from Charlie's desk and balanced it on his knees. Sipping at his coffee he referred to the notes. 'The legal side of Harrison's business was bookmaking,' he stated, 'though even there he was sailing pretty close to the wind. He was prosecuted a couple of years back for supplying incorrect turnover data to the Inland Revenue but his lawyer managed to get him off with a 'not proven' verdict. The Revenue boys are conducting another investigation into his affairs right now and charges are pending. There's a sleeping partner in the business, a bloke called Ronnie McGavigan. He's a bit of a chancer as well. He used to be in the bookmaking business but he lost his licence five years ago because of persistent tax evasion. Harrison ran six betting shops in Glasgow, four of which were in premises owned by McGavigan. It's common knowledge that Harrison was involved in some pretty murky activities – drugs, protection rackets, pimping, hardcore porn and the like – but he was adept at covering his tracks and we never managed to gather enough evidence to prosecute. By the way,' Renton added, turning to Charlie, 'it seems that Billy McAteer joined Harrison's payroll a while back.'

'Billy McAteer?' Charlie scratched at the back of his neck. 'Now there's a name to conjure with.'

'That name means something to me,' O'Sullivan said. 'But I can't place it.'

'He was way before your time,' Charlie said. 'You remember him, Colin?'

'A hard man to forget, sir.'

'A hard man in every sense of the word. Thirty-odd years ago his face was splashed across the front pages of the tabloids,' Charlie said, 'but he's been out of circulation for quite some time. If I remember correctly he got fifteen years for armed robbery with violence.'

'And he picked up a few more years for assault while inside Barlinnie,' Renton said. 'His idea of a Guy Fawkes Night celebration was to pick on a fellow inmate – a defrocked priest who was doing time for molesting altar boys. McAteer and one of his cronies stripped the poor bugger naked, tied him face-down to the bed in his cell, rammed his Y-fronts into his mouth, stuck a Roman candle up his arse and lit the fuse.'

'Jesus Christ!' Tony flinched and screwed his eyes shut.

'It wasn't the first time he'd used that trick,' Renton said. 'Anyone McAteer suspected of being a kiddie fiddler was liable to get the treatment. You can just imagine it. If the victim struggles the flames cascade all over his back and his legs – and if he tries to lie still he gets his bum barbecued.'

'You could spare us the graphic details, Colin!' Tony winced.

'McAteer claims to have invented the punishment,' Renton said.

'Another name to be added to the list of great Scottish inventors,' Tony said. 'How the hell did he manage to smuggle a Roman candle into Barlinnie?'

'Christ only knows!' Renton said. 'I suppose we should be thankful that he didn't have a supply of bangers. He had a motto whittled into a piece of wood that he kept on display in his cell: "*An eye for an eye and an arse for an arse.*"'

'Despite his track record,' Charlie said, 'he got out of prison earlier this year. If there was a vote for Glasgow's number one psychopath of this, or any other, decade Billy McAteer would be right up there with the best of them. How about this for a background? His family emigrated from Belfast to Glasgow when he was about two and he was brought up in Govan, a stone's throw from Ibrox. He was Rangers daft. Even as a teenager he was a complete and utter bampot. When he had a drink in him his party trick was to climb up onto the table in his local and belt out "The Sash", then he'd down a pint in one swallow and announce to the world that he wouldn't rest until every Catholic had been driven out of Northern Ireland. In the meantime, just to keep his hand in, he wasn't averse to taking his razor to the occasional passing Tim.

'When he was in his twenties he signed up for the army – probably hoping to get in a bit of practice at legalised killing. As luck would have it he was posted to Northern Ireland and the reason he made such a splash in the papers was that he'd only been there a few weeks before he was mutilated by an IRA bomb. His regiment was under strict orders not to frequent the local pubs, but taking orders wasn't one of McAteer's strong points. He went for a pint with some of his mates when they were off duty and he ended up with his face lacerated beyond recognition.'

'Dramatic irony at its best,' Renton nodded.

'If McAteer had a chip on his shoulder when he went to Northern Ireland,' Charlie said, 'he came back with a fish supper.'

'Remember what happened to Harry Robertson?' Renton said.

'That's going back a bit,' Charlie said, scratching his head. 'He was related to McAteer, wasn't he?'

'His uncle.'

'Must've been twenty years ago,' Charlie said, 'but you never forget a murder as gruesome as that. Robertson's body was pulled from the Clyde. His hands were tied behind his back and there were several bullets in his skull. He had two six-inch nails protruding from his eye sockets and the skin had been stripped from his buttocks with something like an open-blade razor.'

'The pathologist reckoned that Robertson's eyes and backside had been mutilated while he was still alive.' Renton shivered at the memory. 'No one was ever charged with the murder but the story is that Robertson had taunted McAteer in the pub earlier that evening, referring to him as "arse-features".'

'Nothing about McAteer would surprise me,' Charlie said. 'He had a glass eye for a while but he lost it in a street brawl and never bothered replacing it. Apparently he thought the empty eye socket added to his hard man image. I doubt if he's been out of jail for more than six months at a stretch throughout his entire adult life.'

'According to one of my snitches,' Renton said, 'McAteer phoned Shuggie Morrison's café, looking for Gerry Fraser, the morning Fraser got worked over.'

'Which would go a long way towards explaining Fraser's reluctance to talk,' O'Sullivan said. 'I don't suppose your snitch would be prepared to testify to that?'

'I'll ask him!' Renton smirked.

'Put the word out that we're looking for McAteer,' Charlie said. 'I want him picked up as soon as possible. I want to be there to gauge his reaction when he finds out his boss has been murdered.'

'Did McAteer have any connection with Harrison before he went inside?' O'Sullivan asked.

'Not that I know of,' said Charlie, 'but if Harrison was in the market for a hard man, they don't come any harder.'

Tony raised an eyebrow. 'A hard man, perhaps, but not what you'd call any great shakes as a bodyguard?'

'What can you tell me about Mike Harrison's movements last night?' Charlie asked. Ronnie McGavigan walked over to his

well-stocked cocktail cabinet and poured a stiff measure of
Lagavulin into a crystal tumbler. 'Would you care for a snifter,
Inspector?'

'A bit early in the day for me, thanks all the same.'

'How about a soft drink? Orange juice? Mineral water?'

'Nothing, thanks.'

McGavigan tipped a splash of Highland Spring water into his
whisky and came back to the settee where Charlie was seated,
notebook and pen in hand. McGavigan was small and slimly
built – in his early sixties, Charlie estimated. Charlie studied his
profile as he tilted his head back to pour whisky down his throat.
His hairline was showing signs of receding and his crinkly brown
hair was slicked straight back from his high forehead. Small tufts
of nasal hair protruded from his pinched nostrils. His lips were
thin and his chin was weak.

'Last I saw of Mike was when we packed in playing poker last
night.'

'What time would that have been?'

'About two o'clock in the morning. He was in a good mood
because he'd picked up a few quid. Mike was nothing if not
predictable. When he was winning he was the life and soul of
the party, but when he was on a losing streak he could be a right
miserable old fart. Sorry about that ...' McGavigan broke off and
downed another mouthful of whisky. 'Didn't mean to, you know,
speak ill of the dead and all that ...' His voice tailed off.

'That's all right. I'd rather hear it the way it was.'

'Mike stayed over. He nearly always did after a poker session.
But last night he told me he'd be heading off early in the morning
so not to bother with breakfast.'

'Did he usually leave early when he stayed over?'

'Not at all,' McGavigan said, shaking his head. 'I often had to drag him out of bed after ten o'clock.'

'Can you think of any reason why he would have gone to Kelvingrove Park this morning?'

'I can't think of any reason why he would go near Kelvingrove Park – not this or any other morning. Mike's not – he *wasn't* – what you'd call the outdoor type.'

'Did he say why he was leaving early this morning?'

'Not specifically. He dropped a few hints that he was going to make some easy money, but when I pressed him about it he clammed up. When I got up this morning at the back of eight his car had gone.' Finishing off his whisky, McGavigan crossed to the cocktail cabinet for a refill. 'Are you sure I couldn't tempt you?'

Charlie shook his head. 'Who else was in the poker school last night?' he asked.

'The usual crowd,' McGavigan said, flopping back down on the settee. He put his glass down on a coaster on the coffee table and started counting off on his fingers. 'Besides me and Mike there was John McGill, Willie Grant and Don Higney – they're all regulars – and we try to get someone to stand in for Bill McLelland – usually Jim Amos. Jim was here last night. By the way, your lot haven't done us any favours by taking Bill out of circulation.'

'Sorry about that,' Charlie said, jotting down the names.

'So you should be. It's a real bummer not having Bill in the school. More money than sense – and he couldn't bluff his way out of a paper bag.'

'If he'd been using his own money instead of the Royal Bank of Scotland's he might've been a bit more careful.'

McGavigan guffawed. 'Could you not see your way to letting him out for a few hours every other Friday?'

'I'll have a word with the first minister.'

McGavigan started to laugh again, quickly choking it off with an embarrassed cough as he gazed down into his whisky.

'Did any of these other guys stay over?' Charlie asked, jabbing his pencil at the names in his notebook.

'Apart from Jim Amos, none of them can get an overnight pass.' He pressed his thumb down hard on the coffee table to reinforce the point. 'And Jim stays within staggering distance so he always goes home.'

'What was your relationship with Mike Harrison?'

'What do you mean – *relationship*?'

'Was it just social or were you business associates?'

'We did a bit of business together, but it was mainly social. We were golf partners – we've both been members at Haggs Castle for as long as I can remember – and the poker school's been going for God knows how many years.'

'Did Harrison have any enemies?'

'He upset a few people in his time. Who hasn't?'

'Anyone in particular?'

'If you're asking if I know anyone who might've had a reason for seeing the back of him . . .' McGavigan took a swig of whisky. 'The answer is no.'

Billy McAteer drove through Dumbarton and headed north on the road towards Tarbet, negotiating the tight bends on the west bank of Loch Lomond. Shortly after passing the village of Luss he turned off the road and drove for half a mile up a bumpy, snow-covered track until he came to a copse of tall conifers.

He parked his Volvo in a clearing beside a circle of empty caravans, then got out of the car, opened the boot and lifted out a sheet of heavy-duty waterproof tarpaulin which he spread out on the snow. Pulling on his gloves he took the rifle barrel from his holdall and carefully wiped it clean with a dry duster before placing it on the tarpaulin. He repeated the procedure with the butt, the stock, the silencer and the telescopic sights. Having placed the two boxes of ammunition on top of the gun parts he rolled the tarpaulin into a tight parcel which he bound with rope. Taking a long-handled shovel from the car boot he slung the tarpaulin over his shoulder and marched into the copse. When he came to a patch of recently turned earth between two poplars he buried the tarpaulin in the same spot where it had lain undisturbed for more than twenty years.

Laura Harrison steeled herself as the white sheet was eased back to expose what was left of her husband's head. She'd been warned what to expect. A cloth had been placed over the right side of his face and only his left cheek, one eye, and part of his forehead were visible. His bushy eyebrow was unmistakeable, as was the shrivelled brown mole at his temple. Clasping her hands to her mouth Laura gave a quick nod of the head. The sheet was immediately replaced.

As soon as the formalities had been completed Laura hurried out of the building towards her car. Flinging her handbag onto the passenger seat she fired the ignition. As she drove off she groped in her bag for her phone and when she pulled up at a red traffic light she clicked on the number for Simon Ramsay's mobile.

'Simon?'

'Laura! Thank God! I've been worried sick. Did everything go to plan?'

'We can't talk on the phone. Where are you?'

'At home.'

'I have to see you. Meet me in the Terrace Bar in the Hilton.'

'When?'

'As soon as you can get there.'

Laura pulled off Great Western Road into Grosvenor Terrace, but then had to crawl the length of the terrace and across the Huntly Road intersection before she found a parking place. It was difficult keeping her balance as she made her way back along the unsalted, rutted pavement. The pavement sloped down quite sharply and she gripped the wrought iron hand railing, her flesh stinging as her fingers stuck to the frozen metal. She rubbed the palms of her hands together briskly to try to get some feeling back into her fingers as she approached the Hilton Hotel, a long, three-storey, Victorian terraced building. The white sandstone had recently been cleaned but it was already taking on a grimy aspect from the incessant traffic fumes drifting across from Great Western Road. The steps up to the hotel had been cleared of snow. Laura hurried up the stairs and through the main entrance.

Barely-audible piped music was playing in the open-plan Terrace Bar which ran the length of the hotel. The lounge was empty apart from a middle-aged man in a dark blue business suit who was sitting at a table at the far end of the room, next to the bar. He glanced up from the laptop balanced on his knees when he saw Laura arrive, then huddled down again, peering at his screen. There was an untouched half pint of lager on the table in front of him. Laura sat down on a straight-backed armchair in the alcove near the entrance. When the waitress came across she ordered a gin and tonic.

Ten minutes later Simon Ramsay entered the building through the basement level and climbed to the top of the staircase. Spotting Laura, he waved in acknowledgment and hurried across.

'What happened?' he asked in a hoarse whisper, glancing down the bar as he took the seat opposite.

'Mike was in Kelvingrove Park this morning,' she said quietly. Simon stared at her in disbelief. 'It was Mike who was killed,' she mouthed.

Simon tugged his top shirt button loose. 'For fuck's sake!'

'The police came round to the house this morning,' Laura said, stretching forward and tipping the remains of the tonic into her gin. 'They told me Mike's body had been discovered in Kelvingrove Park, down by the river, near the footbridge. He'd been shot several times,' she said in a whisper.

'Jesus wept!'

'I had to go to the mortuary to identify his body.' A shiver ran the length of her spine. 'It was the most gruesome thing I've ever had to do in my life. What was left of his face was barely recognisable.' Picking up her glass in a trembling hand, she took a long sip.

'You mean – it was Mike who was blackmailing me?' Simon asked incredulously.

'I've been going over and over that in my head all morning, but I can't make any sense of it. Mike couldn't have been the blackmailer, Simon. If he'd seen that photo of us together he'd have killed me. He'd have killed both of us.'

'Maybe he was planning to kill us – after he got his hands on the money?'

Laura shook her head firmly. 'He wasn't that good an actor. I'm telling you, if Mike had seen that photograph there is no way in this world he could have behaved civilly towards me. No way he could've laughed and joked his way through your dinner party last Wednesday.' She broke off as the waitress approached to take Simon's order. He asked for a Peroni.

'Then what in the name of God was he doing in Kelvingrove Park?'

'That's what I've been trying to figure out.'

'Have you spoken to . . . to you know who?'

'Not yet.'

'Does he know –' Simon glanced over his shoulder towards the businessman who was engrossed in typing something into his computer. He turned back to face Laura and mouthed the words. 'Does McAteer know who he killed?'

'I don't know if he recognised Mike. Maybe not. The police have issued a press release saying that a body's been found in Kelvingrove Park, but they haven't given out any details about the victim.' The waitress brought Simon's beer on a tray, placing it on the low table in front of him. Laura waited until she was out of earshot. 'The only thing I can think of is that perhaps Mike was acting as a pick-up for someone else. Is it conceivable that the person who was blackmailing you paid Mike to collect the ransom money without him knowing what it was all about?'

Simon frowned. 'Doesn't sound like Mike's style – acting as a messenger boy.'

'It isn't,' Laura said. 'But he was really strapped for cash. If someone had offered to make it worth his while he might have agreed to do it.'

'If that's the case, it means we still have the blackmailer to contend with!' Simon downed half his drink in one swallow. His 'Fucking hell!' rang out down the lounge.

The typing stopped abruptly, the businessman looking up and staring in their direction. 'Steady on, old chap!' The accent was Home Counties. 'There's no call for that kind of language.'

Simon whipped round in his chair. 'Why don't you mind your own fucking business!'

Flipping the lid of his laptop closed, the man tut-tutted and scrambled to his feet. Bustling past them with a sideways glare he made his way down the staircase, muttering under his breath.

'I'd rather you didn't go out of your way to attract attention to us, Simon,' Laura hissed. She sipped at her gin. 'The only way we'll ever know for sure if Mike was involved,' she said, 'is if we find that video recording. If it's somewhere in the house, then I suppose we'll have to conclude that Mike was the blackmailer, though I still can't get my head round that possibility. I suppose I could have his computer checked out,' she added. 'There must be some way to find out if that photo was sent to you from Mike's PC – though I wouldn't have a clue how to go about doing that. And I don't think Mike knew how to do anything technical either. As far as I'm aware he only ever used his computer as a glorified typewriter. Bjorn would be able to find out for me, I suppose, but I can hardly ask him to check if there's a photo on Mike's computer of you and me screwing!'

'It's not worth busting a gut trying to find out,' Simon said grimly. 'If Liam Black's still out there, I'm sure I'll be hearing from him soon enough.' Getting to his feet he went over to the bar to pay for their drinks.

Laura walked down the staircase and crossed to the reception desk. 'My name's Mrs Petrie,' she announced to the receptionist. 'My husband and I stayed here a couple of weeks ago.'

'How can I help you?'

'I've lost a contact lens. I'm not actually sure if it was here or somewhere else. Would it be possible for me to go up to the room to check if it's still there?'

'Which room would that be?'

'301.'

Simon appeared by Laura's side as the receptionist was keying into her terminal. 'No problem. 301's not occupied right now,' she said. 'But I'll be very embarrassed if you do find it,' she added with a smile as she handed across the key. 'By rights it should've been in a vacuum cleaner ages ago.'

'I know it's a long shot.' Laura returned the smile. 'But since we're here anyway I thought it would be worthwhile taking a look. I remember putting my contact lens carrying case down on the arm of a chair and the lens might've slipped down the side of the cushion.'

'What on earth are you playing at?' Simon asked tetchily as the lift doors closed behind them. 'What's all this crap about losing a contact lens?'

'I want to have a look at the room,' Laura said, leading the way along the corridor.

'What, exactly, are we looking for?' Simon asked as she turned the key in the lock.

'I want to know where the camera was hidden.'

'Why?'

'I just want to know. That's all.'

'From the angle of the shot,' Simon said, pointing towards the top of the wardrobe. 'I reckon it must have been up there.'

Laura dragged across an upright chair and stood on it to peer at the top of the wardrobe. 'There are scratch marks in the wood. They look newish. They could've been made by some kind of clamp.'

'What the hell are you trying to prove?'

'I don't know,' she said, clambering down from the chair. 'Do you think I should bring over a photo of Mike and ask the staff if they've seen him hanging around here?'

'I think that showing the hotel staff a photo of someone who's just been murdered would be a sure-fire way of drawing attention to yourself!'

As soon as she got back home Laura started working her way methodically through the house. Beginning with Mike's study she checked all the bedrooms before searching through the rooms on the ground floor, but found nothing. Darkness was falling by the time she went out to the garage. Flicking on the low-wattage light bulb she found a step ladder and climbed up to check the high shelves. Hidden behind an old car battery she found a shoebox containing a stack of unboxed, unlabelled DVDs. Hurrying back to the house with the discs she switched on the TV in the lounge and loaded one into the player.

Her jaw fell slack when she saw the grainy image.

CHAPTER 8

The black and white recording was of a middle-aged man having sexual intercourse with a young girl who couldn't have been more than ten or eleven. The girl was offering no resistance. Her features were Asian and she was smiling vacantly in the direction of the camera, a hollow look in her glazed eyes. Her lips were forming words but there was no soundtrack. Ejecting the disc, Laura slipped another one into the slot and saw a teenage boy being buggered by a naked, scrawny man who looked old enough to be his grandfather.

It was all she could do to avoid being physically ill as she switched from disc to disc. All the recordings were the same basic format – adults sexually abusing submissive Asian children. Laura forced herself to fast-forward through every DVD in the box, searching in vain for the recording of her and Simon in the Hilton.

By the time she'd skimmed through them all her hands were shaking and her head was reeling. She went to the kitchen to pour herself a stiff gin, then picked up the phone and dialled Ronnie McGavigan's number.

'Have you heard the news, Ronnie?'

'Dreadful business, Laura. I had a visit from the police this morning. I was going to call you later this evening.'

'Could you possibly come round straight away? I need to talk to you urgently. It's very important.'

'I'm on my way.'

*

'Was Mike a paedophile?' Laura asked, handing Ronnie McGavigan a tumbler of malt whisky.

He paused with the glass half-way to his mouth. 'What sort of a question is that?'

'I found a box of discs in the garage – they were all films of children being molested.'

'Oh, those?'

'You know about them?'

McGavigan shifted uncomfortably in his seat. 'Stuff like that goes on all the time, Laura. Especially in places like Thailand.'

'I wasn't born yesterday, Ronnie.' She sat down on the sofa beside him. 'But how on earth was Mike involved?'

McGavigan cast his eyes down, nursing his drink in both hands. 'You and Mike went on a cruise to Malaysia last summer, didn't you?'

Laura nodded slowly. 'We went with my sister and her husband.' She looked at him quizzically. 'What's that got to do with it?'

'And your ship docked in Bangkok?'

'That's right. Jude and I didn't get off the boat. We'd both picked up a stomach bug in Singapore and I didn't risk leaving my cabin for three days. Mike and Simon went ashore, I think. I remember Mike saying something about wanting to sample the local beer.'

'Mike told me all about it when he got back. He and Simon went on a pub crawl but they had a barney about something trivial and Simon stormed off in high dudgeon. Mike had a few more beers as he wandered round the city centre and he stumbled across a brothel offering sex with children.

'I don't know if you know anything about how the underage sex business is organised in Thailand, Laura? It's run by so-called *aunties* – women who act as pimps for the kids. They agree with the clients what services the children will provide and they negotiate the price. The kids get paid peanuts – they're usually spaced out on opium – and the aunties pocket the money. For a few quid extra the aunties will record the sex session for the punter so he can have a disc to take home with him as a souvenir.'

'That's just so sick!' Laura said, getting to her feet and walking towards the French windows, shaking her head in disgust.

'Mike ended up having a drunken chat with one of these aunties and when she realised he wasn't interested in screwing kids she told him that the aunties often made extra copies of the DVDs without the client's knowledge. She offered to sell him a batch of these and he ended up negotiating to buy a job lot and arranging to have them shipped back to Glasgow. The internet used to be the main vehicle for transmitting that kind of material but the cops have made so many successful busts in the past few years that a lot of paedophiles have reverted to using DVDs.

'The consignment arrived a few weeks after Mike got back. He showed me some of them. Not to put too fine a point on it, they were pathetic. Most of the time is taken up with some saddo or other struggling to get it up, then maybe two or three minutes of action. However, Mike was convinced there was a market for the stuff. He had the idea of editing the discs down to the "highlights", as he called it, and selling them as *Asian Babes IV* or some such crap. I don't know how far he got with it. He offered to cut me in if I would help him with the distribution but I didn't want to know.'

'Why would he get involved with this kind of filth?' Laura snapped, snatching up a disc and hurling it across the lounge.

There was a pause. 'Did Mike ever discuss his finances with you?'

'No more that he had to. You can be sure of that! He told me the bookie's business was going through a rough patch. And I know he was worried about how nasty the Inland Revenue might turn.'

'That's not the half of it. Mike had serious financial problems.' Laura gave McGavigan a puzzled look. 'He'd been punting heavily for years and he was losing big time,' McGavigan said, downing the rest of his drink. 'I don't know how often I told him to pack in the gambling but he wouldn't listen. He always thought the next big bet would get him out of trouble, but he just kept digging himself in deeper and deeper. I'm sure that's the only reason he got involved with this paedophile crap. He was hoping to make enough from flogging the DVDs to pay off his gambling debts.' There was an awkward silence. 'Do you want me to get rid of those?' McGavigan waved his empty glass in the direction of the discs scattered on the carpet. 'It's not the sort of stuff you want to have lying around the house.'

'I'd appreciate that, Ronnie. Let me top that up for you,' Laura said, taking the empty tumbler from his grasp and crossing to the cocktail cabinet.

'I could keep an eye on the bookies' shops, if you like. There are always day-to-day problems that need sorting out.'

'That would be very helpful.'

'If there's anything else I can do – funeral arrangements, anything like that – you know you just have to ask.'

'Thanks, Ronnie, but I won't be able to have the funeral for some time. The procurator fiscal told me there will have to be a post-mortem and it will be at least a week before the body will be released.'

'Of course. Whenever.' McGavigan spoke quietly. 'Do you have any idea what Mike was doing in Kelvingrove Park this morning?'

'I was hoping you might be able to fill me in on that,' Laura said, handing him his glass.

'Not a bloody clue!' He clinked the ice round in his drink. 'Last night, Mike was bouncier than I've seen him in a long time. He told me he'd be leaving early in the morning, so not to do breakfast. Gave me the old nod nod, wink wink. Said he was going to meet someone on Saturday morning and make a killing.' McGavigan sipped at his drink. 'Sorry!' He held his hand up in a gesture of apology. 'Poor choice of expression.'

'Did he say anything else?'

McGavigan shook his head.

The sleet had turned to steady rain when Colin Renton pulled up near the junction of University Avenue and Byres Road. 'How do you want to handle it, Sarge?'

'You wait here,' O'Sullivan said. 'I'll bring him out. Always assuming your snitch has got it right.'

'If Bert Tollin says he's drinking in Tennent's, then he's drinking in Tennent's. Do you want a bet?'

'Sod off!' O'Sullivan got out of the car and ran diagonally across the junction, dodging through the heavy traffic.

He scanned the pub from the doorway. There were only a handful of early evening customers: three pensioners, half pints of heavy on the table in front of them, their eyes fixed on a large screen where the rerun of an Italian football match was being shown with the sound turned off; a teenage couple, sitting in an alcove, arguing heatedly; two tall men, propping up the bar.

As O'Sullivan approached the men he could see the reflection of McAteer's scarred features in the mirror. He was leaning with one elbow on the counter, his back to the door.

'Billy McAteer?' O'Sullivan spoke quietly.

'What's your problem, pal?' McAteer responded without turning round.

'Detective Sergeant O'Sullivan, Glasgow CID.' O'Sullivan cupped his warrant card in the palm of his hand and thrust it at arm's length in front of McAteer's face. 'I'd like you to accompany me to police headquarters. Inspector Anderson wants a word with you.'

McAteer studied the badge, then without turning round he pushed O'Sullivan's hand away and picked up his pint glass from the bar. Taking a sip, he resumed his conversation.

O'Sullivan tapped him on the shoulder. McAteer twitched his arm away and spun round quickly, flicking at his shoulder with his fingertips as if trying to dislodge something unpleasant. 'Gauny no' do that, pal,' he snarled. 'I didny pay good money for this jumper for you to wipe your manky paws on it.'

'You heard me, McAteer.' O'Sullivan spoke quietly but forcibly. 'Either you come outside with me right now or I'm taking you out.'

'It's *Mr* McAteer to you,' he spat, thrusting his face to within inches of O'Sullivan's. The exchange had attracted no attention from the bar staff or the other customers.

McAteer took a step backwards and eyed O'Sullivan up and down. 'An' Anderson has the cheek to send a Papist to pick me up. You are a Papist, aren't you, sonny?' he sneered. 'The red heid's a dead giveaway. If there's two things in this world I can smell a mile off it's pigs an' Papists. An' right now the stench of a mingin', Fenian pig is fillin' my nostrils an' makin' me want to boak.'

Realising he was being goaded into reacting, O'Sullivan felt a hot flush redden his cheeks. McAteer took a sudden pace forward, again thrusting his face to within inches of O'Sullivan's. 'What does your Inspector want wi' me, Paddy? Is he gauny make me say three Our Faithers an' three Hail Marys for bein' a naughty boy?'

O'Sullivan's instinct was to grab McAteer by the scruff of the neck and frog-march him out of the pub, but he knew that a public display of unprovoked police violence was exactly what he was angling after. He didn't react to the taunts, but neither did he back off. He didn't concede an inch. If anything, he pushed his face even closer to McAteer's – so close he could taste the stale beer on his breath. For several seconds each held his ground, stock-still, staring unblinkingly. Stags with antlers locked – each defying the other to make the next move.

It was McAteer who made the move. Without lowering his gaze he took a step backwards and tipped the contents of his almost-full pint down the front of O'Sullivan's trousers. 'Oh! Terribly sorry about that!' he exclaimed. He nudged his companion's arm and burst out laughing as he placed his empty beer glass down on the counter. 'My hand must've slipped. Barman! There's been a wee accident. A towel for my friend, if you please.' McAteer lowered his voice. 'Now, if you'll just change your nappy and wait over by the door, Paddy, I'll be with you as soon as I've finished my discussion.' Turning his back on O'Sullivan, McAteer resumed his conversation.

O'Sullivan took the bar towel he'd been handed and dabbed ineffectually at the sticky beer clinging to his trousers. He could feel the cloying liquid seeping through to his skin. Reaching out, he grabbed McAteer by the shoulder. 'Either you walk out of here with me this instant,' he hissed in his ear, 'or I'll fucking-well drag you out.'

'This is harassment.' McAteer stared unblinkingly at O'Sullivan. 'I'm warnin' you, Paddy,' he growled, prodding O'Sullivan hard in the chest. 'You're fuckin' claimed!' With a quick nod to his companion McAteer snatched his leather jacket from the adjacent bar stool and slipped it over his shoulders as he marched towards the pub door, O'Sullivan following close behind.

Steady rain was still falling as they stepped out into Byres Road. O'Sullivan gripped McAteer firmly by the arm and, staying within the shelter of the pub doorway, signalled to Renton who was parked on the other side of the junction. As the car engine kicked into life he grabbed McAteer's wrists and rammed both his arms up his back, holding him in that position while he snapped on the handcuffs.

'So you think you're a right smart-arse?' O'Sullivan grunted. 'I won't forget this in a hurry, you Orange bastard! Before I'm finished with you, you'll be the one who's wetting your pants.'

'Shut your fuckin' geggie!'

Charlie Anderson walked into the ground-floor interview room where O'Sullivan and Renton were standing by the door. McAteer was perched on a chair at the other side of the room, being tended by the police doctor.

Charlie wandered across. 'Afternoon, doc. What seems to be the problem?' he asked, inclining his head in McAteer's direction.

'Nasty cut above the eye,' Dr Kent replied. 'It'll need a couple of stitches.'

'Can you do it here?'

'No problem. I've given him a local anaesthetic.'

Charlie crossed the room to where O'Sullivan and Renton were standing. He raised a questioning eyebrow. 'What happened?' he mouthed.

'McAteer tried to make a break for it when I was leading him to the car outside Tennent's,' O'Sullivan said quietly. 'He banged his head on the car roof.'

'You're a lyin' cunt!' McAteer yelled and struggled to get to his feet.

'Stay still, man!' Kent roared, pushing him back down on to the chair. 'Or I'll have your other eye out with this needle.' McAteer settled back in his seat and Kent held his head steady while he inserted four neat stitches to close the wound. 'There. That should hold it.'

'Managed to change your trousers, I see!' McAteer sneered in O'Sullivan's direction. He turned to Charlie. 'I want a lawyer. This is fuckin' harassment, Anderson. I've done nuthin'. You've no right to pull me in. And I'm filin' a complaint against that bastard for assault.' He jabbed a finger in O'Sullivan's direction. 'Banged my heid on the car roof, my fuckin' arse! That cunt put the heid on me while I was handcuffed.'

Charlie looked enquiringly at Dr Kent who shook his head and shrugged. 'Can't comment, Charlie,' he said, packing away his equipment. 'The wound's compatible with both versions of the story.'

'Thanks for your help. I'll take it from here.' Charlie sat down behind the desk in the middle of the room and indicated to McAteer to take the seat opposite. 'Let's get this over with. Where were you this morning between seven and nine o'clock?'

'I want a lawyer.'

'Hardly the attitude of someone who's got nothing to hide.'

'Go an' fuck yourself!'

'Answer the question, McAteer. Where were you between seven and nine?'

'In my pit.'

'Anyone who can vouch for that?'

'Kylie Minogue.'

Charlie locked his eyes on McAteer. 'When did you last see Gerry Fraser?'

'Who the fuck's Gerry Fraser?'

'The guy you beat up on Thursday morning.'

'Says who?'

'Who are you working for?'

'I'm no' workin'. I'm on the dole.'

'Who told you to give Fraser a doing?'

'I've no idea what you're witterin' on about.'

'Where are you staying?'

'In Govan.'

'Where in Govan?'

'With my brother.'

'Do you know Mike Harrison?'

McAteer hesitated. 'You mean the bookie?'

'That's him.'

'I know him to see.'

'Ever done any work for him?'

'No.'

'Do you know that he's dead?' Charlie held McAteer's one-eyed stare.

'Deid?' Glancing down quickly McAteer raised his fist to his mouth and started gnawing hard on his thumb nail. 'Since when?'

'Since this morning – murdered – in Kelvingrove Park.' McAteer looked up with a start, his one eye flickering rapidly.

'What's that got to do with me?'

'Weren't you supposed to be looking after him?'

'You're mental, Anderson.' McAteer jumped to his feet. 'I've done nuthin'. You canny hold me.'

Charlie pulled himself stiffly to his feet. 'You're free to go.' He gestured to O'Sullivan. 'See him off the premises – and when you've done that, I want to see you and Renton in my office.'

There was a light tap on Charlie's door. He peered over the top of his reading glasses, then put down his pen and pushed the pile of memos to one side as O'Sullivan and Renton walked in.

'Tell me again what happened,' Charlie said, slowly screwing the top back on to his fountain pen. 'How did McAteer's eyebrow get cut?'

Renton glanced sideways at O'Sullivan, inviting him to respond. 'Like I said downstairs, sir, when I came out of Tennent's, Colin was parked at the bottom of University Avenue. I waved him across and when I opened the back door of the car and told McAteer to get inside he tried to make a break for it. I grabbed at him and his head hit the car roof at the top of the door frame.'

'Was he cuffed at the time?'

'Yes, sir.'

Charlie paused. 'You're telling me that McAteer tried to make a break for it?'

'Yes, sir.'

'He tried to run off down Byres Road with his hands cuffed behind his back?'

O'Sullivan's face flushed . 'Yes, sir.'

'That's the way you saw it, Renton?'

Renton shuffled his feet and gazed at the floor. 'Yes, sir,' he mumbled.

'So if I check the car, I'll find blood on the roof and on the door frame?'

'I expect so,' said O'Sullivan. 'Though it's been pissing down all afternoon. It might've got washed off.'

'McAteer mentioned something about you changing your trousers. What was that all about?'

'A pint got spilled on me in the pub. It was an accident.'

'An accident? Nothing deliberate? Nothing that would make you want to get your own back on McAteer?'

'No, sir.'

Charlie removed his spectacles and set them down on the desk. Closing his eyes, he pinched the bridge of his nose between thumb and forefinger and sat motionless for some time. When he replaced his glasses he peered over them at O'Sullivan.

'I don't believe you,' he said quietly.

'But, sir –'

'Don't you fucking-well argue with me!' Charlie roared as he grabbed the sides of his desk and pulled himself up to his full height. 'Do you think I came up the Clyde in a fucking banana boat? I'll say it again, O'Sullivan.' Charlie measured every syllable. 'I don't believe one fucking word of it.' He glared long and hard, first at O'Sullivan, then at Renton, before settling back down on his chair. 'However, as I can't prove anything, it won't go any further this time. But I'm warning you – both of you,' he said, jabbing a crooked index finger at each of them in turn. 'As long as I'm running this show – and that may not be for very much longer – but as long as I'm here you'll do things by the book.

Even with scum like McAteer. Is that clear, O'Sullivan?'

'Yes, sir.'

'That goes for you too, Renton.' Renton nodded. 'Here's a nice wee job to keep you out of mischief on a Saturday night,' Charlie said, taking out his notebook and ripping out a page. 'These are the names of the punters who were playing poker with Harrison last night – along with Ronnie McGavigan, the last people to see him alive. Find out where they live and pay them a visit. I want to know what Harrison talked about last night and I want to know if he gave any indication as to why he was planning to go to Kelvingrove Park this morning. While you're at it, find out where these guys were between seven and nine o'clock this morning. And when you've done that,' Charlie continued, digging through his mail and handing a sheaf of paper to O'Sullivan, 'Niggle wants an explanation as to why violent crime is up by 9.6 per cent this year. As you're well qualified on that subject, you're the ideal person to analyse the data and prepare a report. Have your draft response available to review with me first thing on Monday morning.'

'But I'm not on duty this weekend, sir, and –' Catching Charlie's glare, O'Sullivan choked off his protest and took the proffered papers.

'One more thing,' Charlie called out as O'Sullivan and Renton were heading towards the door. 'In future, if you ever get an uncontrollable urge to stick the heid on someone, make it a fair fight. Don't do it when they're cuffed.'

O'Sullivan's attempt at a protest was cut short by Renton grabbing him by the arm and pulling him out of the office.

Laura Harrison sat in front of her television set watching the news. The gruesome murder in Kelvingrove Park was the lead story and the police were appealing for anyone who had been in the vicinity of the park around eight o'clock on Saturday morning to come forward. Her mind was churning, struggling to make sense of what had happened. She was convinced Mike couldn't have been the blackmailer. She knew him too well. He could never have acted as casually as he had done if he'd seen that photograph of her and Simon. In which case, what on earth had he been doing in the park? Her confused thoughts were interrupted by the ring of the doorbell.

'What in the name of God are you doing here?'

Billy McAteer pushed past her into the hallway and slammed the door behind him. 'Is there anyone else here?' he demanded.

'No.'

He grabbed her by the forearm. 'You've been pullin' my plonker,' he snarled. 'I don't like that.'

'What are you talking about?' she said, wrenching her arm free.

'You set me up to bump off your auld man.'

'I'd no idea it would be Mike.'

'Don't give me that crap!'

'It's true. Honestly!'

'I don't know what game you're playin', but the rules have just changed.'

'What are you talking about?'

'You've screwed me up good an' proper. Your auld man was payin' me five hundred a week in readies. Now I've got nothin' comin' in. I want the ten grand you owe me – and I want it now.'

'You'll get your money, but I'll have to –'

'And don't even think about turnin' me in to the polis,' he said, 'because you're in this right up to your pretty little neck.' He gripped her arm again painfully.

'You'll get your money – but it'll take me time to raise the cash.' Her face creased in pain as he increased the pressure on her arm. 'I told you that already.' He stared at her hard, slowly relaxing his grip. Pulling away from him, she massaged her arm. 'In the meantime don't come anywhere near here,' she said. 'For all we know the police might be watching the house.'

'They're not. I checked. I'm not stupid.'

'In any case it's too dangerous for you to come here. Someone might see you. I'll get in touch with you as soon as I've got the money.'

'We agreed on one week – max. That gives you until Friday – not a day longer.' He turned round and eased open the front door. Peering out, he headed off down the drive.

CHAPTER 9

'It's very good of you to come round on a Saturday, Mr Glancey.' Laura Harrison ushered the tall, slightly stooped figure ahead of her into the lounge. 'And on such a filthy night as well.'

'Under the circumstances it was the least I could do.' Keith Glancey, senior partner of Glancey, Glancey, Layfield and Jackson, perched himself on the edge of the settee and pulled a folder from his attaché case. 'Dreadful business, Mrs Harrison. Quite dreadful. I'm terribly sorry,' he added, fiddling nervously with his bow tie. 'I really don't know what to say.'

'Can I get you something? A cup of tea – or coffee?' He shook his head. 'Perhaps you'd like something stronger?'

'Nothing for me. Truly,' he said, waving his hand in front of his face and clearing his throat. Laura sank down on the armchair facing him. 'I went into the office this afternoon to check the files,' he began as he sorted fussily through his papers. 'I'm afraid things are even worse than I first thought.' Laura moved forward on to the edge of her seat, her hands gripping the arms of the chair. 'Effectively, Mrs Harrison,' he said, coughing into his fist, 'I'm afraid you've got nothing.'

'Nothing?'

'Your husband remortgaged the house last year – to way beyond its current value. I think you'll find you're in negative equity.'

'What about the betting shops?'

'Four of the shops belong to Mr McGavigan. Your husband did own the other two but he sold them to a property developer a year ago and rented back the premises.'

'Don't we have any other assets? Stocks and shares? Investments?'

Glancey took a spotless white handkerchief from his breast pocket and used it to dab his brow. 'There are some, but the value isn't significant and the little that there is will be more than swallowed up by the outstanding claim from the Inland Revenue.'

'Mike had a couple of life insurance policies.'

Glancey shook his head. 'He cashed both of them in some time ago.'

'The bastard!' hissed out from between Laura's clenched teeth. She composed herself quickly. 'What about the cars? They must be worth something?'

'Both your car, and your husband's, are leased.'

Laura got to her feet and walked towards the French windows, staring vacantly out into the darkened garden. 'I need to raise ten thousand pounds urgently, Mr Glancey. In fact, within the next couple of days.' She spun around. 'What would be the best way of going about that?'

Glancey fiddled with his bow tie. 'I'm sorry to be so negative at a time like this, Mrs Harrison, but I really don't see how you're going to be able to do that.'

Simon Ramsay was sitting in front of his computer screen when there was a sharp rap on the study door. 'What is it?' he demanded irritably, reaching for the packet of cigarettes on the desk.

Jude walked in and stood by the door. 'I want an explanation.'

'What are you talking about?' he snapped. 'An explanation for what?'

'I tried phoning you at the office on Thursday morning. They told me you'd taken a few days off.'

'Oh, that.' He pulled a cigarette from the packet and tapped it on the desk. 'I needed a break. That was all. The pressure of work was getting to me.'

'Why didn't you mention anything about that to me?'

'There's no way you'd have understood!' His fingers were trembling as he cradled his cigarette lighter in both hands. 'You don't realise what a bastard your father is to work for.'

Jude stared at him. 'Why did you sneak out of the house at half-past seven this morning?'

Simon got to his feet, pulling hard on his cigarette. 'Jesus Christ! This is worse than the fucking Spanish Inquisition!' He exhaled noisily. 'Anyway, I didn't *sneak* out this morning. I'd run out of fags so I nipped out to get some. I went out quietly so as not to wake you up.'

'Quite a coincidence that Mike was murdered while you were out of the house,' Jude said in a matter-of-fact tone.

His face turned scarlet. 'What the hell are you driving at?'

'Oh, for God's sake! I'm not accusing you of murder. I know you wouldn't have the balls to do anything like that. However, it's still one hell of a coincidence, don't you think? The police are coming here tomorrow to take our statements. Don't expect me to cover up for you.' Jude turned away and gripped the door handle. 'And for your sake, I hope whoever sold you the cigarettes this morning remembers doing so.'

Sunday 19 December

Charlie looked up at the kitchen clock and quickly folded *The Sunday Post*. 'I'd better not hang about. Jamie's expecting me at half-past,' he said, buttering a slice of toast

'Will you be going into the office afterwards?' There was resignation in Kay's voice as she refilled his tea cup.

'I'm meeting Tony O'Sullivan in Pitt Street at ten. He's set up interviews with Mike Harrison's relatives this morning. Got to strike while the iron's hot, love.'

'Just for once, couldn't someone else –' Kay's comment was interrupted by the ring of the phone. Charlie took the call.

'Charlie, it's Hugh,' a breezy voice announced. 'Glad I caught you. I might be able to get my hands on a spare ticket for the match and I wanted to know if you'd be interested.'

'Match? What match?'

'*The* match, of course. Wednesday night. Champions League. Celtic versus Dynamo Zagreb.'

'You know I only go to a football match if there's half a chance of a Scotsman appearing on the pitch.'

'The day Thistle are in the Champions League is the day you can start being picky. Seriously, big brother, are you up for it?'

'Sure.'

'I can't promise about the ticket. I won't know until Wednesday afternoon whether or not I'll be able to get it. I'll give you a call as soon as I know.'

'Thanks, Hugh.' Charlie replaced the receiver. 'Sorry, love. What were you about to say?' he asked.

'I just wanted to know if you'd be home in time for dinner.'

'I'll do my best.'

'It's stovies.'

'You sure know how to tempt a man.' Charlie bent down to give Kay a peck on the cheek. 'I will try to get home at a respectable hour. I'll give you a bell some time in the afternoon and let you know how things are going.' Picking up his gloves and his car keys from the hall table, he pulled on his heavy overcoat.

Charlie drew up outside his daughter's semi-detached bungalow just before eight-thirty. Jamie, already kitted out in his bright yellow goalkeeper's jersey, white shorts and football boots, was watching from his bedroom window. When he saw his grandfather's car approach he ran outside, waving his new football aloft.

'Hello, Grandad!' he squealed as he careered down the path. 'Mum's still in bed so we can start straight away.'

Charlie pulled off his overcoat and rummaged in the car boot for an old pair of gardening shoes. 'How's the birthday boy?'

'Great. Thanks a million for the book you and Grandma gave me. It's smashing. It tells you everything about the World Cup ever since it started.'

'You haven't read it already?' Charlie asked as he was changing his shoes.

'I've flicked through it. There's photos of all the teams and pictures of the best goals. Do you remember Archie Gemmill scoring against Holland in Argentina in 1978?'

'Indeed I do. It was a belter.'

'There's a photo of that goal in the book. I'll show it to you later.'

'What else did you get?'

'These,' he announced proudly, holding up the football in one hand and tugging at his new jersey with the other.

'Have you tried them out yet?'

'I was waiting for you.'

'Let's go then.'

Jamie raced ahead to the back garden where he'd already positioned two dustbins as goalposts in front of the hedge and marked a penalty spot with a handful of dirt. 'The hedge is the goal, grandad.' Placing the ball on the spot, he ran to take up his position on the goal line.

'Are you sure this is twelve yards, Jamie?'

'Grandad! It's eleven metres. Nobody says twelve yards any more.'

'It'll always be twelve yards for me, son. Right. Who's playing?'

'Scotland versus Brazil. World Cup final 1978 in Argentina.'

Charlie guffawed. 'I think we'd better check some of the facts in that book of yours.'

'It wasn't really. It's only pretend.'

'Fair enough. What's the score?'

'Scotland are leading 1–0. There's only a minute to go and the referee's given Brazil a dodgy penalty. It was never a foul, but the referee's English so what can you expect?'

Charlie's grin broadened. 'Who are you?'

'Alan Rough.'

'Who am I?'

'Pele.'

'Pele? He doesn't miss many penalties.'

'But he's never scored against Scotland in a World Cup final, has he?'

'That, I cannot argue with!'

Jamie bent forward, hands wide apart. Charlie struck the ball low and hard to his right, burying it in the hedge. Jamie recovered the ball and ran to replace it on the spot before sprinting back to the goal line.

'Ready!' he shouted. The next shot lodged in the hedge on the other side.

For twenty minutes the game continued unabated, Jamie tirelessly replacing the ball on the spot after each shot. Charlie checked his watch. 'I'll have to be going now. Last one, okay?'

Jamie crouched very low – concentration written all over his face. As Charlie side-footed the ball Jamie flung himself to his right and the spinning ball flicked his outstretched fingertips, struck the dustbin and ricocheted back into his arms as he lay on the ground. 'Does that count as a save, Grandad?' he implored as he scrambled to his feet. 'Does it?'

'Of course, Jamie. That counts.'

Throwing the ball high in the air he danced a triumphant jig. 'That makes six saves,' he yelped. 'That's a record! I've never saved six before.'

'You did really well today, son,' Charlie said, ruffling Jamie's unruly crop of black hair as they walked round the side of the house. 'You're reading the direction of the shots a lot better. Your second save was a real cracker.'

'When can we play again?' he asked excitedly.

'Soon, I promise. Now make sure you take off those muddy boots before you go into the house – and I'm not at all sure what your mother's going to say when she sees the state of your new jersey,' he added, eyeing the mud-splattered mess.

'You can't be a goalkeeper and have a clean jersey. You told me that. Remember?'

'Be off with you!' Charlie smiled, ruffling his hair again. 'Tell your mum I couldn't wait to see her. Tell her I'll call her later in the day.'

'Bye, Grandad.' Jamie kept waving until Charlie's car was out of sight, then he sat down on the doorstep and started to untie his bootlaces.

Tony O'Sullivan was waiting in Charlie's office.

'How did you make out with the poker school crowd?' Charlie asked as he draped his coat on the stand.

'Between us, Renton and I managed to track them all down. Not much joy, I'm afraid. They all claim that the extent of their conversation with Harrison on Friday night was "raise you a fiver". They say he didn't mention anything about going to Kelvingrove Park on Saturday morning.'

'Do they have alibis for the time Harrison was killed?'

'McGill, Grant and Higney all have wives who will vouch for them. Amos lives on his own. He claims he was still in bed at eight o'clock yesterday morning – no reason not to believe him.'

'Give me a rundown on Harrison's relatives.'

O'Sullivan referred to his notebook. 'He had no immediate family, apart from an elderly maiden aunt who lives in a residential home on the outskirts of Stirling. His wife, Laura, is the eldest daughter of a bloke called Jim Cuthbertson. You might have heard of him?'

'The stockbroker?' Charlie rubbed his thumb and forefingers together meaningfully.

'That's the one. He's got offices all over the country. He disowned Laura when she took up with Harrison because he didn't approve of his business activities. Apparently he hasn't spoken to Laura for the past ten years. There are three younger sisters,' O'Sullivan continued. 'Alison's the next in line. She's married to a teuchter called Norman Mitchell. They have two young kids and they run an organic farm near Ballinluig in Perthshire. Then there's Judith. She made her reputation as the editor of a fashion magazine. She's married to a bloke called Simon Ramsay, originally from Greenock. Ramsay dropped out of university and was bumming around on the dole when he hooked up with Judith. The rumour is that the only reason they got hitched was because she got pregnant, but then she miscarried. He's got a couple of previous for cocaine possession during his university days but nothing recent. Cuthbertson gave him a job in his Glasgow office in some sort of administrative capacity. The word on the street is that Cuthbertson doesn't think a lot of Ramsay either, but he tolerates him because he thinks the sun shines out of Judith's backside. The Ramsays and the Harrisons used to socialise a lot together – holidays, concerts, restaurants, dinner parties, that sort of thing. Which leaves Helen. She's quite a bit younger than the others. She was a fashion model – middle of the road – until she packed it in quite recently. She's shacked up with a Swedish computer programmer, name of Bjorn Svensson. They live in a flash pad in Giffnock.'

'What's our schedule for today?' Charlie asked.

'We're seeing the Ramsays at eleven o'clock and Helen Cuthbertson at two.'

'Not Svensson?'

'He's gone to Sweden for the weekend for his mother's sixtieth. He's not due back until tomorrow night so we won't be able to talk to him before then, unless, of course, the expense account will run to a couple of return tickets to Stockholm?'

Charlie grimaced. 'Mileage to Perthshire would be pushing it.'

'I didn't know if you'd want to go up there today. The A9 is open again but the Mitchells' farm is twenty miles from Ballinluig and their road is still cut off. According to the Met Office it might be reopened later this afternoon, but there's no guarantee.'

'I'm too long in the tooth to take up cross-country skiing. Let's see what we get out of the Ramsays and Helen Cuthbertson. We can decide later if it's worth our while making a trip to Ballinluig.'

Charlie reversed into a parking place at the far end of Park Terrace and switched off the ignition. He levered himself out of the driver's seat and leaned with both elbows on the car roof, shielding his eyes from the watery sun as he scanned the city centre and the sprawling conurbations. 'You get a cracking view from up here,' he said. 'Can you see my house?' he asked, pointing a gloved finger towards the specks on the horizon.

O'Sullivan put his forearm in front of his eyes and squinted. 'Is it the one with the pink-flowered lace curtains in the upstairs bathroom?'

'Nice try. But the bathroom's on the other side of the house.'

'Okay, I admit it. It was the garden gnome I recognised.'

'His name's Alan.'

'Named after Alan Rough, by any chance?'

'Might be,' Charlie said defensively.

'My Dad's got a garden gnome,' O'Sullivan offered.

'Called Jinky, by any chance?'

O'Sullivan nodded in affirmation as Charlie slammed the car door and depressed his key to activate the central locking.

Charlie could feel the tension between Jude and Simon Ramsay as they sat facing him at opposite ends of the settee.

'When did you last see Mike Harrison?' Charlie cast his eyes down at his notebook, pen poised, leaving the question hanging to see who would volunteer to respond.

'Last Wednesday.' It was Simon who had spoken.

'Which was the fifteenth,' Jude said. 'Mike and Laura came here for dinner to celebrate Simon's fortieth.'

'Was there anyone else present?' Charlie asked.

'My kid sister, Helen, and her boyfriend, Bjorn Svensson,' Jude said. 'My other sister, Alison, and her husband were supposed to be coming but they couldn't make it because of the weather.'

'How did Mike Harrison behave?' Jude looked puzzled. 'Was he his usual self?' Charlie probed. 'Did he appear worried? Was he distracted? Did he seem preoccupied with anything?'

Jude looked at Simon and puffed out her cheeks. 'Nothing wrong, as far as I could tell,' she said. 'He was the life and soul of the party, as usual.'

'He didn't mention any particular problems?' O'Sullivan inquired. 'Anyone or anything bothering him?'

'Not that I can remember,' Simon stated, lighting up a cigarette.

'He did say something about financial problems,' Jude said, 'but I took that with a pinch of salt. Mike was forever going on about how difficult it was for a bookie to make ends meet these days.'

'Your sister, Laura, how was she?' Charlie asked.

Jude shrugged. 'A bit quieter than usual, perhaps. She was upset because she'd been mugged.'

Charlie glanced up from his notebook. 'Mugged?'

'A couple of thugs tried to snatch her handbag on Monday night.'

'Where did that happen?'

'Outside a cinema in Renfrew Street. Laura managed to hang on to her bag but she got a punch in the face for her trouble,' Jude said.

'When I saw her yesterday, I did notice her face was bruised,' O'Sullivan said.

'I got the impression there was more to it than that,' Simon said.

'More to it than what, Simon?' Jude asked tetchily.

'I don't know. Laura was very quiet all evening. I don't think it was just on account of the mugging. I thought there was something going on between her and Mike. When I let them in I got the impression that they weren't talking.'

Jude looked askance. 'Your imagination is running away with you, Simon.' She turned to face Charlie. 'Mike and Laura were perfectly all right, Inspector. Take my word for it. If there had been anything untoward, Laura would've told me. We're very close.'

Simon drew hard on his cigarette. 'I suppose I might've been mistaken,' he muttered, exhaling a lungful of smoke. 'It was just a feeling I had.'

Charlie broke the silence that followed. 'As far as you know, did Laura and Mike have any marital problems?' Again, he directed the question towards no one in particular.

'No more than most.' Jude smoothed down her skirt. 'They had their ups and downs. Who doesn't?'

'I believe your father didn't approve of their relationship?'

'It's no secret that Dad had no time for Mike. He believed the stories that were being bandied around.'

'Stories? Such as?'

'That Mike was involved in activities less legal than bookmaking.'

'Was he?'

'I would have thought you would be in a much better position to judge that than I am,' Jude said stiffly. She looked pointedly at her watch. 'Do you have many more questions?'

'Just a couple of routine ones,' Charlie said. 'Where were you yesterday morning between seven and nine?'

'In bed. I had a late night at the opera on Friday and I didn't get up until after ten.'

'And you, sir?'

Simon sucked hard on his cigarette. 'I had a lie-in, too.' Jude's piercing eyes stared long and hard at her husband's profile.

Charlie put away his notebook. 'I'll leave my phone number,' he said, taking a card from the breast pocket of his jacket and placing it on the coffee table. 'If you think of anything that might be relevant, don't hesitate to give me a call.'

After showing them out, Jude strode back into the lounge. 'Why didn't you say anything to the police about going out for cigarettes yesterday morning?' she demanded.

'It was irrelevant,' Simon said, waving his hand dismissively. 'They've got enough on their plate without getting bogged down with insignificant details.'

'Where did you buy the cigarettes?'

'I didn't say I *bought* cigarettes. I said I went out to get some. My car windscreen was frozen solid and while I was waiting for it to defrost I remembered I'd left a packet of fags in the glove compartment. I found it, so I came back in.'

Helen Cuthbertson, wearing a cream miniskirt and a matching, figure-hugging angora sweater, sat with her legs crossed on a high-backed chair opposite Charlie and Tony. Her make-up was flawless.

'I really don't think there's anything I can help you with, gentlemen,' she said, blowing on her tapered fingernails to help dry the bright, purple polish. 'It was a run-of-the-mill, boring dinner party. Bjorn hates our family gatherings at the best of times and this one was even worse than usual because Jude had insisted that he wear a dinner suit. He didn't want to go, but I dragged him along. As for the others . . .' She placed her index finger across her lips as she reflected. 'Simon seemed to be having a miserable time – which is par for the course when Jude's around – and Mike's jokes were even cruder than usual. By the end of the evening Mike was pretty much the worse for wear. Not that I've got a lot of room to talk, mind you. I was knocking back wine and Drambuie like they were going out of fashion. I paid for it the next morning,' she added, massaging her forehead tenderly.

'How were your sisters?' Charlie asked.

Helen puckered her lips. 'Laura was moody – nothing unusual in that – and Jude was making no secret of the fact that she was pissed off with Simon.'

'How would you describe the relationship between Laura and her husband,' O'Sullivan inquired.

'I'm not the best person to ask. I haven't spent much time in Glasgow in recent years – I had to do a lot of travelling for my job. And when I was here,' she added, 'I didn't see much of the Harrisons. Bjorn and I have our own circle of friends and we only ever socialised with Laura and Mike on family occasions.'

'I believe Mr Svensson is away just now?' Charlie said.

'In Stockholm. Mummy's sixtieth. I managed to find an excuse to avoid having to suffer the old bat.' She raised her eyes to the ceiling. 'Bjorn says that it isn't fair that he has to put up with my relatives while I avoid his like the plague.' She fluttered her long false eyelashes. 'I must admit – he does have a point.'

'Where were you yesterday morning around eight o'clock?' Tony asked.

'I hope you're not checking up to see if I have an alibi, Sergeant?' Helen placed her hands on her lap and smiled coyly. 'Let me see now. At eight o'clock, I was in bed – with Bjorn. We got up around nine and I drove him to the airport just after ten to catch his flight. It wasn't until later in the day that Laura phoned to tell me the dreadful news about Mike.'

'When will Mr Svensson be back?' Charlie asked.

'Tomorrow evening. Will you need to talk to him?'

'There may be a few questions,' Charlie said, getting to his feet. 'If so, we'll be in touch.'

'Bit of a wasted day, sir?' O'Sullivan said as they drove down the slope into Pitt Street's underground car park.

'Not a lot to go on,' Charlie conceded.

Getting out of the car, they bent into the funnelling wind as they hurried towards the main building. 'Fancy a coffee?' Charlie asked as they were climbing the staircase.

'I'll get them in,' Tony volunteered. 'I've got a pocketful of change.'

When they got to his office, Charlie looked at his watch. 'It looks like I'm actually going to be home in time for dinner. Must call Kay and give her the glad tidings,' he said, putting his coffee down on the desk and stretching for the phone. Kay answered on the first ring. 'You can put the dinner on, love,' Charlie said, 'I won't be late.' Replacing the receiver he asked Tony, 'Do you have anything exciting planned for this evening?'

'I've invited someone round to my place, but I'm going to have to put them off. I'm not half-way through analysing the crime stats for tomorrow's report.'

'Oh, did I not tell you?'

'Tell me what?'

'I got the date wrong. The analysis isn't required until a week on Monday.' Charlie suppressed a grin. ' Who's the lucky girl, then?'

'Chance would be a fine thing!' O'Sullivan let out a snort. 'I've invited Tom Freer round to sample my collection of malts.'

'Do I know him?'

'He's a new guy, up from London. He was with you in the interview room when you were grilling Fraser about the Save the Children box.'

Charlie snapped his fingers. 'Got him! He counted the money for me. Seemed like a decent enough lad.'

'He was working for the Met but he requested a move up north because his girlfriend was transferred to Glasgow by her firm. He knows hardly anybody up here so I thought it would be a nice idea to offer him some traditional Scottish hospitality. He's bringing the Indian takeaway and I'm supplying the bevvy.'

'Sounds perfect!'

'It'll make a change from drinking on my own. Do you fancy stopping off for a quick one on the way home, sir?'

'I sure as hell fancy it, but I'd better not risk it. It would be more than my life's worth to get involved in a session. Anyway, I need to stop off in Sauchiehall Street to pick up a Christmas present for Kay, and I don't want to be late. Sunday night is stovies night,' he added, smacking his lips.

'Shouldn't that be "Rainday" night?' Tony said. Charlie chuckled. 'Which reminds me,' Tony said, getting to his feet. 'There's a call I have to make. I'll be back in a minute.' Nipping into the adjacent empty office he pulled his mobile from his pocket. Having checked the slip of paper in his notebook he tapped in the number. 'Sue? It's Tony.'

'Hi!'

'How did the skiing go?'

Sue had to shout to make herself heard. 'I've got a bruised knee, a sore bum and a twisted ankle – but apart from that it was fine. And now I've got a houseful of kids screaming "Happy Birthday, dear Jamie".' She held the phone away from her ear. 'See what I mean?'

'Lucky you! How are you fixed for tomorrow night?'

Sue shoved a finger into her ear. 'Everything's organised. I've got a babysitter lined up and I've managed to enlist a couple of volunteers to close up the school hall after the nativity play.'

'Great! How about we meet in the Tron Bar at half-seven and wander down from there?'

'That's going to be a bit tight for me. It might be better if we met at Glasgow Green.'

'Okay. How about the park gates at the Clyde Street end? As near to half-seven as you can make it.'

'Fine. I'm really looking forward to the gig.'

'Me too.'

Sue started humming the intro to 'Fake Plastic Trees', but was quickly drowned out by another screeching chorus of 'Happy Birthday, dear Jamie'.

Tony wandered back into Charlie's office. 'What about Ballinluig? Will we need to go up there?'

'Can't see that we'd get a lot out of it,' Charlie said, shaking his head. 'Why don't you give the Pitlochry boys a bell? Brief them on the situation and ask them to drop in and have a chat with the Mitchells when the snow has cleared.'

The phone on Charlie's desk rang. He hesitated, his hand hovering over the handset. 'Picking this up is flirting with disaster,' he said. 'I've just told Kay I'm on my way home.' He let it ring twice more before snatching the receiver from its cradle. 'Anderson!' he barked.

'This is Simon Ramsay, Inspector. I hope I'm not disturbing you?'

'Not at all, Mr Ramsay.' Charlie switched the phone to loudspeaker mode so Tony could listen in. 'What can I do for you?'

'Following on from our discussion this morning, I didn't want to say any more in front of my wife.' Ramsay hesitated. 'But I don't think Laura Harrison's injuries were caused by a bag snatcher.'

'Really? How do you think they were caused?'

'By her husband.'

'Indeed?' Charlie winked at Tony. 'What makes you think that?'

'It's just a hunch. I've had my suspicions for some time that Mike was violent towards Laura, though she never said anything. I hope this isn't out of order, but I thought you ought to know. Perhaps you could find some way to check it out?'

'I'll see what I can do.'

'Please don't mention anything to my wife about what I've just told you – and especially not to Laura. Neither of them would appreciate my interfering.'

'No problem, Mr Ramsay. Our little secret.' Charlie replaced the receiver slowly. 'Maybe today wasn't such a waste of time after all.' He drummed his fingertips on the desk. 'If I was a suspicious person I might think our Mr Ramsay was trying to plant a seed in my mind that Laura Harrison had a good reason for wanting to see the back of her old man.'

CHAPTER 10

Tony O'Sullivan answered the ring on his doorbell and found Tom Freer standing on the threshold, clutching two carrier bags.

'Bang on time, Tom.' Freer transferred both bags to his left hand so he could shake hands. 'Dino would approve,' Tony said, taking his hand in a firm grip. 'Come on in.'

Freer wiped his shoes on the doormat before stepping into the carpeted hallway. Tall and slim, he was wearing a crew-neck sweater and black cord trousers. 'Nice place you've got here, sir,' he said, looking up admiringly at the high, corniced ceiling.

'We're off duty, Tom. It's Tony.'

'Okay, sir ... er ... Tony.' He smiled sheepishly. 'What do you want me to do with these?' he asked, holding up the carrier bags.

Tony rubbed his hands together. 'I'll take care of that lot,' he said, taking the bags and leading the way to the kitchen. 'This smell's driving me crazy. I didn't realise how hungry I was.' Tony slid the four cardboard-covered, tinfoil containers from the carrier bags and left them on the table while he fetched two plates from the rack on the draining board. Help yourself to a drink while I dish this out. Lager's in the fridge, beer's in the cupboard under the sink. What's your poison?'

'Lager for me, please.'

'I can't see past export myself.'

Sitting at opposite sides of the wooden kitchen table they each downed a couple of beers straight from the can while making short work of the curries.

'You canny whack a Shish Mahal takeaway,' Tony said, wiping the back of his hand across his lips. 'How did that compare with London's finest?'

'Chicken vindaloo's the same the world over. Anybody who claims they can taste anything's a bloody liar.'

'Fair comment.' Tony leaned back in his chair. 'How are you settling in to life in the frozen north?'

'We're not really organised yet. Mel and I have rented a furnished flat in Shieldhall. It's a bit grotty but we managed to negotiate a short-term lease and it'll do until we find something better.'

'How's the job panning out?'

'So far, so good. Colin Renton's been a big help – introducing me to everyone and helping me find my feet.'

'Renton's the salt of the earth,' Tony nodded.

'What about Charlie Anderson?' Tom asked. 'What's he like to work for?'

'The first time I came across him was when I attended a graduate trainee seminar about ten years ago. He was a DI at the time and his lecture consisted of trying to convince the class of the benefits of learning shorthand. That was how he acquired the nickname "Dino", after Fred Flintstone's dinosaur. It really was Stone Age stuff, him strutting up and down the room, waving his notebook in the air and ranting on about "The Key Question" – that's his pet theory. He thinks the best way to solve a crime is to ask all the questions you can think of and note down the answers, in shorthand of course, then analyse the data to death until you find an inconsistency. His methods might be out of the ark but his success rate is up there with the best of them.

'He takes a very pragmatic approach. He realises he can't convict every villain he'd like to, so he picks his targets and goes after the ones where he thinks he has a realistic chance of getting a result.'

'He seems to sail close to the wind at times.'

'How do you mean?'

'When he was interviewing Gerry Fraser he had a real go at him – physically.'

'That's typical of Charlie! If you or I tried that he'd tear a strip off us, but he's a law unto himself – very much an advocate of "Do as I say, not do as I do".'

Tony pulled himself to his feet and fetched two more cans. 'Apart from work, how's Glasgow treating you?' he asked, handing across the lager.

'Okay. Though I think I'm going to need to take language lessons. Do you know if Linguaphone do a course in Glaswegian?'

Tony smiled. 'You should try to get your hands on the *Parliamo Glasgow* tapes.'

'What are they when they're at home?'

'An old Stanley Baxter routine – the foreigners' guide to making yourself understood in Glasgow. Foreign includes the east of Scotland, by the way.' Tony flopped back down on his chair. 'I liked the one about the German tourist who asked someone to explain the meaning of the word "breeding". He was told: "It all depends where you come from. In Edinburgh, it means good taste. In Glasgow, it means good fun".' Tom laughed as Tony wiped up the last traces of curry sauce with a piece of folded chapatti and stuffed it into his mouth, washing it down with a long swig of export. He pushed his plate to one side. 'Now it's time to get down to the serious business,' he said. 'Where would you like to start?' He counted off on his fingers. 'I've got Laphroaig, Glenmorangie, Highland Park, Talisker, Balvenie and Lagavulin.'

'When in doubt, I tend to go for alphabetical order.'

'Helen, I need your help.' Laura Harrison's voice sounded agitated.

Helen Cuthbertson transferred the phone to her left hand and picked up her glass of Chablis. 'I'll do what I can, sis. You know that,' she said. 'What's the problem?'

'I need to get my hands on money – a lot of money – and I need it quickly.'

'How much is *a lot*?'

'Ten thousand pounds.'

Helen hesitated. 'I don't know about that. I'd have to talk to Bjorn. He's in Stockholm right now, but he'll be back tomorrow night and –'

'I've got to have it, Helen!'

'Steady on! I don't have that kind of money to hand.'

'You've got five thousand a month going into the Cayman Islands, for Christ's sake! Don't try to tell me you don't have it.'

'Calm down, Laura. The funds in the Caymans aren't readily accessible. I can't just phone up and transfer cash to my Bank of Scotland current account. It doesn't work like that.' Laura started sobbing down the line. 'What's the problem?' Helen asked gently. 'Why do you need the money?'

'Mike stitched me up,' she said between sobs. 'The bastard remortgaged the house, sold the bookies' shops and cashed in his life insurance policies without saying a bloody word. He's left me with debts that have to be cleared.'

'I'm sure we'll be able to sort something out. As I said, Bjorn will be back from Stockholm tomorrow night. He's got a couple of days off. We'll come across to your place first thing on Tuesday morning and talk things through.'

Tom Freer looked at his watch. 'Hey, is that the time? I really ought to be making tracks. Mel will be wondering where I've got to.'

'Give her a bell,' Tony said.

'She's probably asleep by now, in which case she wouldn't appreciate being woken up to be told I'm on my way. Okay if I call a cab?'

'Sure. The number of the nearest rank's on the side of the phone.'

Tom picked up the handset and dialled. 'Fifteen minutes,' he said, replacing the receiver.

'Time for a nightcap, then.' Tony got to his feet, a little unsteadily, and fetched the Talisker bottle from the cupboard. 'Not a lot left in this one,' he said, angling the bottle and holding it up to the light. 'Still, enough for a snifter.'

'Tell me something,' Tom said as Tony was pouring. 'A couple of people at work asked me what school I went to. What's that all about?'

Tony kicked off his shoes and swung his feet up onto the kitchen table. 'Ah ha! They were trying to find out what foot you kick with.'

'Come again?'

'Are you a Billy or a Tim?' He transferred his whisky tumbler from one hand to the other, then back again. 'A blue-nose or a Bhoy? Do you frequent Ibrox or Parkhead? I realise this is difficult for you to get your head round, Tom – you have to be brought up with it. The English don't have a clue about the west of Scotland mentality. They can't begin to understand the bigotry.'

'Bigotry's not something we're short of down south,' Tom stated emphatically.

'There's bigotry . . .' Tony transferred his whisky glass again. 'And there's bigotry. What I'm talking about is inherited, religious bigotry. Let me ask you a question.' He put his glass down on the table and ripped the ring-pull from a can of export. 'How many people did you work with in the Met?'

Tom shrugged his shoulders. 'Twenty, maybe – perhaps thirty?'

'Of those, how many were Catholics and how many were Protestants?'

'How on earth would I know something like that?'

'Exactly! That's my point. I can tell you what foot everyone in Pitt Street kicks with. And I mean everyone – from the chief constable down to the cleaners. In this part of the world you have to know everyone's religion. It's as much a part of their identity as their name. No one will ask you outright, of course – that would be unsubtle. So when you first meet someone, they'll josh you about what football team you support. If you admit to Celtic or Rangers they've got you pigeon-holed. If you claim to support Partick Thistle, and you weren't born in Maryhill, they'll suspect you're trying to duck the issue so they'll pick their moment to slip the killer question into the conversation: "What school did you go to, pal?" Bingo! If it begins with "Saint" or "Our Lady" you're a Tim, if not, you're a Hun. No point in trying to qualify your response, by the way: "I went to such and such a school, but I'm an atheist, an agnostic, a Jew, or I've recently converted to the Church of Scientology." None of that'll wash. The rules don't allow for opting out.' Tony took a long swig of beer from his can. 'You're not going to believe this but a few years back a Sikh applied for a job as a trainee constable and the interviewer asked him if he was a Catholic Sikh or a Protestant Sikh.'

Tom burst out laughing. 'You cannot be serious!'

'It would be hilarious if it wasn't the God's honest truth. Let me explain how things work in this part of the world. From the age of four, children are segregated.' Tony separated out the empty cans. 'Protestants to one school.' He slid the lager cans to the far end of the table. 'Catholics to another.' He wrapped his arms round the export cans and pulled them towards him. 'Thus ensuring that everyone you're in contact with during your formative years is of the same religious persuasion. This, in turn, defines the football team you'll support, who your mates will be and, if your family has its way, who you'll marry and how you'll bring up your kids. It's no exaggeration to say that the primary school your mammy sends you to defines the label branded on your forehead for the rest of your life.' With a sweep of his arm Tony sent all the cans clattering to the floor.

Tom looked incredulous. 'Surely that's all a thing of the past?'

'Don't you believe it!'

'I didn't realise things were as bad as that.'

'Just once, while you're up in Glasgow, try to get your hands on a ticket for an Old Firm match and see what you make of it. The raw hatred between the rival sets of fans is almost tangible. The powers that be try to keep a lid on things but I can remember being at games, not all that long ago, when half the fans, the majority of them pissed out of their brains, were belting out

"The Sash My Father Wore" and rejoicing in the slaughter of the papists at the Battle of the Boyne while the other lot were chanting "The Soldier's Song" and wallowing in the glories of the 1916 Easter Rising.'

'It sounds like a completely different world.' Tom said.

'The Met might have a monopoly on institutionalised racism, but we've cornered the market when it comes to religious bigotry.' Tony broke off to tip the dregs from the Talisker bottle into Tom's glass, then drained his can. 'And things aren't a lot better at work,' he added with feeling.

'How do you mean?'

'Pitt Street might as well be a branch of the Orange Lodge. If you don't do the handshake and roll up your trouser leg at the appropriate time you might as well forget about having a career. I got knocked back for promotion to sergeant first time round because the high heidyins didn't like the school I went to.'

'How can you know that was the reason?' Tom asked incredulously.

'Because I know!' Tony snorted. 'Look at Charlie Anderson. One of the best cops in the division, yet left to fester at the rank of DI for God knows how many years. The only reason he eventually got a step up on the ladder was because there was nobody else. I'm telling you, the foot you kick with around here is a damned sight more important than any ability you might or might not have.'

Tony held the Talisker bottle up to the light. 'This one's dead. Okay with you if we go back to the Balvenie?'

'As long as you're not expecting me to go through the alphabet again,' Tom said, holding out his glass.

*

Jude Ramsay lay quietly in bed listening to her husband's steady breathing. After waiting until it had developed into a regular snore she slipped from underneath the duvet and tiptoed along the hall to his study. Closing the door quietly behind her she switched on the light and eased open the bottom drawer of the desk. She saw the half-full carton of Marlboro.

Monday 20 December

Tony O'Sullivan was waiting for Charlie when he arrived in the office. 'We've arrested Tommy Hemphill,' he announced. 'He's the junkie who tried to have Councillor Mullen's eye out. We've also picked up Tosh McCulloch. How do you want to play it?'

'You take care of Hemphill, Tony,' Charlie said as they strode down the corridor. 'I want my pound of flesh out of McCulloch. Where is he being held?'

'Over in Partick.'

'Phone across and let them know I'm on my way.'

Charlie circled slowly round behind the nervous, scrawny figure hunched on the chair. Tosh McCulloch twisted round in his seat, his eyes following Charlie's every move.

'What are you playing at, Anderson?'

'I'm weighing up if you're worth losing my pension for,' Charlie growled. McCulloch's tongue flicked over his dry lips. 'Tell you what,' Charlie said. 'How about if *you* start something?' He kicked hard at the leg of McCulloch's chair, causing it to almost topple over. 'That would really make my day.'

McCulloch wrapped his arms over his head and cowered down. 'I know my rights. Somebody else should be in here.'

'Who should be in here?'

'Anybody. I want a witness.'

'You want a witness?' Charlie snorted. 'Well tough titties, sunshine. We're understaffed. Everybody's gone for lunch. So for the next hour, you miserable little runt, it's just you and me.'

'You can't do that!'

'Try me.'

'What do you want?' McCulloch whimpered.

'I want names. I want to know who you buy from – and who you sell to.'

'I'm sayin' nothin'.'

'The fuck you are!' Charlie roared, grabbing him by the shirt collar and twisting hard. 'I said I want names, you little shitbag – and I want them now!' He ground his fist hard into McCulloch's windpipe.

'Get a fuckin' grip!' McCulloch gasped.

'Anything to oblige.' Charlie dug his knuckles in deeper.

McCulloch tried unsuccessfully to prise his fingers between his shirt collar and his neck. 'I buy from Gerry Fraser,' he spluttered.

'Fraser's small beer. Who does he work for?'

'How the hell would I know? For Christ's sake, Anderson! You're chokin' me!'

Charlie relaxed his grip. 'Who do you sell to?'

'Nobody in particular,' McCulloch wheezed, twisting his head and massaging the bruise forming on the side of his neck.

'How many of those nobodies are children?'

'I don't sell to kids.'

Charlie's raised his fist high above his head and brought it hammering down on the table. 'Wrong answer!' McCulloch cowered down, holding up both hands in a gesture of surrender. 'A ten year-old boy is dead because of you. Did you know that?' Charlie roared at the snivelling figure. 'Do you even know his name?' Charlie thumped his fist down on the table again. 'It's John O'Hara – remember that name – because it's going to haunt you for the rest of your life. I'm going to make sure you get put away for a long time, McCulloch. When you eventually get out I'll be long retired. But I've got a good memory – and I've got contacts – and I'll be keeping in touch. And if I ever find out that you've been seen within a mile of a school playground, I'll come after you, you miserable wee nyaff, and there won't be a badge standing in my way.'

When Charlie arrived back in Pitt Street he found Tony O'Sullivan waiting for him in his office.

'How did you get on with McCulloch, sir?'

'I'm going to have that bastard,' Charlie growled, the colour rising in his cheeks. 'I know he sold cocaine to John O'Hara.'

'That reminds me,' O'Sullivan said. 'There was a phone call while you were out from a Miss Appleton – she left her mobile number and asked if you would call her back as soon as possible. She said it was to do with John O'Hara, but she wanted to speak to you personally.'

Charlie picked up the phone and dialled, switching to loudspeaker mode so O'Sullivan could listen in. 'Miss Appleton?' he enquired to a background of childish chatter. 'This is DCI Anderson. You left a message for me to call?'

'Hold on a minute, Inspector, while I go out into the corridor. That's better,' she said as the hubbub died away. 'This morning one of the boys in my class told me he had information for you,' she said, 'but he made me promise not to tell you his name.'

'Go on.'

'There's a café called Trento's, about two hundred yards from the school. He says he saw John O'Hara in there a couple of times talking to a scruffily dressed guy in his thirties.'

'Would he be able to ID the guy?'

'Probably, but he's too frightened to talk to the police. However, I know Trento has a CCTV system installed so he can identify kids who try to steal stuff. I thought that information might be useful?'

'Very useful, Miss Appleton. Thank you. We'll follow it up.'

'Check it out, Tony,' Charlie said as he replaced the receiver. 'See if you can get your hands on Trento's footage for the month preceding John O'Hara's death. And when you've done that,' he added, 'nip over to Glasgow airport and meet Bjorn Svensson off the Stockholm flight. It's due in at half-past five.'

'What's the score with him? Do you reckon he's got something to hide?'

Charlie shrugged. 'Just a gut feeling. It might be nothing, but I'd like to get a statement out of him about where he was on Saturday morning before his wife gets the chance to prime him.'

'If she wanted to do that surely she'll have phoned him in Stockholm?'

'Possibly – but she might not have bothered if she assumed she'd be seeing him before we got to him.'

O'Sullivan was sitting in the café near the airport arrivals' area, stirring sugar into his coffee, when the announcement came over the public address system that there had been a further delay to the incoming flight from Stockholm. The latest ETA was given as 18.45. He cursed under his breath as he did the calculation. On the ground at 18.45, passengers disembarking by 19.00. Assuming he could get into the baggage retrieval area it would take him five minutes to get a statement out of Svensson, which would leave him twenty-five minutes to get to Glasgow Green. He fingered the tickets in his inside jacket pocket, then cursed again when he burned his tongue on the scalding coffee. Digging his mobile out he checked Sue's home number and dialled. A cheerful female voice answered.

'Hello!'

'I assume I'm talking to Sue's babysitter?'

'You most certainly are.'

'My name's Tony O'Sullivan. I'm supposed to be meeting Sue at half-past seven to go to the Radiohead gig but I'm running late. Do you know if she has a mobile and if so, do you have the number?'

'The good news is that she does have a mobile and I do have the number. The bad news is that her phone's sitting on the coffee table in front of me. She put it on charge and forgot to take it with her.'

'Wonderful!'

'Can I take a message in case she calls home?'

'No. Thanks all the same. I'll do my best to get there on time.'

CHAPTER 11

Tuesday 21 December

'I'm not kidding. I thought I was going to have a heart attack when that cop marched up to me in the arrivals hall waving his warrant card.' Indicating right for the Bearsden Switchback, Bjorn Svensson drifted into the outside lane on Great Western Road. 'I was sure my programming changes must've come to light. I couldn't think of any other reason for the reception committee.' Bjorn applied the Mercedes' brakes smoothly as the Anniesland Cross traffic lights up ahead changed to red.

Helen Cuthbertson tugged down the sun visor to check her make-up in the vanity mirror. 'I can imagine. A bit strange that Mr Plod went to all the trouble of going out to the airport to meet you, don't you think? What was there that couldn't have waited until this morning?'

'Search me. It's not as if he had any earth-shattering questions to ask. Where was I at eight o'clock on Saturday morning? Who was I with? That was about it.'

When the lights changed, Bjorn turned right and accelerated up the hill. Stretching her hand across, Helen started caressing the front of his jeans. 'Just as well he didn't insist on knowing what you were doing at eight o'clock on Saturday morning.'

'Stop it, Helen! Not when I'm driving!' He pushed her hand away. 'Anyway, I thought you were supposed to be in mourning?'

'For my dear departed brother-in-law?' Helen pouted her lips. 'Pull the other one.' She pawed again at his trousers. 'Though I'd rather pull this one,' she squealed. Bjorn tried to drag her hand away while at the same time wrestling one-handed with the steering wheel. Helen unclipped her seat belt and plunged across, burying her face in his lap. When she started blowing loud raspberries against his crotch they both dissolved in laughter.

Laura Harrison carried a tray with three cups of coffee into the lounge where Helen and Bjorn were seated. 'What happened to you, Helen?' she asked as she put the tray down on a side table. 'You look like you've been dragged through a hedge backwards.'

Helen tossed back her hair. 'I came out in a bit of a rush, sis.'

'That's not like you.'

'My fault, Laura,' Bjorn said. 'I insisted on leaving early to beat the rush-hour traffic.'

'There was no need to do that. You could've waited until the traffic eased off and come across later in the –' Laura broke off, tears welling in her eyes.

Helen sprang to her feet and wrapped a comforting arm around her sister's shoulder. 'Everything's going to be all right,' she whispered in her ear.

Laura knuckled away a tear. 'God knows, it's not as if I'm heartbroken because Mike is dead. I don't have to tell you that. It's the sheer frustration that he made such a bloody mess of things. He gambled away everything, you know – and I mean everything.' Helen and Bjorn exchanged glances. 'Even the mortgage is more than the value of the damned house!' Laura took a deep breath to try to control her breathing.

'Christ, I need a drink! Anyone care to join me?' she asked, lifting the gin bottle from the drinks trolley and holding it up.

'It's a bit early in the day, sis. Even for me.'

'How about you, Bjorn?'

'No thanks, Laura.'

Laura poured herself a stiff measure, adding a splash of tonic. 'Will you be able to lend me the money?' she asked quietly. 'I'll pay you back as soon as I can.'

Helen made eye contact with Bjorn. 'I'm not sure we can.'

'You know I wouldn't ask you unless I was desperate. I've nobody else to turn to.' She pleaded with her eyes. 'I've got to have ten thousand pounds by Friday.'

'We'd like to help you,' Helen said. 'We really would. But we can't do anything as quickly as that. All our assets are tied up in investments. Even if we were to accept early withdrawal penalties it would be at least a fortnight before we could transfer the money to you.'

'That's no use.' Laura's teeth sank into her quivering bottom lip. 'I must have it by Friday.'

'We could probably come up with a banker's order or a post-dated cheque by Friday. Would that do?'

Laura looked away to avoid her sister's eyes. 'It has to be in cash,' she said in little more than a whisper.

'In the name of God, Laura! What sort of trouble have you got yourself into?' Laura turned her back and stared out of the window. 'Won't you tell me what this is all about?' Helen insisted.

'I can't.'

'Why don't you talk to Dad?'

Laura spun back round. 'No way!'

'Tell Dad what's happened. Explain to him that Mike has left you with nothing. Now that Mike's no longer ...' Her voice tailed off. 'You know what I'm driving at. One conciliatory gesture from you and Dad would welcome his prodigal daughter back into the fold with open arms – and he'd sort out your financial problems in no time.'

'I couldn't go to him. Not after ten years.'

'Then let me talk to him. I'll act as the go-between.'

'No! I don't want you to do that.'

'What other options do you have?' Silent tears were seeping down Laura's cheeks. Helen took her in her arms and cuddled her in close.

Tony O'Sullivan rapped on Charlie's open office door and walked in.

'No luck at Trento's, I'm afraid,' he said. 'There is a CCTV system in the café but he doesn't keep the data for more than a week.'

Charlie let out a world-weary sigh. 'How did you make out with Svensson?'

'His plane eventually landed the back of nine. The runway in Stockholm was iced up and they took off four hours late.'

'What did he have to say for himself?'

'Not a lot. Basically, he confirmed everything his wife had told us.'

'Did he sound convincing?'

O'Sullivan shrugged. 'He was pretty relaxed about it all.'

'Bit of a wasted evening, then?'

'You could say that.'

'Well, look on the bright side. At least it saved you from pissing your money away in the pub.'

Billy McAteer watched from the corner of Canniesburn Road as Bjorn Svensson's Mercedes pulled out of the drive. Turning his back on the traffic as the car sped past he hurried towards the house, then checked to make sure he wasn't being observed before striding up the drive and pressing the bell push.

'I told you not to come here!' Laura tried to push the door closed but McAteer had already inserted a blocking foot. Forcing the door wide, he stepped inside and slammed it behind him.

'I want my money tomorrow.'

'Tomorrow's Wednesday – you said Friday!'

'Now, I'm sayin' tomorrow. I'm goin' to have to make myself scarce an' I need the cash.'

'How many times do I have to tell you? I don't have the bloody money!'

Grabbing Laura's jaw in his fist McAteer squeezed hard, forcing her onto her tiptoes. 'I know how you got your sore face.' His manic eye drilled into her. 'Your auld man telt me he had to teach you a lesson from time to time because you had a nasty habit of chattin' up other blokes. Well, if you think he gave you a hard time, you ain't seen nothin'.' McAteer pressed his fingers so hard into Laura's cheeks that her eyes bulged. 'You've got until tomorrow afternoon to come up with the money. That's enough time if you put your mind to it. I'll be here at four o'clock sharp.' Producing a flick knife from his jacket pocket he snapped open the blade. 'You'd better have the money by then,' he said, slowly rotating the tip of the blade an inch from her eyeball. 'Because if you don't come up with the cash . . .' The blade stopped turning.

'There won't be a single bloke in Glasgow who'll be interested in chattin' you up.'

Charlie walked up to the desk in Partick Police Station and spoke to the duty officer. 'Are you still holding Tosh McCulloch here, Andy?' he asked.

'Yes, sir. He's due in court this afternoon.'

'I'd like a word with him.'

'No problem,' he said, stretching for the cell key and handing it across. 'You know the way. Cell number four. Let yourself in.'

McCulloch scrambled to his feet when he heard the cell door opening, then cowered against the far wall when he saw Charlie enter.

'There's a change in the charge sheet for this afternoon, McCulloch,' Charlie announced. 'As well as buying drugs in Argyle Street we're going to do you for supplying cocaine to John O'Hara – and that's a murder charge.'

'I telt you already, Anderson. I don't sell to kids.'

'That won't wash, McCulloch. We have it all in glorious Technicolor. You didn't know there was CCTV in Trento's café?' McCulloch stared open-mouthed. 'The whole café is covered. I've just been across to see the footage of you and John O'Hara together, including a clear shot of you handing the stuff across.' McCulloch's jaw tightened. 'If you're going to stick to your half-arsed story you're looking at a life sentence,' Charlie continued. 'On the other hand, if you make a full confession the procurator fiscal might be prepared to negotiate a charge of manslaughter. What's it to be?'

All the colour drained from McCulloch's features. 'You're bluffing, Anderson.'

'Fine! Have it your own way.' Charlie snorted and turned to leave. 'I don't know why I'm even wasting my time.'

'Wait a minute!' Charlie paused with his hand on the door. 'I telt the kid . . .' McCulloch said hesitantly. 'I telt him how much he should take.'

Charlie fixed McCulloch with a glare. 'You told him how much he should take?'

'Aye,' McCulloch said in little more than a whisper.

'You told him how much he should take?' Charlie repeated the words slowly, measuring every syllable.

'It's no' ma fault the stupid wee eejit overdosed,' McCulloch whimpered.

Grabbing McCulloch by the shirt collar, Charlie yanked him up on to his tiptoes, their noses almost touching. 'So that's your defence? The boy was ten years old, for fuck's sake!' Charlie's features were florid. 'You told a ten-year-old kid how much cocaine he should fucking-well take!'

'It's no' ma fault he's deid,' McCulloch spluttered, trying unsuccessfully to twist from Charlie's grip. 'There's no way you can ca' that murder!'

Slowly relaxing his fists Charlie released his grip, allowing McCulloch to sink to his knees, sobbing heavily. Without a backward glance Charlie spun on his heel and strode from the cell, slamming the door behind him and turning the key in the lock. Exhaling loudly, he removed the microphone from under his lapel and switched off the recording device in his jacket pocket.

Tony O'Sullivan found the number he was looking for in the telephone directory.

'I'm afraid we don't have any teacher called Anderson, sir,' the school secretary said in reply to his query.

'Susan Anderson was her maiden name. I don't know her surname. She was married to someone called Paul who taught in your school, but she's a widow now.'

'That'll be Susan Paterson.'

'Would it be possible for me to speak to her?'

'I'll check her timetable.' There was a short pause. 'Sorry. Mrs Paterson takes her class to the swimming baths on Tuesday mornings. Can I take a message?'

'No, thanks all the same. I'll try to catch her at home this evening.'

CHAPTER 12

Tony O'Sullivan kicked off his shoes and walked down the hall to collect a can of export from his kitchen cupboard en route to the lounge. Flicking on the light he flopped down on the settee, picked up the phone and dialled Sue's number. As the call was ringing out he ripped the ring-pull from the can.

'Sue?'

'It was my fault entirely,' she stated.

'Come again?'

'I forgot the first rule of going out with a copper.'

'Which is?'

'Always make sure you've got the tickets. You might end up at the gig on your own, but you can impress everyone around you by telling them you paid for an extra seat for your coat to avoid having to queue for the cloakroom.'

'Ouch! I had that coming! I really am sorry, Sue. I got tied up. You know how it is . . .'

'Don't I just?'

'I tried calling you at school this morning to apologise but I was told you'd taken your class to the baths.'

'The secretary told me someone had called looking for me – someone who didn't even know my surname. I figured that had to be you.'

'What did you end up doing last night?'

'I hung around the park gates at Glasgow Green until well after eight. When you didn't show I went to the ticket office and asked if there was any chance of a spare ticket – which at least raised a giggle. Not wanting to waste a babysitter, I stopped off at my local to see if there was anyone in I knew. There wasn't, so I came back home.'

'Your local?' Tony said. 'I thought you were TT?'

'Typical pisshead's attitude! My local happens to do a mean line in tomato juice and angostura bitters. As I was saying, I went back home and Amanda, my babysitter, told me you'd called to say you were running late. For lack of anything better to do I challenged her to a game of Scrabble. How was your evening?'

'I spent over four hours at Glasgow airport waiting for a plane that was frozen to the tarmac in Stockholm.'

'You probably had a marginally better time than I did. I lost at Scrabble to a sixteen-year-old, with the added indignity of paying her ten quid an hour for the privilege of being hammered. By the way, did you know that "alizarine" is a word?' she stated indignantly. 'It's in the dictionary. Some sort of dye, apparently. Triple word score, no less.'

'Any chance of me making it up to you?'

'That will not be easy.'

'How about dinner? You get to choose the restaurant.'

'Lucky for you that the Chardon d'Or's booked up solid at this time of year.'

'How about the Ubiquitous Chip?'

'Hmm . . . I suppose I might be open to persuasion.'

'What night would suit you best?'

'Hold on a minute. Let me check my engagements.' Sue rustled some papers. 'If we could avoid December the nineteenth next year,' she said. 'That's the date of the next nativity play.'

Tony chortled. 'How did the play go?'

'Mary forgot her lines and one of the wise men farted, which nearly cleared the hall. Apart from that everything went well.'

'How are you fixed for tomorrow night?'

'Sounds good.'

'I'll ring the Chip straight away and see if I can get a table. I'll call you right back.'

'Before you hang up, to avoid any repetition of last night's fiasco, how about we exchange mobile numbers?'

'Not much point if you forget to take yours with you.'

'Cheeky beggar!'

Simon Ramsay drew up in Laura Harrison's driveway and switched off his headlamps. Steady drizzle was falling as he hurried towards the front door. He pressed his finger hard to the bell-push and kept it there until Laura answered.

'Simon! What in the name of God are you doing here?'

'Are you on your own?'

'Yes.'

'I had to see you.' He stepped inside. 'I couldn't risk talking on the phone.'

'I'm in big trouble,' Laura blurted out. 'McAteer's threatening to cut up rough if he doesn't get his money by tomorrow.'

'It gets worse.'

'What could possibly be worse?'

'Jude suspects something.'

'Did you hear what I just said? McAteer's threatening to slash my face to ribbons if I don't come up with ten thousand pounds by tomorrow afternoon. I don't know where to turn. I've been sitting here all day.' She waved her gin glass in front of his nose. 'Drinking myself into oblivion while trying to pluck up the courage to phone my father and beg him to let me have ten thousand pounds – and all you have to worry about is that Jude might suspect something!'

'She knows I was out of the house at the time Mike was killed. She suspects I was involved somehow. If she finds out what we've been up to she'll hand me to the cops on a plate – you know how vindictive she can be. We'll have to find a way to deal with her.'

'Deal with her! *Deal with her!*' Laura's voice went up an octave. 'The same way we dealt with Mike?' She poured gin down her throat. 'I don't know how I ever let you talk me into getting involved with McAteer. Look at the fucking mess that's landed me in!'

'Get a grip of yourself,' he said, grabbing her by the shoulders and shaking her hard.

'Not to put too fine a point on it,' she said, twisting herself free from his grasp, 'Jude's your problem. If I manage to get McAteer off my back – and God only knows how I'm going to be able to do that – then I might have to suffer the ignominy of having been caught shagging my sister's husband. But at least I no longer have Mike to contend with. You, on the other hand, are going to have a lot of explaining to do to Jude.' Turning her back on him, she drained her glass.

Simon stormed from the room and out of the front door, slamming it behind him. Laura heard the squeal of tyres spinning in the loose gravel as he slewed backwards down the driveway. As she buried her face in her hands, sobbing uncontrollably, the phone rang. Rubbing away her tears, she tried to control the tremble in her voice as she picked up the receiver.

'Hello,' she stammered.

'Laura?' The phone froze in her hand. She hadn't heard his voice in ten years, but she recognised it instantly. 'Helen called me earlier this evening.'

'She shouldn't have done that. I told her not to.'

'She and Bjorn couldn't come up with any way of getting ten thousand pounds for you quickly so she decided to phone me. It was the right thing to do.'

Laura choked back her tears. 'Will you help me, Dad?'

'Will you tell me what this is all about?'

'I can't.'

There was a brief pause. 'Helen said you need the money by Friday.'

'That was the situation this morning, but things have changed. I have to have it by four o'clock tomorrow afternoon.'

Jim Cuthbertson sucked hard on his teeth. 'You don't make things easy, Laura.' Laura felt a huge sob welling in her throat. 'However, if it has to be tomorrow, then it has to be tomorrow,' he stated in a matter-of-fact tone. 'I'll need some time in the morning to get things organised. If I bring the money over to your place around lunchtime, would that be okay?'

'Oh, Dad!'

'You need ten thousand in cash, if I understand the situation correctly?' Laura's pent-up sob came bursting forth. 'There's one condition,' Cuthbertson said.

'What's that?'

'You come over to our place for Christmas lunch.' He replaced the receiver before she could blurt out her thanks.

*

Tony O'Sullivan dialled Sue's number.

'We're on for the Chip tomorrow night,' he said.

'Great!'

'The table's booked for eight. How about we meet at half-seven in the upstairs bar?'

'If you're not there by nine o'clock, would you like me to order for you?'

'Just watch it! By the way, what *is* your mobile number?'

Wednesday 22 December

Charlie Anderson was in his office early, ploughing through his paperwork, when Colin Renton stuck his head round the door.

'Have you got a minute, sir?'

'Sure.' Charlie slid a memo into his out-basket and put down his pen.

'I followed up on a hunch last night,' Renton said, a self-satisfied smirk plastered across his features. 'Remember Harry Robertson – McAteer's uncle?'

'Of course. Shot in the head and his body dumped in the Clyde twenty-odd years ago – on the same day he taunted McAteer in the pub about his "arse-features".'

Renton nodded. 'The murder weapon was never found so I dug out the ballistics report and checked it against the bullets that were lodged in Mike Harrison's skull.'

'And?'

'In both cases 5.56 millimetre shells were used and, according to the boffins, there's a ninety-nine percent probability that the shots were fired from the same gun.'

'Nice one, Colin!'

'From the striations on the bullets the lab guys told me the weapon was an SA80 assault rifle, which was the standard army combat weapon when McAteer did his tour of duty in Northern Ireland.'

'How the hell would he manage to get his hands on a combat rifle?'

'Bribe the quartermaster? Maybe claim the IRA had nicked it?' Renton suggested. 'Your guess is as good as mine.'

Charlie depressed his intercom button. 'Pauline, find O'Sullivan and tell him to come to my office right away. It's time we did a bit of brainstorming.'

Charlie rolled up his shirt sleeves and turned over to a fresh sheet of paper on the flipchart board. Picking up a marker pen he lobbed it in Renton's direction. 'You be the scribe, Colin. No one can read my shorthand.' Tony O'Sullivan rocked back in his chair and swung his feet up onto Charlie's desk. .

'Let's summarise what we've got.' Charlie strode up and down the office as he spoke. 'Billy McAteer seems to be the common thread in all of this. Harrison hires him as his muscle and not long after that Harrison is killed by McAteer's gun – not in a fit of temper, but in a cold-blooded, well-planned assassination. Someone must've been paying McAteer big time to get him to bump off his source of income.'

'Always assuming McAteer knew who he was killing,' Renton said.

'What are you driving at?' O'Sullivan asked.

'I've been studying the forensic report,' Renton said. 'From the angle of the shots, the rifle bullets were fired from underneath the archway of the bridge and Harrison was shot in the back. The sniper might never have seen his victim's face. Maybe he didn't know it was Harrison he was firing at? Perhaps he was expecting someone else to be in the park at that time?'

'Good point! A nice wee bit of lateral thinking there.' Charlie clapped his hands enthusiastically. 'That would go a long way towards explaining something that's been nagging at the back of my mind ever since you told me Harrison had been shot with McAteer's gun.'

'What's that?' Renton asked.

'If McAteer wanted to do away with Harrison, why make such an elaborate production of it? He had easy access to him. A bullet in the back, drop his body in the Clyde with a couple of lead weights attached and Bob's your uncle – no one would ever have been any the wiser.'

'Should we pull McAteer in for questioning?' O'Sullivan asked.

'That is an option.' Charlie settled down on his chair. 'But I'd rather not show our hand right now. We wouldn't be able to hold him for long, unless, of course, we could persuade Gerry Fraser to press charges. What do you think, Tony? Now that Harrison's out of the way, what do you think the chances would be of getting Fraser to testify against McAteer?'

O'Sullivan looked dubious. 'I reckon Fraser's a lot more terrified of McAteer that he ever was of Harrison.'

'Okay,' Charlie said. 'For now, let's settle for putting a round-the-clock tail on McAteer. Colin, get a rota organised as soon as we've wrapped up here.'

'To follow up on Colin's idea,' O'Sullivan chipped in. 'Assuming McAteer didn't know who he was firing at, then whoever hired him to carry out the hit presumably knew the score. He must have set Harrison up to be in the park on Saturday morning.'

'He – or she,' said Renton.

'Is that another bit of lateral thinking, or do you have someone specific in mind?' Charlie asked.

'Wife beating has been known to drive people to extremes.'

'Laura Harrison paying her husband's hit man to do in her old man?' Charlie mused. 'Nice touch of dramatic irony – and stranger things have happened. Definitely worth our while having another chat with Mrs Harrison. We should also probe her about the mugging incident outside the cinema. For one thing I'd like to know if she reported the assault at the time and, if not, why not.' Charlie got to his feet. 'Tony, you nip across to Bearsden and have a chat with Mrs H. I'm going to have another go at Simon Ramsay. He seemed awfully keen to let me know that he suspected Mike Harrison was a wife beater. How would he know something like that?'

'And was he acting as a concerned bystander,' O'Sullivan said, 'or was he trying to point the finger at Laura Harrison?'

The sun was struggling to filter through the high clouds when Tony O'Sullivan pulled up in the Harrisons' driveway. Laura hurried to the door when he rang the bell but she was clearly taken aback when she saw who it was.

'Is this a bad time, Mrs Harrison?'

'No . . . Sergeant,' she stammered. 'It's just . . .'

'You were expecting someone else?'

'My father said he'd drop over this morning. I thought it would be him.'

'I won't keep you long. Just a couple of questions.' O'Sullivan took out his notebook and pen.

'I'd appreciate it if you would be as quick as you can.' Laura fiddled nervously with her hair.

'We're trying to establish your husband's movements last Friday in case he might have mentioned to someone why he was going to Kelvingrove Park the following morning. We know he arrived at Ronnie McGavigan's place around eight-thirty for the poker school. Can you tell me where he was before then?'

'He left for work on Friday morning as usual – around nine o'clock. He never came home for dinner on poker nights. He usually picked up a fish supper or a pizza and ate it in one of his betting shops.'

'Did he have a set routine?'

'What do you mean?'

'Did he always go to the same betting shop on Fridays?'

'He tended to base himself in Bishopbriggs but I can't be sure if he was there last Friday. I'm sorry I can't be more precise.'

'That's okay. I'll have a word with the Bishopbriggs staff. Perhaps one of them might be able to cast some light on the matter.' Tony put away his notebook and slipped his pen into his pocket. 'By the way,' he added casually as he was turning to leave, 'we're still trying to track down the yobs who tried to snatch your handbag. There's been a spate of that sort of thing recently. Could you give me a description of them? Age, height, clothes, make of bike? Anything at all might be useful.'

Laura shook her head. 'It all happened so quickly.'

'Did you report the assault at the time?'

'Didn't seem much point. I hadn't actually lost anything and I couldn't even begin to identify them.'

'The chief constable will be pleased.' Laura looked puzzled. 'If you'd reported the incident you would have added another unsolved crime to his statistics.' Tony smiled at Laura but his smile wasn't returned. 'Were there any witnesses?' he asked.

'The cinema had just come out and there were a lot of people milling around. I suppose someone might have seen what happened but I was so upset at having been punched in the face that I just wanted to get into a taxi and get away from there as quickly as possible.'

'Outside which cinema did this happen?'

'I can never remember the name.' She twisted her fingers into her hair. 'The multiplex near the top of Renfield Street.'

'The UGC?' Tony suggested. 'In Renfrew Street?'

'I think that's what it's called.'

'What film did you see?'

Laura hesitated. 'An American cop thing. Can't remember the name of it. Not at all my type of movie but Mike was a big fan.'

They both turned round when a white Rolls-Royce came into the driveway and pulled up behind O'Sullivan's car. Jim Cuthbertson stepped out. Short, thick set with improbably black, short-cropped hair, he was wearing a sports jacket and a pair of light brown trousers. A mat of grey chest hair protruded from his open-necked shirt.

'Will there be anything else, Sergeant?' Laura asked.

'Not for now.'

Cuthbertson strode towards them. 'Good morning, Laura.' His voice boomed out.

'This is a police officer, Dad,' she said, nodding towards Tony. 'He's investigating Mike's murder.'

Cuthbertson took Tony's proffered hand. 'Terrible business, officer.' Tony felt the tentative, probing thumb of the Masonic handshake as Cuthbertson's fingers slid across his palm.

'Detective Sergeant O'Sullivan, Mr Cuthbertson.' Tony delivered his name in a lilting, Irish accent. Cuthbertson's groping fingers froze, then withdrew to give a limp handshake, fingertips only.

'Do you have any idea who murdered Mike, Sergeant?'

'Nothing much to go on yet, I'm afraid.' Tony turned to Laura. 'Thanks for your time, Mrs Harrison. I'll be in touch.'

'My car's not blocking you?' Cuthbertson looked back over his shoulder.

'No problem, sir.'

Jim Cuthbertson followed his daughter into the lounge. 'Won't you tell me what this is all about?' Avoiding eye contact, Laura stared at the wall. Cuthbertson pulled a thick brown envelope from his inside jacket pocket and weighed it in his hand. 'You know, there may be a better solution.'

'There isn't, Dad,' she said quietly, struggling to hold back her tears.

He handed her the envelope. 'Are you sure this is going to solve your problem?'

Laura threw her arms around her father's neck and sobbed into his jacket collar.

As Billy McAteer parked his Volvo in Maryhill Road, opposite Cluny Park, an unmarked police car pulled up fifty yards further down the road.

'It would be better if I tailed him, sir,' Tom Freer said. 'There's no chance of him recognising me.'

'Okay, but no matter what happens, don't confront him,' O'Sullivan said. 'The guy's a complete psycho. Don't hesitate to radio for backup if you think you might need it.'

Freer got out of the car and fell in behind McAteer as he headed towards the roundabout at the end of Maryhill Road. Crossing from there into Canniesburn Road, Freer watched him stride up a gravel drive and ring the front door bell. Laura Harrison answered and ushered him inside.

Laura led the way to the lounge. 'Glad to see you've come to your senses,' McAteer said, opening the envelope he'd been handed. He pulled out the thick wad of notes and started thumbing through it.

'There's no need to count it.' Laura stood by the lounge door with her arms folded. 'It's all there.'

'It's better that I check it now.' He grinned at her coldly. 'You wouldn't want me havin' to come back because you were a few quid short, would you?'

'Count it quickly, if you must,' she fumed. 'Then get out of here.'

McAteer stopped counting and stuffed the money back into the envelope. Slipping the envelope into his pocket, he moved towards Laura. 'I was hoping there might be somethin' else in it for me.'

'Get out of here at once!' She pointed towards the front door.

Gripping both her arms, McAteer twisted them behind her back and pulled her body towards him. 'How about a wee bonus for your business partner?' He pressed his deformed mouth against her lips and tried to force his tongue into her mouth. Laura struggled to twist her head away and lashed out with her foot, the point of her toecap catching McAteer full on the shin bone. He cursed as he released his grip.

'Get out of here right now!' she screamed.

McAteer rubbed hard at his bruised shin, then rushed at Laura and grappled her to the ground, one hand groping for her breast, the other tugging at her skirt.

'Let go of me!' she yelled.

'Mike told me you liked playin' the field,' he said, breathing heavily as he knelt astride her body. Grabbing both her wrists, he pinned them to the floor above her head and held them there with one hand. 'That was why he had to slap you about, wasn't it?' He leered at her as he cuffed her violently back and forward across the face. Reaching under her skirt, he grabbed at her pants and started tugging them down. Laura screamed as loudly as she could. Suddenly the front doorbell rang. McAteer clamped his hand tightly over her mouth. 'Not a peep out of you,' he hissed, 'or you'll go the same way as your auld man.' The bell jangled again.

Whipping his knife from his jacket pocket he flicked open the blade and pressed the tip against her temple. Slowly, he dragged the razor-sharp point down the side of her face, the blade coming to rest flat against her throat. 'The slightest noise,' he said in a hoarse whisper, 'an' I'll finish you off right now.' Drops of blood, seeping from the yawning wound in her cheek, were dripping onto the carpet. Laura felt her head start to spin. When the doorbell rang again McAteer scrambled to his feet. Looking round the room he flung open the French windows and sprinted outside, vaulting the low, stone wall at the bottom of the garden. Laura staggered to her feet, her hand clasped to the side of her face to try to stem the flow of blood. She lurched along the hallway leaving a trail of blood splattered on the carpet. When she threw the front door open there was no one there.

CHAPTER 13

When Freer saw McAteer's Volvo start to pull away from the kerb he raced the last twenty yards to the waiting car. Seeing him coming, O'Sullivan flung open the passenger door and fired the engine. As soon as Freer had scrambled inside he set off in pursuit.

'What happened back there?' O'Sullivan demanded.

'He went into a house in Canniesburn Road,' Freer panted, 'which I assume was Laura Harrison's place. He rang the bell and a woman let him in. I made my way round to the back of the house and saw them together in the lounge, through the French windows. She gave him an envelope and he started counting what seemed to be a lot of money. Then he had a go at her.'

'Meaning what, exactly?'

'He flung himself at her and wrestled her to the ground. I could hear her screaming through the closed windows. It looked as if he was about to rape her. You said not to confront him but I couldn't just stand there and do nothing so I raced round to the front of the house and kept ringing the doorbell. I heard the French windows being thrown open and when I looked round the side of the house I saw McAteer clambering over the garden wall. I followed him back here.'

'Quick thinking, Tom.' The traffic was comparatively light and O'Sullivan had no difficulty keeping the Volvo in sight as it turned right at Anniesland Cross and headed out Great Western Road towards Drumchapel. 'So, Mrs H. was paying McAteer off, was she? That can only mean one thing – she hired him to bump off her old man.' O'Sullivan pulled up, several cars behind the Volvo, at a set of traffic lights.

'And it would appear that he fancied his chances of taking advantage of the situation,' Freer said. 'Mrs Harrison is hardly in a position to report a rape. Looks like she might've bitten off a lot more than she can chew.'

'Radio in,' O'Sullivan said. 'Let them know we're tailing McAteer. Give them his licence number and a description of the vehicle in case we lose him.'

McAteer drove through Drumchapel and headed north towards Balloch, O'Sullivan staying as far back as he could without letting the Volvo out of his sight. When he saw McAteer indicate left just beyond the village of Luss, O'Sullivan pulled over at the side of the road.

'Are we not going to follow him?' Freer asked.

'I know that track. It doesn't lead anywhere. I don't know what he's up to but we might as well wait for him here. He has to come back down the same way.' O'Sullivan slipped the car into first gear and drove slowly past the turn off, then kept going for another hundred yards until he spotted a gap in the trees. Reversing off the road, he cut the engine.

Charlie was about to call Simon Ramsay when his phone rang.

'Turnbull here, Anderson. Drop whatever you're doing and come to my office straight away.'

Charlie replaced the receiver. He got to his feet and lifted his jacket from the back of his chair. It was the first time he'd ever been summoned by the chief constable. When he got to Bill Turnbull's office he was ushered straight in by his secretary, who closed the door behind him. Turnbull was sitting behind his wide desk, talking on the phone. Acknowledging Charlie's presence with a wave, he indicated a chair. To Charlie's surprise it appeared that the meeting was going to involve only the two of them.

When he'd finished his call Turnbull pressed his desk intercom. 'No interruptions, Margaret.' Boxing the edges of the papers in his hand, he slipped on his reading glasses and peered over the top of them. 'I've had a call from the first minister. Bit of a tricky one here, Anderson.' Turnbull's reputation went before him. When he resorted to understatement it invariably meant trouble. 'The conversation we are about to have is in the strictest confidence. We have received information about a planned bomb attack at Celtic Park tonight.'

Charlie inched forward onto the edge of his chair, his mouth tight. 'You mean – during the match?'

Turnbull nodded. 'An Ulster loyalist splinter group is going for a high-profile spectacular.'

Charlie felt the palms of his hands turn clammy. 'How good is the information?'

'Rock solid. The anti-terrorist boys have infiltrated a loyalist paramilitary organisation in Derry and their man managed to get a message out yesterday. Jack Craig, an explosives expert, crossed on the ferry from Larne to Stranraer last night carrying seven kilos of Semtex. He caught a train to Glasgow where he was met by a driver. Unfortunately, the unit assigned to tail them lost them in the city-centre traffic.'

Charlie held his breath as Turnbull adjusted his spectacles and referred to the sheet of paper in his hand. 'From the information we've received it appears that the paramilitaries have an insider in Celtic Park. Special Branch have reason to believe he's a contract security guard but they haven't been able to pinpoint his identity. The plan is that Craig will turn up at Parkhead tonight with the Semtex. He's got a rendezvous with his contact inside the ground at six o'clock and he's going to plant the bomb in a cistern in one of the toilets underneath the main stand.'

'Jesus wept!'

'My first instinct was to contact the Parkhead management,' Turnbull continued, 'and instruct them to replace all the security guards who are scheduled to be on duty tonight. However, the first minister has told me that is not an option.'

'Why not?'

'Any action that shows that we're on to them would result in the elimination of the anti-terrorist squad's agent. It's taken him four years to get accepted and the powers that be think he's been told more than he needs to know about tonight's operation as a test. If Special Branch intercept Craig, the Loyalists will realise there's been a leak at their end and the agent would be compromised. That's where we come in. Special Branch have asked the first minister for our support in fronting the operation. The idea is that we can justify a police presence at the ground by saying we have reason to believe drug dealers are going to be operating at Parkhead tonight.'

'How much detail do we have of their plans?' Charlie asked.

'They're going to plant the bomb around six o'clock and trigger the explosion to go off during the match. I've talked it through with the first minister and we've concluded that the only avenue open to us is to let Craig plant his device and allow him to leave the stadium unmolested before we neutralise the bomb.'

Charlie shook his head in exasperation. 'Does the first minister realise how many lives he's putting at risk?'

Turnbull glared over the top of his spectacles. 'What sort of a damn fool question is that?'

'Sorry, sir. It's just that – my brother's going to be at that match.'

Turnbull paused. 'So is my son.'

Charlie's mind was racing. 'Can we at least arrange for someone to monitor the toilets so we know where the device has been planted?'

Turnbull shook his head. 'We can't run the risk of doing anything that might spook them. The best we can do is have someone in the vicinity of the toilets who'll be able to recognise Craig and tip us the wink when he and his crony have left the area.'

'Do we have anyone who knows what Craig looks like?'

'No, but we've got some good mug shots of him, taken on the ferry last night.' Turnbull slid a sheaf of photographs across the desk. 'I want you to take charge of the operation at Parkhead. You'll need someone with you to act as a lookout for Craig – someone you can trust to keep his mouth shut.'

Charlie thought quickly. 'I'll take Renton.'

Turnbull nodded. 'I've arranged with the army to provide a bomb disposal expert and a sniffer dog,' he continued. 'You'll have the support of a dozen officers but you won't make a move until you're sure that Craig and his accomplice have left the area – which should be around six-thirty. We need a rationale to justify our presence to the Parkhead management so the official line is that we've reason to suspect drug dealing is going to take place in the toilets and we need to cordon off the area. However, no one apart from you, Renton and the bomb disposal expert will know the true nature of the operation. The back-up officers will be told it's a drugs bust.'

'Is that really necessary?'

'I would love to be confident that there's not an officer on this force who would leak information to the loyalist paramilitaries – but I'm not prepared to bet an agent's life on it.'

'What if something goes wrong? What if we don't find the bomb?' Charlie adjusted his tie knot nervously.

'You'll have half an hour to find the device and defuse it. If, for whatever reason, you haven't succeeded in neutralising it by seven o'clock we'll announce over the public address system that there's been a bomb warning and that the stadium has to be evacuated. An hour should be sufficient time for that. We know the device won't be triggered to go off before eight o'clock. However, if we have to resort to that course of action I wouldn't give a monkey's for the agent's chances,' Turnbull said grimly.

'What about the houses around the ground, sir? What's the range of seven kilos of Semtex?'

'Not my field. Discuss that with the bomb disposal expert. If we have to clear the stadium it'll be his decision as to whether or not we need to evacuate the surrounding area. But let's hope it doesn't come to that. One more thing,' Turnbull said, referring to his briefing papers. 'Special Branch are keen to identify the rogue security guard, so ask the Parkhead management to let us know if any of their staff go AWOL during the match. Take my mobile number,' he said, jotting it down and handing across the slip of paper. 'You're reporting directly to me on this, Anderson. You can call me at any time.'

*

Darkness fell quickly, shrouding Loch Lomond in a shadowy mist. 'Are you sure that isn't a through road?' Freer asked, peering at his watch through the gloom as he huddled into his jacket.

'Of course I'm sure!' Freer caught the tetchiness in O'Sullivan's voice.

'We've been here almost an hour,' Freer said. 'How much longer are we going to wait for him?'

'What the hell can he be playing at?' O'Sullivan rubbed the palms of his hands together to try to get his circulation moving. 'Come on,' he said, flinging open the driver's door. 'We'll go in on foot and find up what he's up to. It's half a mile at most to the far end of the track and anything's better than sitting here freezing to death.'

Moving at a brisk pace, they followed the tyre tracks up the snow-covered, rutted path until they came to a clearing in which there were several caravans. McAteer's Volvo was the only car in sight, parked in the middle of the clearing. There was a light shining from the windows of one of the caravans.

'This is a summer resort,' O'Sullivan said quietly. 'No one in their right mind comes within a mile of this place in winter.'

'What now?' Freer asked.

O'Sullivan stopped to consider. 'With what you witnessed at the Harrison's place, we've got enough evidence to put McAteer away – and I don't want to risk him slipping through our fingers. It's a long walk back to the car to call out back-up – and I certainly don't fancy freezing to death for another hour while we wait for them to arrive. How about we get McAteer to give us a lift back to our car en route to Pitt Street?' he said with a grin. 'Are you up for it?'

'You're calling the shots, sir.'

They moved silently across the camp site towards the caravan. 'You wait here,' O'Sullivan whispered. 'I'll go inside and bring him out.' O'Sullivan tiptoed up the five iron steps, handcuffs at the ready. He turned the handle as quietly as he could, then put his shoulder to the door and barged inside, the caravan door rebounding on its hinges and slamming closed behind him. Billy McAteer was stretched out on a bench seat, dozing. O'Sullivan dropped on one knee and managed to cuff McAteer's wrists in front of him before he fully realised what was happening. 'You're under arrest, McAteer. Don't try anything stupid,' O'Sullivan warned as McAteer struggled to get to his feet. 'I've got armed back-up outside.'

McAteer glowered at him. 'If it isn't the Fenian cunt!' He spat in O'Sullivan's face.

O'Sullivan brought his knee up sharply, catching McAteer full in the groin and causing him to fold at the waist with an agonised grunt. 'That's for the pint of beer in Tennent's.' Pulling him up straight, he drew back his right arm and slammed his fist into McAteer's solar plexus. 'And that's for the "Fenian cunt".' The caravan rocked on its wheels as McAteer toppled over. O'Sullivan grabbed him by the shoulders and tugged him to his feet. 'Let's go.'

The sound of the caravan toilet being flushed caused O'Sullivan to spin round and in the same instant McAteer let out a roar and flung his cuffed arms over O'Sullivan's head and yanked his body towards him in a bear hug. Lifting O'Sullivan clean off his feet he crushed the breath from his lungs and held him suspended in mid-air for several seconds before hammering his body downwards and driving his kneecap into O'Sullivan's coccyx.

As O'Sullivan lay moaning on the floor, McAteer pulled a flick knife from his jacket pocket and held the blade to O'Sullivan's throat. 'Undo the cuffs, Paddy,' he commanded.

'I didn't bring the keys with me,' O'Sullivan croaked.

McAteer stabbed the point of the blade into O'Sullivan's throat, drawing blood. 'The keys, you smart-arsed bastard, or it's your jugular next.'

O'Sullivan reached slowly into his trouser pocket and produced the handcuff keys. McAteer thrust his hands forward, the tip of the blade still pressing into O'Sullivan's throat. 'Open them,' he demanded. When O'Sullivan had unlocked both cuffs McAteer twisted him onto his face, yanked his arms behind his back and snapped the cuffs closed around his wrists. He shoved the keys into his pocket and dragged O'Sullivan to his feet, spinning him round to face him. There was a wild look of triumph in McAteer's eye as he smashed his forehead into the bridge of O'Sullivan's nose, the sharp, cracking sound ringing round the enclosed space. 'That's us quits, you fucking Papist bastard,' he panted. O'Sullivan dropped to his knees, blood from his broken nose spurting down his jacket.

'What the hell's going on?' A squat, dark-haired figure came striding out of the toilet, buckling his belt.

'It's the filth.' McAteer gestured towards O'Sullivan. 'He must've followed me out here.'

'Shite! That's all I need! Is he on his own?'

'He says he's got armed back-up outside.'

'Fucking hell!'

'He's probably bluffing. Come on.' McAteer picked up his car keys from the table and lobbed them across. 'You drive, Jack. I'll take care of this one.' Jack Craig caught the keys, then lifted his anorak and his heavy briefcase from the bed.

McAteer dragged O'Sullivan to his feet and held him in front of him. He kicked open the caravan door, the knife blade pressed hard against O'Sullivan's throat, drawing more blood.

'Whoever's out there,' he yelled. 'Back off, or Paddy cops his lot!'

Tom Freer stepped back silently into the shadow of the trees. McAteer moved down the caravan steps slowly, giving his eye time to adjust to the gloom, Jack Craig following close behind. They made their way across to the Volvo, McAteer's blade pressed against O'Sullivan's windpipe. He opened the passenger door and got inside, forcing O'Sullivan to sit on the door sill. Craig placed his briefcase carefully on the back seat, then slipped in behind the steering wheel. Firing the ignition, he depressed the clutch and nudged the car into gear. McAteer locked his elbow around O'Sullivan's throat as the car inched forward, O'Sullivan's heels dragging a rutted track through the snow. When they started to gather pace McAteer pushed O'Sullivan's body clear of the car and slammed the door.

Just after half-past five Charlie and Colin Renton walked into the office they'd been allocated, adjacent to the Parkhead hospitality suite. They were greeted by two Celtic directors. A police sergeant and a dozen uniformed officers, most of whom Charlie recognised, were waiting in the office.

'This is a large-scale operation,' Charlie announced to the assembled company. 'We have reason to believe that several hundred thousand pounds' worth of drugs will be changing hands in the west toilets underneath the main stand in about an hour's time.'

'Why would anyone choose to deal in drugs here, Inspector?' one of the directors enquired.

'Our information is that two dealers, posing as Dynamo Zagreb supporters, have brought a large quantity of heroin into the country and they've set up a rendezvous with their contacts at six-thirty in the toilets to sell it on. When you're given the signal to move in,' Charlie said, turning to the sergeant, 'assign two of your men to cordon off the area and direct anyone trying to approach the toilets to the loos at the other end of the stand. The rest of your team will body search everyone coming out of the west toilets. What we're looking for is serious quantities of heroin and large sums of money.'

'What's "a large sum of money", sir?' one of the officers asked.

'Twenty quid, if you're on my salary,' someone chipped in, to the accompaniment of whistles and hoots of derision.

Charlie waited for the banter to die away before continuing. 'Use your common sense. Wads of notes in brown envelopes would be a good starting point. And talking of using your common sense, we need to do everything we can to ensure cooperation for the body searches, so make it clear that you're not interested in personal use stuff. If anyone refuses to cooperate, cuff them and take them to the Black Maria that's parked outside the South Stand. It's important that we do this with the minimum of fuss and aggro,' Charlie stated. 'We don't want rowdy arguments going on outside the toilets in case that spooks the dealers into flushing the evidence down the pan. Any questions?'

There was a sharp rap on the office door and a girl popped her head round. 'There's someone from the drugs squad here to see you, Inspector.'

'Send him in,' Charlie said. 'If there are no questions,' he said, looking round the room. 'I need to brief this guy.'

As the police officers and the directors were filing out of the room, a diminutive figure in jeans and a polo-necked sweater walked in. He had a large rucksack strapped to his back and he was holding a jet-black Labrador on a leash.

'Warrant Officer Pete McIntyre, Inspector,' he announced, taking a firm grip of Charlie's proffered hand. He acknowledged Renton's presence with a wave. 'Ammunitions Technical Officer to the army cognoscenti,' he said with a toothy smile. 'One-man bomb disposal squad to the rest of the world.' McIntyre had the wiry frame of a jockey. There wasn't an ounce of spare flesh on his angular features and his tousled brown hair flopped down over his forehead.

'Am I glad to see you,' said Charlie.

'What's the situation?'

'How much have you been told?'

'Only that I'm here to disarm an explosive device and that you two are the only people I'm allowed to discuss it with. As far as everyone else is concerned I'm with the drugs squad.'

Charlie nodded. 'We've reason to believe that a bomb is going to be planted in the toilets downstairs in about half an hour's time – Semtex, about seven kilos of the stuff. What sort of damage would we be looking at if that went off?'

'It all depends where the device is positioned. To put it into perspective, a few grams of high explosive packed into a radio cassette player was enough to bring down the Lockerbie plane, whereas when the IRA tried to take out Thatcher and her cabinet in Brighton in the nineteen eighties we reckon they used about nine kilos of gelignite. Seven kilos of Semtex, expertly placed, could make one hell of a mess of the stadium.'

'What about the surrounding area?'

'The nearest houses are on the other side of London Road?'

'That's right.'

McIntyre shook his head. 'The blast might take out a few windows, but nothing more by way of collateral damage. Anyway,' he added, 'that's all theoretical. It's my job to make sure the device doesn't go pop.'

'I must say I find your confidence reassuring. We should be able to have the toilets cordoned off by about six-thirty. How do you want to play it?'

'How many searchers do we have?'

'You're looking at us.'

'I assume there's no problem with me using my dog?'

'As long as you con it into believing it's looking for drugs. You're not allowed to tell it about the Semtex.'

'I'll try,' he whispered, tapping the side of his nose. 'But Sheena's nobody's fool.' McIntyre's top teeth stuck out when he grinned. 'In which case I suggest you leave the search activity to me and the two of you concentrate on keeping any nosy parkers at bay. There isn't a better sniffer dog in Scotland than Sheena, but we can't rely on her. One of the reasons Semtex is so popular with terrorists is that it has only a faint signature odour and the dogs have a problem with it. But I've got my bag of tricks.' He shrugged off his heavy rucksack. 'I've got a trace detector to take air samples and that'll pick up just about any explosive material in the vicinity, including Semtex, and if the bomb's been placed somewhere inaccessible I've got a robot that will let me have a close-up look at the device before I decide how I'm going to disarm it.'

'Anything in particular we should be doing?' Charlie asked.

'Switch off your mobiles, just in case the device is radio

activated. I'd hate to go through the roof because one of your wives called to say your dinner was ready.'

'Can we use walkie-talkies?' Renton asked.

'No problem – different frequency entirely.'

When McAteer and Craig reached the other side of Luss village they pulled into a lay-by and swapped over, McAteer taking the wheel.

'What the hell were you thinking about – leading the cops to the caravan?' Craig complained as he clipped on his seatbelt. 'The last thing we need is the fuzz on the lookout for this car.'

'It's nothin' to get worked up about. It'll be hours before anybody finds him, an' with a bit of luck he'll be frozen to death by the time they do.'

'Where was his car? I didn't see it.'

'Probably hidden in the trees.'

'Odds-on there was someone else with him. He wouldn't have followed you out here on his own. The cops are probably on the lookout for this car right now.'

'Well, if it's botherin' you that much . . .' They were on a straight stretch of road on the approach to Arden and McAteer started flashing his headlights at the dark green Renault in front of him. When the car slowed down, McAteer pulled alongside and rolled down his window to flag down the driver.

'You've got a problem, pal!' McAteer yelled, pointing towards the rear of his vehicle. The driver looked across in confusion as McAteer accelerated in front of him and, indicating left, pulled in at the side of the road. When the Renault tucked in behind McAteer got out of his car and walked back. The driver wound down his window and stuck his head out.

'What's the problem, Jimmy?' he asked.

'Your exhaust's hingin' off, pal. You're about to lose it.'

'Bloody hell!' The driver got out and marched round to the back of his vehicle, McAteer following him. 'I've just had this bloody car serviced,' he complained. As he bent low to examine his exhaust McAteer brought the side of his hand slamming down in a rabbit punch on the nape of his neck. Lifting the unconscious body, he dropped it over a low hedge.

'Get your gear,' he shouted. Craig reached over to the back seat for his briefcase and anorak and hurried towards the Renault, McAteer getting into the driver's seat and Craig climbing into the back.

On the approach to the city, Craig took a body harness from his briefcase and strapped it around his shoulders before lifting the Semtex carefully from his case and fitting it snugly inside the harness. Having tested the harness straps he tugged on his anorak.

McAteer drove across the city centre and made his way along Duke Street as far as Parkhead Cross, then cut across the junction into Springfield Road. When he saw the green and white structure of Celtic Park loom into view he pulled up outside The Oak Bar. 'I'll park round the corner and wait for you there,' he said, indicating the empty parking bay he'd spotted in West Whitby Street. 'Walk down to the bottom of the hill and turn right into London Road. You can't miss it.'

'Okay. We'll meet you back here,' Craig said, adjusting the straps of the harness under his anorak.

'Are you sure you've got your ticket?' McAteer asked.

Craig produced a match ticket from his inside pocket and examined it. 'Cracking seat. Pity I won't get to see the match.'

'You could always stay for the first half,' McAteer grinned.

'You've got a lot more confidence in the accuracy of this timing device than I have,' Craig said, tapping his anorak pocket. Craig produced a Celtic scarf from his case and wound it round his neck.

'Never thought I'd see the day!' McAteer guffawed. 'What wouldn't I give for a photo!'

'If word got out I wouldn't dare show my face in the Shankill Road ever again,' Craig said as he got out of the car and slammed the door. Heading down Springfield Road, he turned into London Road where there were already a fair number of singing, flag-waving, can-swilling supporters walking past the school and drifting up the slope, past the Celtic Superstore, towards the stadium – the Irish tricolours heavily outnumbering the Scottish saltires. He moved at a brisk pace through the crowd and joined a short queue at a turnstile in front of the main stand. When he got inside the ground he made eye contact with a security guard leaning against the wall. Archie Glen nodded in recognition as Craig walked towards him. Their hands met, thumbs probing, fingers sliding past each other. Nothing was said as Glen limped along in front, dragging his club foot. When they arrived at the West Stand toilets there were several people using the urinals. Glen went into a cubicle with an OUT OF ORDER sign pinned to the door. Taking a long black coat from the door peg he slipped it on over his security guard's uniform. 'The cistern's empty an' the water's turned off,' he whispered as he came out. Craig nodded and went into the booth, bolting the door from the inside while Glen stood guard.

A drunk-looking figure, a dirty Celtic scarf draped around his shoulders, was slouched on the stairs leading down from the main stand. He slipped a miniature walkie-talkie from his pocket and concealed it in his fist as he connected with Charlie. 'I've spotted Craig, sir,' Renton whispered into his fist. 'He and a bloke wearing a security guard's uniform have just gone into the loos.'

Ten minutes later Craig and Glen emerged from the toilets and headed for a wooden door set into the red-brick stadium wall. Glen glanced over his shoulder to check they weren't being observed before using his pass key to unlock the door. They stepped outside, Glen locking the door behind them.

Charlie's walkie-talkie connected again. 'Craig and his accomplice have just left the stadium.'

'We're not going anywhere in a hurry, Archie,' Craig said, casually pulling a packet of cigarettes from his pocket and offering it to Glen. 'It would look odd if we were to be seen hurrying away from the ground.' Taking out a book of matches he lit both their cigarettes. 'Bugger!' he exclaimed in a loud voice. 'I promised Malky a scarf for his Christmas and I forget all about it. Do we have time to get one before kick-off?' he asked, pointing in the direction of the Supporters' Superstore.

Glen took his cue. 'Sure,' he said, glancing at his watch. 'We've got plenty of time.' Craig led the way down the slope.

Having gazed in the shop window for a few minutes, Craig tugged at Glen's sleeve. 'It's time we were making ourselves scarce,' he whispered. Moving against the flow of supporters they edged their way down towards London Road, Craig repeatedly calling out: 'Any spare tickets, lads?'

'I've got one for the North Stand.' The voice came from the other side of the road, a man waving a ticket above his head.

'We're looking for two together, pal,' Craig called back, continuing on his way. 'Thanks all the same.'

McAteer was waiting for them at the pick-up spot in West Whitby Street. Ripping off the Celtic scarf, Craig spat on it and threw it over a low wall before climbing into the back seat of the Renault along with Glen.

'Where to?' McAteer asked.

'Drop us off somewhere near Central Station, then dump this car.'

Charlie ordered his team into position at six-thirty and as soon as the toilets had been cleared he went inside with McIntyre and his dog. On McIntrye's command, Sheena sat down, her head cocked to one side, her eyes never leaving her master. 'Think they're trying to give us a hint?' McIntyre nodded towards the OUT OF ORDER sign pinned to a cubicle door.

'Might be the break we need,' Charlie said. 'If that's where the device has been planted it would make sense for them to discourage anyone from trying to use that booth.'

'I'll have a look.' McIntyre twisted the handle slowly and eased open the cubicle door. 'It's probably in here,' he said, carefully lifting the cover from the cistern and peering inside. 'Bingo!' His tuneless whistling of 'Flower of Scotland' as he examined the device did nothing to soothe Charlie's nerves. Replacing the cistern cover he came out of the cubicle. 'It looks straightforward enough,' he said, opening up his rucksack and taking out his blast-resistant protective clothing.'

'How will you go about disarming it?' Charlie asked as McIntyre was getting dressed.

'With one of these.' McIntyre pulled a two-foot long metal tube from the side pocket of his rucksack and showed it to Charlie. 'This is what the army boys call a pigstick. Despite what you see in the movies, I'm not about to select a wire and snip it with a pair of cutters. For a start, I'm colour blind – and even if I wasn't, the odds on picking the right wire aren't all that great. With this little beauty,' he said, holding up the pigstick, 'I position it a few inches from the device and when I press the trigger it fires an explosive jet of water into the bomb which will disrupt the circuitry before the explosive material has time to detonate. At least, I think that's what it says in the instructions.' He handed the pigstick to Charlie. 'Would you check that for me?'

'Are you taking the piss?'

McIntyre grinned. 'I've defused twenty-odd bombs in my time with one of these. So far, so good.' He took the pigstick back. 'I won't need Sheena for this operation,' he said, clicking his fingers to get the Labrador's attention. He pointed at Charlie. 'Sheena – go with him,' he instructed, picking up the end of the leash from the floor and handing it to Charlie.

'I want you well out of the road before I go in,' McIntyre said as he was pulling on his helmet. 'Go upstairs and wait at the far end of the corridor. If the device were to explode, the walls would tend to channel the blast vertically, so whatever you do don't stand above the toilets.'

'Thanks for the tip.'

'Don't take this personally, Inspector,' McIntryre said with a wry smile as he lowered his visor. 'It was Sheena I was worried about.'

Charlie felt the hairs on the back of his neck crawl as he wiped the palms of his clammy hands down the sides of his trousers. Sheena sat patiently by his side, ears pricked.

Fifteen minutes elapsed before McIntyre came up the staircase and walked along the corridor towards Charlie. He had changed back into his jeans and polo-necked sweater.

'The Semtex is in here.' He held up his rucksack. 'Harmless as a baby.' When he snapped his fingers Sheena trotted across to nuzzle into his hand.

'Well done!' Charlie exhaled noisily.

'We have to be alive to the possibility of secondaries, Inspector. Not much point in disarming a device only to find it was a decoy and the mother-lode's in an adjacent cubicle.'

'I doubt if they'll have gone to those lengths. They didn't have a lot of time and I'm reasonably sure they don't suspect we're on to them.'

'You're probably right – this lot feels like seven kilos.' McIntyre weighed his rucksack in his hand 'But it won't do any harm to have a quick butcher's in the other booths, just in case. I'll go back down now and do that. You can never be too careful in this line of work.'

'I really don't know how you do your job.'

'Neither does my wife.'

Charlie made his way back to the directors' hospitality suite. 'Looks like it was a false alarm, gentlemen. Either that or the dealers got wind of the fact that we were on to them and called the operation off.'

'No harm done, Inspector – apart from a few crossed legs, I imagine.'

Charlie forced a smile. 'There is one thing I'd like you to do for me,' he said.

'Yes?'

'Could you check if any of your staff are missing? We suspect that one of your security guards might have been in cahoots with the drug dealers and he might've taken off in fright when he saw the police presence.'

'Of course.'

'I'd appreciate it if you would give me a call me as soon as you have that information,' Charlie said, writing down his mobile number and tearing the page from his notebook.

Sleet was starting to fall as Charlie and Colin Renton made their way down the slope, away from the stadium, to where they'd parked their car. Charlie turned up his coat collar and pulled his hat tightly down on his forehead to the accompaniment of the burgeoning chant of 'Hail! hail! The Celts are here' drifting down the hill. He turned back and gazed up at the freezing night air, shimmering in the iridescent floodlights. Beyond the lights the clouds were low, grey and menacing. 'We'll have to take their word for it that the Celts are here, Colin,' he said, 'but I can sure as hell vouch for the hail!' Plunging his hands deep into his coat pockets he felt for his mobile. His numb fingers fumbled to switch it on and he saw he'd missed one call. When he checked the message he recognised his brother's cheery voice: 'This is Hugh, Charlie. I managed to get you a ticket for the South Stand. I'll leave it in an envelope with your name on it at the players' entrance – and I'll let you buy me a pint after the match.'

With a wry smile, Charlie deleted the message.

'The first minister is delighted with the outcome, Anderson,' Chief Constable Turnbull announced. 'He asked me to give you his personal congratulations.'

'It's Warrant Officer McIntyre who deserves the plaudits, sir. He did all the work.'

'I'll make sure that message gets passed on.'

'How does that leave the situation with the undercover agent?'

'He can hardly be held responsible for the fact that Craig cocked up the timing mechanism.'

'Won't their tame security guard be back in the morning, looking for the Semtex?'

'A cleaner came across it – didn't you know?'

Charlie furrowed his brow. 'When?'

Turnbull looked at his watch. 'Oh, in about an hour's time, I reckon. Cleaning the toilets after the match, he'll see something suspicious in one of the loos and inform the Parkhead management. It'll be reported in the papers tomorrow as an attempted atrocity that backfired because of a faulty timing device.'

An ashen-faced Tom Freer stood in front of Charlie's desk and explained what had happened.

'In the name of Christ! What got into O'Sullivan?' Charlie snapped. 'Surely he knew what McAteer was capable of?'

'I don't really know, sir,' Freer said. 'He seemed determined to bring him in.'

'You said there was someone with McAteer?'

'Yes, sir. A smallish, bloke – I couldn't see much more in the dark. He was carrying a briefcase.'

'What's the news from the hospital?'

'Sergeant O'Sullivan's got a broken nose, two cracked ribs and a nasty wound to his throat. He's lost a lot of blood, but his life's not in danger. They've got him under sedation.'

'That's all I need!' Charlie grunted. 'Hospital visits to fit into my schedule. Are you on duty tomorrow, son?'

'Yes, sir.'

'Be in my office at eight o'clock sharp. I'm going over to Bearsden for a chat with Mrs Harrison and I'd like you to tag along.'

Charlie felt his mobile start to vibrate in his jacket pocket. Pulling it out he took the call.

'Inspector Anderson?' the caller inquired.

'Speaking.'

'This is Frank Collins from Celtic Park. I've got the information you were looking for. One of our contract security guards, a guy called Archie Glen, turned up for duty before the game but he wasn't present at the end of the match. He didn't tell anyone why he was leaving.'

'Do you have his address?'

'Yes.'

Charlie tucked his phone under his chin and unscrewed the top from his fountain pen. 'Fire away.' Having noted the details, he thanked the caller.

Charlie called Turnbull's mobile. 'I've got the info you were looking for about the Parkhead security guard who went AWOL.' He read out Glen's name and address. 'How you want to play it?'

'Leave it with me. I don't want to tread on any toes on this one. I'll pass the information on to Special Branch and they can decide how they want to handle it.'

Sue swilled down her third tomato juice in the upstairs bar at the Ubiquitous Chip and tried Tony O'Sullivan's mobile for the umpteenth time. There was still no reply. Getting to her feet she tugged on her coat and wrapped her scarf twice round her neck as she trudged down the tiled staircase. At the foot of the stairs she popped into the restaurant and asked the waiter to cancel the table for two booked in the name of O'Sullivan. Making her way down Ashton Lane she stopped on the corner of Byres Road and took out her phone to call home. 'Amanda, it's Sue. I'll be home in about twenty minutes – get the Scrabble board ready. By the way, what kind of takeaway do you prefer – Indian or Chinese?'

'What was the score?' Kay asked as Charlie was stripping off his overcoat.

'The score?'

'Don't try to kid me you were working,' she said with a smile. 'I know you were at Parkhead enjoying yourself.'

'What are you talking about?'

'Hugh phoned the back of six to say he'd managed to get you a ticket. I told him to call you on your mobile. Oh, don't tell me he didn't manage to get in touch with you?'

'I had my phone switched off all evening, love.'

'What's the point in carrying it around with you if you're not going to switch it on?'

'Anyway, I was busy. I wouldn't have had time for the match. Bit of bad news, by the way,' he added as he draped his coat over the hallstand. 'Tony O'Sullivan got on the wrong side of Billy McAteer and ended up in hospital.'

'That's terrible! Is he all right?'

'Nothing life threatening, but bad enough. A broken nose and a couple of cracked ribs. He's in the Southern General. I'm going over to see him in the morning.'

'Fancy a cup of tea?' Kay asked.

'I certainly do. And a very big hauf to go with it,' Charlie added with a heavy sigh.

Archie Glen got off the train at Paisley Gilmour Street station. It was dry but bitterly cold as he limped the length of Moss Street and made his way up the High Street, into the teeth of the wind, as far as the Bruce Arms. When he went into the pub there was the usual buzz of conversation, but not the level of animation he'd expected to find. He checked his watch. Well after ten. Surely news should have filtered through by now?'

'The usual, Archie?' the familiar voice from behind the bar called out.

'Make it a large one, Andy. It's fuckin' freezin' out there. Anythin' on the news?' he asked casually as a large Famous Grouse and a jug of water were placed on the bar in front of him.

'The news?' Andy chortled. 'Since when have you been interested in the news, apart from the racing results?'

'Just thought there might've been somethin',' Glen mumbled. He paid for his whisky and downed it in one gulp before hurrying outside. Lighting a cigarette in the shelter of the pub doorway he cupped it in both hands to try to warm them as he limped along the pavement towards his tenement close. He made his way slowly up to the top floor, gripping the handrail and dragging his club foot up each step behind him. Unlocking his front door he went straight to the kitchen to pour himself another stiff belt of whisky which he threw down his throat. He considered making a phone call to find out what had happened, but thought better of it. Shivering, he stripped off his clothes in the unheated bedroom and changed into his pyjamas. He shuffled down the hall to the bathroom. As he stepped inside, the door closed behind him and the butt of a handgun crashed into the back of his head.

Glen's unconscious body was carried back to the bedroom and placed between the sheets. A jerrycan of petrol was used liberally to soak the bedclothes, curtains and carpet, then a match was struck and dropped onto the bed.

*

Gerry Fraser was curled up in bed when he heard a sharp rap on his front door. He switched on his bedside lamp and squinted at his watch. It showed half-past twelve.

'Who the fuck can that be?' he muttered under his breath as he switched the lamp off. The knocking became louder and more insistent. 'You can piss off, whoever you are!' he shouted out, turning over and pulling the bedclothes over his head. The knocking turned to hammering and then there was a loud bang, followed by the sound of splintering wood. Fraser sat bolt upright in bed, trembling fingers clutching the blankets to his chin. His whole body broke out in a cold sweat when he saw the tall figure framed in the bedroom doorway.

McAteer flicked the bedroom light switch on. 'You would save yourself a lot of money in repair bills if you answered your fuckin' door, Fraser.'

'What do you want?' he bleated.

'No need to wet yourself. I huvny come to gie you a doin'. I just need somewhere to kip down.'

CHAPTER 14

Thursday 23 December

'I don't believe this!' Kay Anderson hurried down the hall to the kitchen clutching the *Daily Record* that had just dropped thorough the letter box. 'You were nearly at that match, Charlie.' Her hand was shaking as she handed him the newspaper. 'Hugh was at that match.'

Charlie grabbed the paper from her grasp and scanned the front page story. 'An attempted bomb outrage at Celtic Park last night was thwarted when an anonymous phone caller tipped the police off about the planned atrocity.'

Charlie snatched up the phone and called Bill Turnbull's mobile. 'I've just seen the *Record*. What the hell happened to the press release about the faulty timing mechanism and the cleaner coming across the Semtex after the match?' he demanded.

'That's the story Special Branch were planning to go with, but it was far from ideal. For one thing, Craig's a pro. It's highly improbable that he would've messed up the timing device. In addition to that, what's the likelihood of a cleaner actually looking inside a toilet cistern? If they'd gone with that scenario there was a risk the loyalists might put two and two together and suspect that there was an informer in their midst. However, when we managed to get a fix on Glen, that all changed.'

'In what way?'

'If you turn to page ten in the *Record* you'll see a story about a tragic accident. Archie Glen, a security guard, burned to death in his flat in Paisley last night. The story goes on to say that the police suspect that Glen had too much to drink and that he set his bed alight with a cigarette.'

'For Christ's sake! Glen's loyalist colleagues are never going to buy that! There's no way in this world they're going to think his death was an accident!'

'Of course not. But they'll never know for sure if he tipped off the police – and if he did – did he then top himself or did Special Branch take him out once he'd outlived his usefulness? Information has been leaked to the paramilitaries that Glen was on Special Branch's payroll and when they check up they'll find a large sum of money was paid into his bank account last week.'

'How the hell could that have happened last week when we didn't discover his identity until last night?'

'It's called transaction backdating, Charlie. It's a Special Branch speciality.'

Charlie, accompanied by Tom Freer, rang Laura Harrison's bell just after half-past eight. She came to the door in dressing gown and slippers.

'You might have warned me you were coming, Inspector.'

Charlie studied her bruises and the ugly scar down the side of her face. 'Don't tell me,' he said, stepping across the threshold. 'You had an accident.'

'I . . . I walked into a glass door.' Laura's fingers traced the scar.

'I thought it was open. I . . . I didn't have my contact lenses in,' she stammered.

'This must be the most accident-prone city in the world,' Charlie said, tugging off his coat. 'People knock their teeth out when changing light bulbs and they walk face-first into glass doors. But there's one amazing coincidence. These things only seem to happen when Billy McAteer's in the vicinity.'

As Laura's knees started to buckle, Freer stepped forward and grabbed her by the arm to steady her.

'I think it's about time you came clean with us, Mrs Harrison,' Charlie stated, taking her by the elbow and guiding her along the corridor towards the lounge. Laura settled on the settee, Charlie sitting down beside her.

'This is Detective Constable Freer,' Charlie said. 'He was watching through the window yesterday afternoon when you gave Billy McAteer a large sum of money.' Laura's body stiffened visibly. 'He saw McAteer slap you about and if it hadn't been for his presence of mind you probably would've been raped.' Gazing wide-eyed at Freer, Laura buried her face in her hands, silent tears running down her bruised cheeks and seeping through her fingers. 'We know your husband was shot with McAteer's gun, Mrs Harrison. But what I want to know,' Charlie said, 'is why you paid McAteer to kill him?'

Laura let out an involuntary yelp and started sobbing violently, rocking back and forth on her seat.

'Find the kitchen and make her a cup of tea, son,' Charlie said quietly to Freer. 'Lots of sugar.'

'Has school broken up?' Tony O'Sullivan squinted sideways at Sue as she dragged the visitor's chair from underneath his hospital bed.

'Today's the last day of term. The heidie's taking a special assembly this morning to deliver his traditional Christmas message.'

'Which is?'

'Anyone caught stealing during the holiday period will get the living daylights kicked out of them in the New Year. I can afford to give it a miss. I've heard it all before. Anyway, I'm not planning to pinch anything over Christmas.'

'What about Jamie?'

'As far as I'm aware he's not planning to nick anything either.'

Tony held on to the bandages around his ribs. 'Don't make me laugh, Sue. I meant, how is Jamie getting to school?'

'My neighbour's giving him a lift.'

'It can't be easy bringing up a kid on your own.'

'It certainly isn't,' Sue said with feeling. 'Especially when he's at that difficult age – born, but not yet left home.'

Tony smiled. 'How did you find out about this?' he asked, pointing towards his face.

'Mum called me first thing. You just can't let anything get past you, can you?' she said, tapping the side of her nose with her index finger. 'I had a broken hooter, so you had to have one too. I realise imitation's the sincerest form of flattery but this is taking things a bit too far. Anyway,' she pouted, angling her head and studying his face, 'my break's much more subtle. It's only a few degrees off the vertical. I reckon yours is closer to a right angle.'

Tony touched his nose gingerly. 'They're going to reset it later when the swelling's had a chance to die down.'

Sue pulled a bunch of black grapes from the paper bag she was carrying and placed it in the bowl on the bedside table. 'Nothing if not original, that's me!'

'Grapes of wrath, I presume?'

'I must admit, at nine o'clock last night you were not my favourite person in the whole wide world. I'd spent an hour studying the menu, salivating between the roast guinea fowl and the braised duck – only to end up back home tucking into lukewarm chicken chop suey and egg fried rice. Still, it wasn't all bad news. I stuffed Amanda at Scrabble.'

'I really am sorry, Sue. I'll make it up to you as soon as –'

'Sssh,' Sue whispered, reaching across to place her index finger across his lips. 'How are you feeling?'

'Battered and bruised, but it's the blow to my pride that hurts the most. I still can't believe I let the bastard duff me up. I even had him cuffed, for God's sake!' Twisting his whole body round so he could face her, Tony winced when a twinge of pain pulsed through his ribcage. 'However, a broken nose and a few cracked ribs is nothing compared with the bollocking I'm going to get from your old man.'

'Mum told me he's coming in to see you later this morning.'

'I can feel a coma coming on.'

'That'll only postpone the evil hour.' Sue switched to her parade ground voice. 'Take your punishment like a man, Sergeant O'Sullivan!' she boomed.

Several heads in the ward turned towards them.

Laura Harrison had stopped weeping but she continued to dab at her puffy eyelids with a soggy tissue as she nursed a steaming mug of sweet tea.

Charlie took out his notebook and pen. 'Would you like to tell me all about it?'

Pulling a fresh tissue from the box on her knee, Laura used it to wipe her nose. She took a deep breath, trying to compose herself. 'I hired McAteer to deal with a blackmailer, but I'd no idea it would turn out to be my husband.'

'Your husband was blackmailing you?'

'Not directly. He targeted Simon Ramsay, my brother-in-law.' She blew on her tea before taking a sip, screwing up her face at the unwelcome sweetness. 'Simon and I have been having an affair.'

'How long has that being going on?'

'A couple of years. It all started off innocently enough, meeting up for the occasional drink in Rogano's and a mutual bitching session about our respective spouses. From there it developed into a bit of drunken groping in the car on the way home and before I really knew what was happening we were booking into the Hilton as Mr and Mrs Petrie every other Friday night when Mike stayed over at Ronnie McGavigan's place after his poker school.'

'What about Mr Ramsay? What excuse did he have for staying out all night?'

'He didn't need one. Jude doesn't give a damn what he gets up to as long as he doesn't flaunt it. She's got plenty going on the side herself. But Simon screwing with me is a completely different kettle of fish,' Laura added, forcing a sip of tea between her lips. 'If Jude finds out about that she'll go ballistic.'

'How was Mr Ramsay being blackmailed?'

'It would appear that someone found out about our Friday nights in the Hilton and managed to conceal a camera in the bedroom. He got all the sordid details on film and sent Simon an email with a sample photograph attached. He was demanding fifty thousand pounds or else he threatened to sell the story to the tabloids.'

'And the blackmailer was your husband?'

Laura crinkled up her face. 'Logically, I suppose it had to be him, but I still can't make any sense of that. Mike was the most insanely jealous person you could ever meet, Inspector, and he had an extremely violent temper. If he thought for one minute that I was even looking at another man he'd go berserk.'

'Did he ever resort to violence with you?'

'Sometimes.' Her hand strayed towards her cheek. 'Normally only when he had a drink in him. I used to worry myself sick about what he would do if he ever found out about Simon and me. I really thought he would kill us both.' Laura broke off to dab her eyes with a tissue. 'It's completely out of character for Mike to plot a cold-blooded revenge like blackmail,' she continued. 'Having said that, he was desperate for money. He'd run up significant gambling debts and, unknown to me, he'd sold off everything we owned. And he was in Kelvingrove Park at the time the handover was supposed to take place, so I can only assume he was the blackmailer.'

'And you hired Billy McAteer to kill him?'

'I hired McAteer to deal with an unknown blackmailer, who turned out to be my husband.'

'By "deal with", you mean "kill"?'

Laura sunk her teeth into her quivering bottom lip. Fighting to hold back the tears, she gave a quick nod of the head.

'How much did you pay McAteer?'

'Ten thousand pounds.'

'If your husband had sold off everything, how were you able to lay your hands on that kind of money?'

Laura hesitated. 'My father gave it to me,' she said in a little more than whisper.

Charlie put away his notebook. 'I'll have to ask you to accompany me to Pitt Street and make a full statement. You will be formally charged with conspiracy to murder.'

'Is it all right if I get changed first?' she asked, tugging on the lapel of her dressing gown.

'Of course. Is there anyone you want to phone?'

'My father, I suppose,' she stammered, a shiver running the length of her spine. 'I don't *want* to phone him, but I think I'd better.'

When Laura called Jim Cuthbertson's Glasgow office she was told he was on a business trip to Aberdeen. She asked for the number of the Aberdeen office and dialled again.

'This is utterly ridiculous, Inspector!' Charlie, notebook and pen in hand, was seated on an upholstered leather chair in Simon Ramsay's office. Opposite him, Ramsay sat behind a wide desk, an unlit cigarette dangling from his nicotine-stained fingers. 'I admit Laura and I were having an affair, but everything else is a complete fabrication on her part. I can only assume that this is her twisted way of getting her revenge. Either that or she's having some kind of breakdown.'

'Why would she be looking for revenge?'

'Last week I told her our affair was over. She took it very badly. Screaming tantrums and all that.'

'And you weren't being blackmailed?'

'Blackmailed? I've never heard anything so preposterous in all my life!'

'So you didn't go to Mrs Harrison and ask her for help to pay off a blackmailer?'

'Of course not!'

'In her statement she said that a blackmailer, who she thinks was her husband, sent you an email with a compromising photograph attached, threatening to expose you. She claims you showed her this photo and talked her into hiring a hit man to murder the blackmailer.'

'What am I supposed to say to that?' He raised his eyes to the heavens and spread both arms wide. 'Hell hath no fury...' He shook his head slowly from side to side. 'I don't know what's got into Laura lately,' he said with an exaggerated sigh. 'I told you that I suspected Mike was beating her up. I can only conclude that it all got too much for her and she hired this *hit man*, as you call him, to solve her problems.' He paused to suck on his unlit cigarette. 'I don't imagine for one minute that she has given you a shred of evidence to substantiate her wild claims? After all, how could she? For example, has she produced a copy of this so-called "compromising photograph"?'

'In her statement she said she set fire to it in Rogano's.'

'How very convenient! It would appear that Laura hired someone to kill her husband and, out of spite, she's trying to drag me down with her. I haven't spoken to her since last week when I told her our affair was over.' Charlie put away his notebook and pen. 'Inspector,' Ramsay said slowly, 'the fact that Laura and I were having an affair . . .' He hesitated. 'I don't suppose it would be possible for that to be . . .' He broke off.

'To be what?'

'To be hushed up, is what I was about to say, but I didn't mean it like that. What I wanted to know is – does my wife have to find out about the affair? I mean, it's not as if it has any relevance to the murder investigation?'

'I can't comment on that. What comes out in a court of law is a matter for the prosecution and the defence lawyers.'

'Of course, of course, I understand that.' He coughed harshly into his fist. 'I realise everything will have to be out in the open eventually. I was just hoping to be able to break the news to Jude myself – before she hears it from someone else.'

'I wouldn't leave that too long if I were you, Mr Ramsay,' Charlie said, rising to his feet. 'Once the press get wind of an arrest, things tend to move pretty quickly.'

Tony O'Sullivan heard Charlie's voice before he saw him. He slipped the paperback he was reading under his pillow and feigned sleep as Charlie's footsteps came clomping down the ward.

'I know you're awake.' Charlie pulled out the visitor's chair, turned it round and straddled it. 'If you don't open your eyes right now, Sergeant O'Sullivan,' he said in a mock stage whisper, 'I'm going to tickle you in the ribs.'

Tony's puffed-up eyes opened slowly. 'How did you know I was awake?'

'The ward sister told me you were sitting up in bed reading. Don't worry, I'm saving up my tirade until you're back on your feet. That way I won't feel so bad about sticking the heid on you.'

'Ouch!' Tony touched the splint on his nose.

'Nice wee Glasgow kiss you've got there,' Charlie said, stroking his chin approvingly as he examined Tony's bruised face.

'The bastard nutted me while I was handcuffed.'

'Now where have I heard that before?'

'He only got a split eyebrow,' Tony protested. 'Not that I'm admitting anything,' he added quickly. 'This one's a real cracker, though.' He fingered the splint carefully.

'I can't wait to hear all about it.' Charlie dragged his chair closer to the bed.

'Freer and I followed McAteer from Laura Harrison's place to a deserted caravan park near Luss,' Tony said. 'I went into the caravan to arrest McAteer while Tom waited outside. I actually had the bastard cuffed when my attention was distracted by someone flushing the toilet – I've no bloody idea who he was! McAteer grabbed me and stuck the heid on me, then he and this other bloke dumped me outside in the snow and drove off. Freer saw them leave, but he didn't show himself.'

'Thank God someone around here showed a modicum of common sense!'

'The worst indignity was that McAteer had cuffed me with my own handcuffs. Freer had a look round in the caravan for the keys but he couldn't find them, so I had to navigate him to the Southern General with congealed blood in my eyes and my hands cuffed behind my back. I'm telling you, I felt a right pillock when the doctor had to send out for bolt cutters before he could treat me.'

'If it's sympathy you're after you're barking up the wrong tree. You deserve everything you got for going in after McAteer without back-up.'

'I realise that.' Tony slumped his head back on the pillow. 'Any news of him?'

'Just before I left the office I heard that his Volvo's been found abandoned on the A82, somewhere near Arden, along with some poor sod lying unconscious in the ditch. The forensic boys are on standby to give his car the once over as soon as it's brought in. It seems McAteer commandeered another vehicle, which was found abandoned in the city centre late last night. We've no idea where he is now. It's unlikely he'll go within a mile of the caravan site or his brother's flat in Govan – but we've got both places under surveillance just in case.

'However, things are hotting up on the murder enquiry front,' Charlie continued. 'Laura Harrison has admitted to hiring McAteer to bump off a blackmailer – though she claims she didn't know it would turn out to be her old man. According to her, Simon Ramsay was being blackmailed and he came to her for help – apparently, they've been having an affair for the past couple of years. I've just been to see Ramsay. He denies all knowledge of any blackmail attempt and claims to know nothing about McAteer being hired as a hit man. His version of events is that Laura is trying to drag him down with her out of spite because he ended their affair.'

'Who do you believe?'

'Mrs H. hasn't produced any concrete evidence that would implicate Ramsay, but I've got a feeling in my guts that he's involved. He was bending over backwards to appear cooperative this morning but at the end of the day he seemed more concerned with stopping his wife finding out about his shenanigans than about his girlfriend being arrested as an accessory to murder.' Charlie gave a knowing wink. 'Mr Ramsay would appreciate it if we could keep the news of his extra-marital affair from his wife for as long as possible.'

Noticing the grapes on the bedside table, Charlie helped himself to a handful. 'I'm not your first visitor, then?'

'A secret admirer dropped by earlier.'

'Anyone I know?'

'It wouldn't be a secret then.'

'Be like that,' Charlie said, stuffing grapes into his mouth.

'Nice grapes, these – seedless – my favourite.'

'Help yourself.'

'Any idea how long they're planning to keep you in?'

'The doc's coming to see me on his rounds this afternoon. I'm hoping he might let me out later today.'

'No chance! The ward sister told me it would be at least another twenty-four hours before they'll even let you get out of bed.' Charlie tugged off another stem of grapes. 'I wish you'd tell me who your secret admirer is. I'd like to know where she got these.'

When he got back to his office Charlie found a message waiting for him, telling him to call Superintendent Hamilton. He sighed as he picked up the phone.

'I've got a press briefing in a couple of hours,' Hamilton stated. 'What's the latest news on O'Sullivan?'

'I've been over to the Southern General to see him. He'll be out of action for a few days but there doesn't appear to be any permanent damage.'

'Why in the name of Christ did he try to tackle McAteer on his own?'

'I have to concede it wasn't the brightest thing he's ever done.'

'I warned you about that one, Anderson. He's a hothead. I'm still not convinced we did the right thing in promoting him to Sergeant.'

When Hamilton disconnected, Charlie turned his phone sideways and mimed playing the flute, quickly coughing into his fist and fumbling to replace the receiver when Renton walked into the office.

'Forensic report on McAteer's Volvo,' Renton said, waving a document. 'Hot off the press.'

'Anything of interest?'

'Pebbles found in the treads of the Wellingtons in the car boot are a match for those underneath the bridge in Kelvingrove Park. There are also traces of cordite ground into the carpet in the boot.'

'Get your snitches working flat out on this one, Colin. Someone must know where McAteer's hiding out. With his handsome kisser it's not as if he can melt into the background.'

'How long are you goany be hangin' around here?' Gerry Fraser asked hesitantly.

'Until I decide to go.' McAteer was stretched out on the settee in front of the television, using the remote control to flick through the channels. 'What's your problem?'

'I'm supposed to be meetin' Johnny Devlin in the pub at twelve.' Fraser pointed at his watch. 'If I don't turn up he'll wonder where I've got to.'

'Let him fuckin' wonder. Why is there nothin' on the telly about Parkheid?' McAteer furrowed his scarred brow as he kept switching channels.

'Celtic won two nothin', if that's what you're lookin' for.'

'Are you tryin' to take the piss?'

'Naw!'

McAteer pulled himself stiffly to his feet and crossed to the window to look up and down on the street. 'What is there for eatin'?'

'Nothin'. I was goany get a sanny doon the pub.'

'Go an' get some stuff,' McAteer said, pulling the brown envelope from his inside jacket pocket and fishing out a twenty-pound note.

'What do you want?' Fraser asked, taking the money.

'A fry-up. Eggs, bacon, sausages. Get rolls an' cheese as well. I don't suppose you've got any booze?'

'There's a couple of cans of lager in the fridge.'

McAteer produced another two twenties and handed them across. 'Get a bottle of Bells and a dozen cans o' heavy. An' pick up the papers while you're out. An' be quick about it,' he added, 'I'm starvin'.' As Fraser was heading towards the door he felt McAteer's hand on his shoulder. 'I'm warnin' you, Fraser, if you try anythin' smart-arsed I'll have your guts for garters.'

As soon as Fraser turned the corner into the Gallowgate he broke into a trot and he kept running until he reached a phone booth outside the Forge shopping centre. Grabbing the receiver he dialled 999. 'Police! CID!' he panted. 'Quick as you can!'

'What's your name, sir? Where are you calling from?'

Fraser gabbled the information. 'I have to speak to Anderson or O'Sullivan in Pitt Street – it's an emergency.'

Charlie Anderson was in conversation with Renton when the switchboard connected with his extension. 'Will you take a 999 call from someone called Gerry Fraser, sir? He seems highly agitated.'

'Put him through.' Charlie switched the phone to loudspeaker mode as the line clicked twice. 'Anderson here!' he barked.

'It's Gerry Fraser, Mr Anderson,' the voice blurted out. 'McAteer's hiding out at my place.' Charlie's grip tightened on the receiver.

'I know where he lives, sir,' Renton mouthed. 'He's got a flat in Whitevale Road.'

'Are you calling from your flat?' Charlie demanded.

'You must be fuckin' jokin'! I telt you, McAteer's there right now. I'm in a phone box. He sent me out to get grub.'

'Do what he told you and go straight back to your flat. We don't want to arouse his suspicion.'

'Do you think I'm saft in the heid, Anderson? So he can drop me oot the fuckin' window while your lot are batterin' down the door? You can do whatever the hell you like! I'm offski.' Fraser dropped the receiver onto the cradle.

Jude Ramsay chewed slowly on the tuna sandwich she had prepared for her lunch, her face like thunder as she waited for her husband to come home.

When Simon walked through the front door he headed straight for the kitchen. 'We need to talk, Jude.'

'At least that's one thing we agree on,' she said, putting down her sandwich and folding her arms across her chest.

'You know?' he said quietly.

'Laura phoned Dad. Dad phoned me. It's a small world.' Simon slumped down on the chair at the opposite end of the table. 'How could you?' she fumed. 'Of all the people in the world you could have chosen to shag, why did it have to be my sister?'

'I didn't plan it like that. It just happened. I'm sorry,' he mumbled.

'Sorry! And now the two of you are mixed up in a murder!'

'Mike's murder's got nothing to do with me. The police told me what Laura said in her statement, but none of it is true.'

'Why would Laura make up something like that?' Jude asked incredulously. 'She's already admitted to hiring McAteer to kill a blackmailer. Why would she drag you into it if it wasn't true?'

'Out of spite, I suppose, because I told her our affair was over. You remember how moody she was at the dinner party last week? That was because I'd told her the previous day that I wasn't going to be seeing her any more. She pleaded with me to change my mind, but I was adamant. I haven't spoken to her since last Wednesday.'

Jude stared at him hard. 'I don't believe a single word of it. Laura would never make up a story like that.' Jude paused. 'By the way, I also happen to know that you didn't need to go out for cigarettes the morning Mike was murdered,' she added slowly. 'I saw the half-full carton of Marlboro in your study drawer.'

The colour rose in Simon's cheeks. 'You can believe whatever you fucking-well want to!' Springing to his feet he stormed from the kitchen and took the stairs two at a time. He slammed his study door behind him and turned the key in the lock. Switching on his computer he lifted the stopper from the whisky decanter on his desk and poured a large measure into a crystal tumbler, sipping at the drink while he waited for the machine to boot up. As soon as the Windows desktop appeared he started to go through his files, meticulously checking each one in turn and deciding what to delete, then he accessed his mail folder and deleted the email from Liam Black. Noticing that there was one new message waiting he dragged the mouse to click on the 'Inbox' icon, then froze when he saw the message he was downloading had been sent by Liam Black.

CHAPTER 15

The crystal tumbler slipped from Ramsay's grasp and bounced from the keyboard onto the floor. He scrabbled for a cigarette and lit up with twitching fingers as he clicked on the message:

> *That wasn't very clever, Pervert. However, I'm prepared to give you one last chance. Just call me Mr Nice Guy. You've got until tomorrow afternoon to come up with the money. I'll phone you tonight and tell you how I want it handed over. Don't fuck up again.*
>
> *Liam Black*

Ramsay drew hard on his cigarette, repeatedly mouthing 'for fuck's sake' as he read and reread the text. Having deleted the message he closed down his computer.

Charlie Anderson stood in front of Superintendent Hamilton's desk. 'What's the latest on McAteer?' Hamilton demanded.

'We've received information that he's holed up in a flat in Whitevale Road. Shearer is on his way across with an armed unit to try to bring him in.'

'What's the situation with Laura Harrison?'

'We've charged her with conspiracy to murder. She's confessed to hiring McAteer to kill a blackmailer, though she claims she didn't know the victim would be her husband. According to her, she and Simon Ramsay concocted the plot together, but he denies all knowledge of it. Harrison's father has instructed her to say nothing more until she's seen a lawyer. He's cut short his business trip to Aberdeen and he's on his way back to Glasgow.'

'Are you planning to pull Ramsay in?'

'Not at this stage. It's her word against his and we don't have enough to hold him.'

'Jim Cuthbertson has a lot of friends in high places,' Hamilton stated. 'You better make sure you get this one right.'

Charlie glanced at his watch and moved towards the door. 'My priority right now is finding out what's happening with McAteer.'

'Keep me posted.'

Simon Ramsay parked in the underground car park beneath his office block and took the lift to the fifth floor. Closing his office door he unlocked the top drawer of his desk and took out the company chequebook. Office procedures for transferring funds to a client required the signature of either Mike Todd or himself on a cheque for less than ten thousand pounds, both signatures being mandatory for any sum greater than that. It was now or never. Laura had told her father about their affair so he knew he'd be out on his ear as soon as Jim Cuthbertson got back from Aberdeen. He considered writing several cheques, made out to different names, for amounts under ten thousand pounds, but he dismissed the idea as impractical as there was no way he could create fictitious bank accounts to pay the cheques into. One cheque was the only solution. He studied an example of Mike

Todd's signature on a letter; a short enough name, but at least a dozen loops and whorls. He tore up his first three efforts but was reasonably satisfied with his fourth attempt – at least he didn't think he'd be able to improve on it. Using a different pen he appended his own signature and wrote the amount of fifty two thousand four hundred pounds in words and figures. A cheque made out to himself wouldn't be negotiable as a signatory couldn't also be a beneficiary. He filled in the name 'Bjorn Svensson' on the payee line.

Charlie's phone rang. 'Shearer here, sir.'

'What's the status?' Charlie demanded.

'We drew a blank. When we got to Fraser's flat there was no one there. We didn't have to break the door down – someone had already done that for us. The place was deserted. If McAteer had been there it looks like he left in a hurry – the television was still on.'

'What on earth are you doing here, Simon?' Bjorn Svensson had been summoned from the computing department to the foyer of the bank.

'Is there somewhere we can talk in private?' he asked furtively.

'Not really.'

'Come outside for a minute. There's something I need you to do for me. It's urgent.' Despite Bjorn's protestations, Simon guided him through the door and led the way along the street towards the Italian café on the next block.

'What the hell is this all about? I'm supposed to be working.'

'It won't take long.' Entering the café, they sat down at a table near the window. 'I need you to do me a favour,' Simon said, producing the cheque from his pocket and sliding it across the table. 'Pay this into your account and transfer the funds to me.'

'What!'

'It's okay. It's all perfectly legal. I had a bit of luck in the currency markets.'

'Hold on a minute!'

'It's not insider dealing or anything like that, if that's what you're worried about. We're not supposed to dabble in the markets at work but I had a strong fancy that the euro would fall against the dollar so I went for a put option. In three days the euro plummeted and I cashed in. I couldn't have the cheque made payable to myself without arousing suspicion so I arranged for it to be made out in your name. All I'm asking you to do is pay it into your bank account and transfer the funds to me. It's as simple as that.'

'That is not simple! For a start, how am I supposed to justify this amount of money hitting my account?'

'Nobody needs to know anything about it and if you transfer the money to me this afternoon it won't even be in your account overnight. If any questions are asked you just have to say you had a bit of luck on the currency markets.'

Bjorn ran his fingers through his gelled hair. 'This is crazy. Even if I agreed to go along with it my account wouldn't be credited until the cheque had been cleared. It would be at least three days before I could transfer the funds to you.'

'You can transfer money quicker than that when it suits you!'

'What are you talking about?'

'The fucking Cayman Islands.'

'Shut up!' Bjorn grabbed Simon by the arm and glanced

anxiously round the café. 'Will you please keep quiet about that!' he said in a hoarse whisper.

'We all have our little secrets we'd prefer our employers not to know about, Bjorn. I'm only in breach of internal company procedures. I'm not breaking the law,' he added forcefully.

Bjorn narrowed his eyes. 'Is this some kind of threat?'

'Spare me the melodrama. All I'm asking you to do is pay a cheque into your account and do whatever you have to do to the computer programs to make sure the money's transferred to me today. I don't want to know about having to wait three days for the cheque to be cleared.'

'I can't touch the programs that deal with cheque deposits. They're classified as "sensitive", which means written management authorisation is required before any software changes can be made.'

Simon stared long and hard at the cheque, then ripped it into shreds. 'I'm in the shit, Bjorn. Right up to my fucking neck. I have to find a solution. I've got to have fifty thousand in my account by lunchtime tomorrow.'

'There's no way I can get my hands on fifty grand as quickly as that. It's just not possible!'

'You've been salting away five thousand a month for years,' Simon hissed. 'Make it possible.'

Bjorn rubbed hard at his dimpled chin. 'I'll get in touch with the Cayman Islands this afternoon and see what can be done.'

'That's more like it.'

'I'll give you a call this evening and let you know.'

'I won't be at home. Call me on my mobile when you've spoken to your contact in the Caymans. And if you want your little secret to remain safe,' he added as he got to his feet, 'you'd better come up with a solution.' Turning on his heel he stomped out of the café.

Billy McAteer checked to make sure he wasn't being followed before pushing open the door of Shuggie Morrison's café.

'Give me the works, Shuggie,' he called out to the squat figure behind the counter. 'I'm starvin'.'

'Tea or coffee, Billy?'

'Tea.'

The conversation at the table by the window stopped and the three customers on the bench seat craned round to see who had come in. Bert Tollin looked casually at his watch. 'Is that the time, boys?' he said, rising to his feet. 'I'd better be on my way. See you tomorrow.'

'Where the hell do you think you're goin'?' The Red Hand of Ulster was pointing straight at Tollin.

'To the bookies, pal. I've got a cert for the three-thirty at Kempton.'

'Plank your arse back down there. Nobody's goin' anywhere until I say so.'

Tollin hesitated. 'I need a pee. I'm burstin'.'

'On you go, then,' McAteer said, jabbing his thumb in the direction of the toilet as he sat down at the table nearest the door.

Tollin hurried to the toilet and went into the solitary cubicle, locking the door behind him. Fishing his mobile from his inside pocket he paged down to Colin Renton's number. He held the phone hard against his ear as it rang out and as soon as a voice answered he flushed the toilet. 'Billy McAteer is in Shuggie Morrison's café, Mr Renton,' he gabbled over the sound of rushing water. Disconnecting immediately, Tollin scuttled back to the café and took his seat on the bench.

Sue Paterson dropped into the Southern General on her way home from school. Climbing the two flights of stairs she traipsed the length of the ward with Jamie holding onto her hand, a book clutched tightly to his chest. When they came to Tony O'Sullivan's bed they found him lying on his back, snoring gently through a heavily bandaged nose.

'Is that Mr O'Sullivan, Mummy?' Jamie asked, standing on tiptoe to peer over the bedclothes.

'Yes,' she whispered.

'What happened to his nose?'

'As far as I know it was a clash of heads.'

'Is he a forward or a defender?'

'I don't actually know, Jamie,' she said, smiling.

'Can I show him my book now?'

Sue put a finger across her lips. 'It would be a shame to disturb him while he's sleeping,' she said quietly. 'Maybe we could show it to him later?' Sue stopped a male nurse who was walking past. 'Can you tell me anything about Mr O'Sullivan's condition?' she asked.

The nurse lifted the clipboard from the end of the bed. 'His nose was reset this afternoon. No complications. The doctor will see him on his rounds in about half an hour and he'll probably let him out later on today. We like to clear as many beds as possible before the weekend,' he explained. 'A&E gets overrun when the pubs come out. Especially so near Christmas,' he added with a grimace.

'Okay if I leave a note for him?' Sue asked.

'Of course. Do you need something to write on?'

'No thanks, I've got a notebook,' she said, tapping her handbag.

Lifting the visitor's chair noiselessly from beneath the bed, Sue sat down, took her notebook out of her bag and began to write:

> *Assuming you've got nothing more exciting planned for this evening, how about coming round to my place for a bite to eat? It's just chilli con carne. Ever since Dad told Jamie that you were a football fanatic he's been dying to impress you with his book on the World Cup. But I'm warning you – there are liable to be some rather tricky questions to test you out!*
>
> *I'll expect you any time after seven. Give me a bell if you're not able to make it.*
>
> *Sue.*

Having added her address and phone number at the bottom of the note Sue tore out the page, folded the sheet of paper and propped it among the discarded grape stalks in the bowl on the bedside table. Getting to her feet she shepherded Jamie back down the ward.

Sergeant Andrew Shearer deployed his resources: two men round the back of the building and two at each end of the block containing Shuggie Morrison's café. All six were wearing bullet-proof body armour and had hand guns strapped to their waists. One man in each pair carried a walkie-talkie.

Shearer directed operations from his car parked at the end of the street from where he had an unobstructed view of the café entrance. His walkie-talkie crackled into life.

'Unit A in position round the back, sir. There appears to be only one door at the rear of the building and it's closed.'

'Stay in position and await further instructions,' Shearer ordered. He watched as an animated group of half a dozen men and women crossed the road away from the café – they looked like workers making their way back to the office after a very long Christmas lunch. A teenage girl, pushing a pram, turned the corner where two of his officers were leaning casually against the wall and she headed along the pavement in the direction of the café. 'Units B and C,' he barked into the mouthpiece. 'Hold position.' The pram stopped outside the café and the girl studied the menu in the window. 'For Christ's sake, don't go in!' Shearer muttered under his breath, willing the girl to move on. Glancing at her watch, she used the pram to nudge open the door and went inside. 'Shit!' Shearer's men heard the exclamation reverberate through their walkie-talkies. They'd also seen the girl go into the café and four pairs of expectant eyes turned towards the parked car.

'We still have to bring McAteer out, boys.' Shearer spoke into his mouthpiece. 'The girl and the pram are just an added complication. Maximum speed and maximum caution will be required. Units B and C, approach the café rapidly, staying as close to the wall as you can.'

Shearer watched his men hug the buildings as they closed in on the café from both sides, stopping when they got to within a couple of yards of the entrance, their bodies flattened against the brick wall. 'Unit B,' Shearer said, 'withdraw firearms and go in when you're ready. Unit C, hold position and don't make any move unless you hear shots fired.'

A solid shoulder almost took the door off its hinges as Unit B went through the café door together, arms outstretched, pistols levelled. Billy McAteer scrambled to his feet and pulled out his flick knife. He froze when he saw the guns, one aimed at his head, the other at his chest.

'Police! Drop the knife, McAteer.'

McAteer spun round to face the counter. 'Which one of you fuckin' bastard shopped me?' he roared, lancing his knife across the room, the blade whipping over the pram by the counter and burying itself in the wall above Shuggie's head, bringing down a cloud of white plaster.

McAteer glowered in Shuggie's direction, but offered no resistance to being handcuffed.

'Unit B, sir,' crackled in Shearer's ear. 'Subject has been subdued and apprehended. No rounds fired. No police or civilian casualties.'

Simon Ramsay was sitting on his own outside The Rock, nursing a Budweiser and smoking a cigarette, when a call came through on his mobile.

'Simon, it's Bjorn.'

'Did you manage to get it organised?'

'You'll have your fifty thousand pounds tomorrow.'

'That's great, Bjorn! I knew you'd be able to do it if you put your mind to it.'

'I'll need your bank account details to transfer the funds.'

Pulling his chequebook from his jacket pocket, Ramsay read out the relevant information. 'How soon can I have access to the money?' he demanded.

'By lunchtime tomorrow.'

'Thanks, Bjorn. That's one I owe you.'

It was two hours and several Budweisers later when Ramsay's mobile rang again.

'Good evening, Pervert,' the familiar, Dalek-like voice intoned.

'I'll have the money tomorrow,' he whispered into the mouthpiece.

'Excellent!'

'There's just one problem.'

'That's not what I want to hear, Pervert.' The tone was menacing.

'The money will be in my account by lunchtime tomorrow but I can hardly walk into my bank with a suitcase and ask for fifty thousand pounds in cash in small-denomination notes, can I?'

'That's for you to sort out,' he snapped. 'Either I get the fifty grand tomorrow or the world and his wife – which includes your wife, by the way – will get to hear about your little indiscretion.'

'Be reasonable, for Christ's sake! How about if I pay you in instalments over the next few days? Say, a few thousand at a time?' There was an ominous silence at the other end of the line 'There's no way the bank will let me withdraw fifty thousand in cash all in one go. How about it?' he pleaded.

'You're leaving me with a difficult decision, Pervert.'

'What's that?'

'Whether your photo will appear in the papers tomorrow – or whether I should save it for a big splash on Sunday.'

'Hold on a minute!'

The communication was cut.

CHAPTER 16

Friday 24 December

When Charlie Anderson arrived at Pitt Street early the following morning he found someone waiting for him at reception. Having introduced himself, Jim Cuthbertson followed Charlie up the stairs.

'How bad is this, Inspector?' Cuthbertson asked as they were entering Charlie's office.

'It couldn't be much worse. Your daughter has confessed to hiring a hit man to murder a supposed blackmailer. However, we have yet to establish whether or not any blackmail attempt was actually made.'

'What has she been charged with?'

'Conspiracy to murder.'

'Where is she being held?'

'Cornton Vale.'

'Will you oppose bail?'

'That won't be my decision.'

'Have you arrested Simon Ramsay?'

'No.'

'Why the hell not?' Cuthbertson exploded. 'Laura told you he was the instigator of all this!'

'Mr Ramsay claims to know nothing about it.'

'I don't give a shit about what he claims! He put Laura up to it, for Christ's sake! Why is he not under arrest?'

'I'm not prepared to discuss Mr Ramsay's situation with you, Mr Cuthbertson.'

'You mean to say you're going to charge my daughter with conspiracy to murder and let that miserable little bastard walk away scot-free!'

'That's not what I said. If Ramsay's implicated he'll be charged in due course.'

'That's not good enough!'

'Mr Cuthbertson, your daughter has confessed to hiring McAteer to commit a murder. Instead of getting hot under the collar about Simon Ramsay you would be well advised to direct your energies towards ensuring that she gets the best possible legal representation.'

'When I want your advice on what's in my daughter's best interests, I'll ask for it!'

Charlie bristled. 'And when I want your advice on who I should be arresting, I'll be sure to let you know!'

Cuthbertson stared hard at Charlie. 'Have you tracked down this McAteer character?'

'He's in custody.'

'Surely he'll be able to point the finger at Ramsay?'

'I realise I'm in danger of repeating myself, Mr Cuthbertson, but forget about Ramsay! If there's a case for him to answer, we'll deal with it.'

'Laura is sensitive and impressionable. She would never have got herself mixed up in anything like this unless that bastard had pushed her into it.'

'Perhaps you should try to find out who gave your daughter the money to pay off McAteer, Mr Cuthbertson? Whoever it was certainly didn't do her any favours. If he'd come to us instead we might have been able to apprehend McAteer *before* he had the chance to scar your daughter for life.'

'I don't like your attitude, Anderson,' Cuthbertson snarled. 'I'll have you know I'll be taking this up with Superintendent Hamilton!'

Charlie shrugged. 'Your prerogative.' Jim Cuthbertson cursed under his breath as he stomped out of the office.

A young girl nervously approached the main reception desk in Pitt Street. 'Is this where I come to give information about the murder in Kelvingrove Park last Saturday?' she asked hesitantly.

PC Lillian McArthur looked her up and down. Early twenties, she reckoned. The girl had a fair complexion, deep-green, intelligent eyes, and her shoulder-length blonde hair was fastened back with a wooden clasp. She was wearing a light blue anorak and had a Glasgow University medical faculty scarf wrapped round her neck.

'It's as good a place to start as any,' Lillian said reassuringly. 'What have you got for us?'

'I saw a car pull up at the bottom of Kelvin Way just before eight o'clock on the morning of the murder. I know the registration number – or at least, part of it.'

'Hold on a minute.' Lillian picked up the desk phone and tapped in Colin Renton's extension. 'What's your name?' she asked as the phone was ringing out.

'Lesley McDougall.'

'Lillian McArthur at reception, Colin,' she said when Renton picked up. 'There's a young lady here called Lesley McDougall who thinks she might have some useful information on the Harrison murder. Can you talk to her?'

'Sure. Send her up.'

'I think it was a Jaguar.' Lesley McDougall twisted nervously on a strand of loose hair as she took the seat opposite Renton. 'I can't be a hundred per cent sure of that but the registration definitely contained the letters LAM. I'm certain of that.'

'How come you're so sure?'

'LAM. Lesley Anne McDougall. My initials. I'd been at Daft Friday. Have you heard of it? It's an all-night ball in the University Union.'

'I tend not to mix in those circles, Ms McDougall.'

Lesley blushed, twisting harder on her hair. 'Lindsay – she's my flatmate – and I came out of the Union about eight o'clock on Saturday morning. The guys we had gone to the dance with were both the worse for wear and they'd crashed out in the Beer Bar so we decided to leave them to it and head off home. We were standing at the top of the Union steps, trying to flag down a cab, when I noticed a car driving past and pulling up at the bottom of Kelvin Way. It caught my eye because the registration was the same as my initials. I thought it was a sign.' She blushed even deeper. 'I was at the giggly stage, I'm afraid. So was Lindsay. I was, like – let's go across and chat up the driver, but Lindsay wasn't having any of it. She was, like – no way! Let's get a taxi and go home. I tried to pull her across the road but a cab came by and she flagged it down and dragged me into the back seat.'

'Did you notice any of the numbers on the Jag's licence plate?'

Lesley shook her head. 'Sorry.'

'Why did it take you so long to come forward with this information, Ms McDougall?' Renton asked.

'I don't listen much to the news. It was only when some of my friends were discussing the murder in the pub yesterday that I realised it took place round about the time Lindsay and I came out of the Union.'

'Hold on a minute, Dad.' Helen Cuthbertson transferred the phone to her other hand and closed the kitchen door to drown out Bjorn's strident singing which was emanating from the shower. 'Okay, go on. I can hear you now.'

'Brace yourself for a shock,' Jim Cuthbertson said tersely.

'Shock?'

'Laura has been arrested for conspiracy to murder her husband.'

'What!'

'She's apparently been having an affair with Simon Ramsay for the past couple of years.' There was a stunned silence at the other end of the line. 'It appears that Mike found out about their affair,' Cuthbertson said, 'and resorted to blackmail. It seems that he managed to get his hands on a photo of Laura and Simon in bed together and he contacted Ramsay, threatening to expose him if he didn't come up with fifty thousand pounds. Simon told Laura about the threat and he talked her into hiring someone called McAteer to kill the blackmailer, though at that stage they had no idea that Mike was involved.'

'My God!'

'To make matters worse,' Cuthbertson continued, 'Ramsay is now claiming he knows nothing about any blackmail attempt and he's told the police that Laura was acting on her own when she hired McAteer to kill Mike. The little shit is trying to wash his hands of everything and leave Laura to carry the can.'

'The bastard! What kind of state is Laura in?'

'I haven't seen her. I was up in Aberdeen when she phoned me yesterday. She sounded frightened – and very confused. She can't reconcile the fact that Mike knew about her affair with Ramsay – yet he carried on at home as if nothing was wrong.'

'Given what Mike's temper was like, I can see what she means. You say she's been arrested?'

'Yes.'

'Where are they holding her?'

'Cornton Vale. I'm going up to see her this morning. Do you want to come along?'

'Of course.'

'I'll pick you up in half an hour.'

Bjorn Svensson pulled on his knee-length, Paisley pattern dressing gown as he came out of the bathroom, whistling and towelling his head briskly. 'You look stunned,' he said, eyeing Helen's glazed expression as she sat at the kitchen table with the phone still clasped in her hand. 'Is everything all right?'

'You're not going to believe this!' she said, wide-eyed.

Bjorn sat down and listened in silence while Helen recounted the conversation she'd just had with her father. When she'd finished, he got to his feet. 'Come through to the lounge,' he said, retying the cord of his dressing gown and draping his towel around his shoulders. 'There's something I need to tell you.'

The large lounge was sparsely furnished: beige fitted carpet, a rectangular, chrome and glass coffee table and a white leather four-piece suite with several black scatter cushions. Helen sat down on the low-backed settee while Bjorn remained standing.

'Simon Ramsay tried to shaft me yesterday,' he stated.

'What?'

'He turned up at the bank and threatened to expose my fiddle if I didn't help him out.'

'The bastard! What kind of help was he looking for?'

'Fifty thousand quid's worth.'

Helen sprang to her feet. 'What the hell does he think he's playing at –'

'Let me explain,' Bjorn said, easing her back down onto the settee and sitting beside her. 'This is a lot more complicated than you think.'

'More complicated?' Helen looked totally confused.

'You remember Mike and Laura went on a cruise to Thailand last summer?'

'How could I forget? Laura almost bored me to death with her interminable holiday snaps.'

'They went on that cruise with Simon and Jude,' Bjorn continued. 'When they put into Bangkok, Mike and Simon went ashore to have a few beers, but they had an argument and split up. Mike wandered around the city centre on his own and he stumbled across a brothel. The woman in charge tried to interest him in having sex with underage kids, but he didn't want to know. They got talking and she told him that her clients liked to have their sex sessions recorded as a souvenir and she told him that she often made additional copies without the clients' knowledge. She offered to sell some of these to Mike and he ended up negotiating to buy a batch of DVDs and arranging to have them shipped back to Glasgow. He saw it as an opportunity to make a killing by editing the recordings and selling them on to paedophile organisations. However, when the discs arrived a few weeks later, Mike was astonished to find that one of them was a film of Simon having sex with a young Asian girl.'

'What on earth are you talking about?' There was total disbelief in Helen's voice. 'How on earth do you know all this? How are you involved?'

'Mike came to me for technical advice. He was desperate for money and he'd decided to screw Simon for every penny he could get out of him – there was no love lost between those two, let me tell you. Mike offered to cut me in for ten percent if I'd show him how to transfer images from a DVD to a PC-compatible format so he could send Simon a sample image by email.'

'And you agreed to help him?'

'When he showed me what Simon was doing to that kid I didn't even ask for a cut. That bastard really is sick. I went round to Mike's place one night when you were in Rio and I transferred a few images from the disc to his computer. I also set up a Hotmail account for him in the name of Liam Black and showed him how to include an image as an attachment to an email. I even knocked up a voice synthesiser for him to use when he phoned Simon so his voice wouldn't be recognised.

'To really get Simon going,' Bjorn continued, 'Mike sent him an email from the Hotmail account, including an image of him interfering with the young girl, just before he went to the birthday dinner. Simon must've been at his wits' end. He phoned me at work the following day and asked me if an email could be traced back to the originator and I scared the living daylights out of him by offering to go round to his house to check it out for him.'

'Laura didn't say anything about this to Dad.'

'She doesn't know about it.'

'Then how on earth did she get mixed up in all this?'

'Simon needed to get his hands on some serious money to stop the blackmailer blowing the whistle – Mike was demanding fifty thousand quid – so I reckon he went to Laura for help in raising the money.'

'But Laura told Dad that a blackmailer had sent Simon a photo of them in bed together.'

'I reckon Simon must have invented that story because he knew there was no way Laura would help him if she knew the real reason he was being blackmailed.'

'But Laura told Dad that Simon showed her the photo of them screwing in the Hilton – the one the blackmailer was supposed to have sent. Where on earth could that have come from?'

'I've no idea.'

'But . . . of course!' Helen said, snapping her fingers. 'That would explain why Mike didn't go ballistic with Laura. Mike was blackmailing Simon because he had a recording of him interfering with a young girl in Thailand, but he knew nothing about Simon and Laura having an affair. But Simon wouldn't want the blackmailer to be paid off,' she continued. 'With a recording like that in his possession he knew the blackmail demands would never stop. He needed to have him killed, so he talked Laura into hiring a hit man. This is incredible!'

'It was almost me who got killed.'

'What!'

'I'd agreed with Mike that I'd go to Kelvingrove Park to pick up the money. Mike wanted to stay on at Ronnie McGavigan's place for breakfast after the poker school so he would have a cast-iron alibi for the time the money was handed over. However, I opted out because the handover clashed with my mother's birthday party. Mike tried to talk me out of making the trip to Sweden, but when I told him I was adamant he decided to pick the money up himself. When you phoned me in Stockholm and told me Mike had been shot in Kelvingrove Park I nearly had a heart attack.'

'Jesus Christ!' The colour ebbed from Helen's cheeks. 'Is there any way this can be traced back to you, Bjorn?'

'I don't think so. Mike and I exchanged a few emails. Nothing incriminating, just arranging times and places to meet. To be on the safe side I told Mike to delete those emails, as well as the one he sent to Simon, and I showed him how to erase the DVD images completely from his computer.'

'What happened to the DVD?'

'I've got it. Mike didn't want to keep it in the house in case Laura stumbled across it.'

'So Simon talked Laura into hiring someone to kill Mike – and now he's leaving her to carry the can?'

'That's what it looks like. Once the blackmailer had been dealt with Simon thought his problems were over, so he washed his hands of Laura.'

'He really is a first-class prick!' Helen seethed. 'But that doesn't explain why he was threatening to blow the gaff on your fiddle.'

'I couldn't bear to see the smug bastard get away with it so, to scare the living daylights out of him, I sent him another email yesterday morning, purportedly coming from Liam Black, demanding fifty grand. Mike told me he'd nicknamed Simon "Pervert", so I used that name in the message. When he got my email he came scuttling round to the bank and tried to talk me into paying a dodgy cheque from his firm into my bank account and transferring the money to him. When I poured cold water on that idea he turned nasty and demanded that I give him fifty thousand quid or else he threatened to expose my scam.'

'Did you give him the money?'

'You have got to be joking! I played along with him and told him he'd get the money today in order to give me time to unravel my program changes and make sure they couldn't be traced, then I phoned him last night, using the voice synthesiser. He tried to persuade me to accept the money in instalments but I said that wasn't good enough and I told him I was going to expose him in the newspapers. I wouldn't imagine he got much sleep last night.'

'I've got to tell Dad and Laura about this, Bjorn. They have to know what Simon's been up to. And so does Jude. I'll call her straight away.'

Charlie Anderson had to drive round the block twice before he found a parking place at the bottom of Woodlands Terrace. Rummaging around in the glove compartment for change, he fed a few coins into the parking meter before trudging up the hill to Park Terrace. When he rang the Ramsays' bell Jude came to the door, a cup of coffee in one hand, a cordless phone in the other.

'I'll have to go now, Helen,' she said into the mouthpiece. 'Inspector Anderson has just arrived. I'll call you later. Thanks for letting me know about that.' She cut the connection.

'Sorry to disturb you so early, Mrs Ramsay,' Charlie said. 'I was hoping I might catch your husband before he left for work.'

'Simon didn't come home last night.'

'Where was he staying?'

'I've no idea.' She shrugged. 'And, to be quite honest, I couldn't care less.'

'Perhaps I could come in for a minute?' Charlie said, blowing into his gloved fists and huddling into his overcoat.

'Of course! How rude of me.' Jude stood to one side to allow him to step across the threshold before closing the door behind him. 'Would you care for a coffee? I've just made a pot.'

'That sounds like an excellent idea.'

Charlie tugged off his overcoat and gloves as he followed Jude into the kitchen. Presented with a mug of coffee, he sat down, blowing on the piping liquid and warming his hands on the mug.

'I don't know who I'm upset with more, Inspector, Simon or Laura.' Jude took a seat on the opposite side of the table. 'You sort of expect it of husbands, don't you?'

Charlie raised an eyebrow. 'Do you?'

'But not of sisters. I could perhaps have accepted a drunken one-night stand, but the fact that the two of them have been going at it hammer and tongs for the past couple of years is more than I can stomach.'

'Have you spoken to Laura about it?'

'I heard her side of the story from Dad.' Jude averted her eyes. 'I've no wish to talk to her about it.'

'Do you believe her version of events?'

'If by that you mean, do I believe Simon put her up to hiring McAteer to kill Mike, the answer is yes.'

'Is that based on feminine intuition?' Charlie enquired as he stirred two lumps of brown sugar into his coffee. 'Or hard facts?'

Jude paused. 'Simon was out of the house at the time Mike was killed.'

Charlie froze in mid-stir. 'Really?'

'He told me he'd nipped out to the shops to buy cigarettes because he'd run out, but that was a lie. I found a half-full carton of Marlboro in his desk drawer.'

'Why didn't you mention this before?'

'My sister wasn't under arrest before.'

'If Laura's telling the truth, then your husband received an email from a blackmailer. On the other hand, if he's telling the truth, no such email exists.'

'What are you driving at?'

'If we had access to your husband's computer we might be able to establish the facts once and for all.'

'If Simon had received such an email I'd credit him with having enough nous to have deleted it by now.'

'It's still worth checking.'

'Do you know how to do that?'

'Quite frankly, I wouldn't have a clue where to start. I'd need to take his computer back to Pitt Street and let one of our boffins loose on it. Of course, I don't have a warrant.' Charlie broke off and sipped at his coffee. 'I couldn't remove a computer from these premises without the owner's permission.'

'This house, and everything in it, Inspector, belongs to me.'

As soon as he got back to his car Charlie phoned O'Sullivan . 'Get a search warrant authorised for the Harrisons' house, Tony. I want Mike Harrison's computer shipped to Pitt Street as soon as possible.'

'Hi, Sue – just calling to say thanks for the grapes.' Tony held the mouthpiece of the phone down low to avoid it brushing against his nose.

'It would appear that my chilli con carne's reputation has spread further than I thought.'

'Come again?'

'Or were you just too scared to pit your measly football knowledge against Jamie's?'

'How about I hang up and call back and we start this conversation again?'

'You could at least have phoned to say you couldn't make it, Tony,' she said tetchily.

'I'm not with this.'

'You mean – you mean you didn't get my note?'

'What note?'

'I left a note for you in the fruit bowl on your bedside table, inviting you round for dinner last night. I asked you to give me a call if you wouldn't be able to make it.'

Tony exhaled noisily. 'I never saw any note. They woke me up in the hospital at five o'clock and told me I could go home. Everything had been cleared away, including the fruit bowl. As far as I remember the only thing on the bedside table was my watch.'

'Sod's law strikes again! What did you get up to last night?'

'I picked up a takeaway and went back to my flat to watch the telly. By the way, have you ever tried the pakora from The Balti Club in Woodlands Road? It's fantastic! There must be at least twenty different fillings to choose from.'

'You're not doing my chilli con carne's complex any favours.'

'Sorry, Sue. I don't suppose . . .' Tony hesitated. 'It's a silly question, but I don't suppose you're free tonight by any chance?'

'Afraid not. Christmas Eve is panto night. Family tradition. Big treat for Jamie. We're going to see *Jack and the Beanstalk* at the King's.'

'Do you like pantomime?'

'I love anything to do with the theatre. I used to be involved in amateur dramatics before Jamie came along and panto is a great excuse to let your hair down. There's nothing I like better than sitting near the front in the stalls and screaming out "Behind you!" with the best of them. How about you?'

'When I was a kid the panto at Ayr Gaiety was the highlight of my Christmas – until I got disillusioned. When I was eight, the Principal Boy turned down my proposal of marriage. I haven't been back since.'

'One ticket – for tonight, you said?' Tony nodded in confirmation. 'It's virtually a sell-out,' the girl at the King's Theatre box office said as she checked her computer screen, 'but I should be able to find you something. There are always a few singles dotted around. Stalls or circle?

'Stalls, please.'

'Here we are, front stalls, row Y. Would that be okay?'

'Anything nearer the front?'

She scanned her screen. 'Sorry. That's as good as it gets.'

'I'll take it,' he said, handing over his credit card.

'You didn't have to lug across the whole kit and caboodle, sir. The hard drive would've been enough.'

Charlie eyed the serious-looking, bearded constable who had just walked into his office. 'I wouldn't know a hard drive if I found one in my porridge, Donald.' He indicated the seat opposite. 'Did you find anything of interest?'

'All the data that's readily accessible is innocuous enough,' he said as he sat down. 'A few spreadsheets, emails, business letters, family photos. But some of the images that had been deleted are dynamite. A veritable pornographer's paradise – most of it, but not all, paedophile in nature.'

'How did you manage to access the images if they'd been deleted?'

'When you issue a "delete" command on a computer all that happens is that the entry on the file allocation table, effectively the pointer to that particular file, is suppressed and the space is flagged as available for re-use. The data itself isn't removed until it's overwritten by another file. If the storage on a PC isn't heavily used, deleted files can remain on the hard drive for some considerable time.'

'How can you access the files without the pointers?'

'It's all a bit technical. If you've got a spare couple of hours I could take you through the basics.'

'Aye, right!' Charlie waved his hand back and forth in front of his face. 'Will you be able to print out the stuff he tried to delete?'

'The images are being run off downstairs even as we speak. I'll bring them up as soon as they're ready.'

Tony O'Sullivan walked into the office as Donald Porter was getting to his feet. 'Looks like you've been in the wars, sir,' Porter said, eyeing Tony's face.

'If you're hoping to pick up observation credits for your sergeant's exam, Donald, forget it!'

'No need to take it out on Constable Porter, Sergeant,' Charlie said. 'It's not his fault you got cuffed with your own handcuffs.'

'Why don't you announce that over the tannoy, sir? One of the cleaners might not have heard the story.'

'What do you think, Donald?' Charlie winked at Porter. 'Would that be worthwhile?'

'Shouldn't think so, sir. I'm pretty sure all the cleaners know by now.' Porter left the office with a smirk on his face.

'How much longer am I going to have to put up with this snash?'

'I'm thinking of including the incident in my "things not to do" section in the next graduate trainees' seminar. An excellent case study – you could be immortalised.' O'Sullivan let out a snort. 'Should you be here?' Charlie asked. 'Are you not still signed off?'

'The doc said I could go back to work as soon as I felt up to it. But if I'm going to have to suffer this crap I think I might have a relapse.'

'Stop feeling sorry for yourself. Get the coffees in and I'll fill you in on what's been happening. By the way, we got a breakthrough. A student has come forward to tell us she saw a Jag with LAM in the licence plate – which matches Ramsay's car registration – parked in Kelvin Way at eight o'clock on the morning of the murder. And the icing on the cake is that Mrs Ramsay is prepared to testify that her hubby was out of the house at the time of the murder.'

Charlie was briefing O'Sullivan when Donald Porter arrived back in the office carrying an armful of photographs. He spread them out in two rows on the desk.

'That lot,' he said, indicating the top row, 'are downloads from paedophile internet sites. Disgusting – but we've seen most of them before. These,' he said, pointing to the bottom row, 'seem to be the same guy screwing several different women.'

'This is our friend, Simon Ramsay,' Tony said, picking up one of the prints and examining it.

'He seems to be a fan of home movies,' Charlie said. 'Do you recognise any of the women?'

O'Sullivan studied each photo in turn. 'This one's Laura Harrison,' he said, holding up a print. 'I don't know any of the others. He seems to be the type who likes to watch himself perform,' Tony added drily.

'And this particularly nauseating specimen,' Porter said, dangling a print from his fingertips at arm's length, 'was attached to an email sent to him on the fifteenth of December by someone calling himself Liam Black. The email was a barely coded blackmail threat.'

Charlie took the photo and examined it. 'This explains a lot,' he said. 'This is the photo the blackmailer sent to Ramsay, but he knew if he showed this to Laura Harrison there was no way she'd get involved. So he printed off a different photo from his collection – one of Laura and him in bed together – knowing there was nothing she wouldn't do to avoid her husband seeing it – even to the extent of hiring a hit man to kill the blackmailer.'

'What a charming guy!' Tony said.

'What age do you reckon that lassie is?' Charlie asked, shaking his head in disgust as he handed the print across.'

'At a guess, about eleven or twelve,' Tony said. 'She looks Asian.'

'Check with the airlines, travel agents, the passport office etc. Find out if Ramsay's been to Asia anytime in the past few years and, if so, when it was and who he went with. Anything else for us, Donald?' Charlie asked.

'I did a scan to see if there were any more deleted emails from Liam Black on Ramsay's computer. I found one – sent yesterday. I've printed it out for you. This time the blackmail threat was spelled out in no uncertain terms. I've done a trace on the source of both these emails via the service provider,' Porter added. 'The first one was straightforward enough. It was sent from the computer that was brought across from the Harrison's house. However, the second email sent yesterday was routed through Serbia and Georgia and the trail fizzles out somewhere in Latvia. Whoever sent that one certainly didn't want it to be traced.'

'What about Harrison's computer? Did you find anything incriminating on it?'

'No, but that's a different kettle of fish. It looks like a lot of stuff has been deleted recently, but by someone who knew what he was doing. He didn't just suppress the file allocation table, he overwrote the data on the hard disk several times with a random binary series of zeroes and ones. I'll have another go at it, but I'm not optimistic about being able to re-create any of the files.'

'Issue a warrant for Ramsay's arrest, Tony,' Charlie said, 'and tell them to let me know as soon as he's apprehended. I want to spoil his Christmas personally. Christ, is that the time?' he said, glancing at his watch and getting quickly to his feet. 'I'd better get my arse in gear. There's something I have to do this afternoon and it's more than my life's worth to be late home tonight. Kay and I are taking Sue and Jamie to the panto.'

'What's on?'

'I haven't a clue. Pantomime isn't at all my cup of tea. I could well do without spending the evening surrounded by a bunch of screaming kids, but such are the joys of a family Christmas,' Charlie said, pulling on his coat. 'What are you up to tonight?'

'Tony hesitated before answering. 'Not a lot'. He gave a shrug. 'I think I might take a wander down the pub.'

'Lucky so-and-so!'

*

Charlie Anderson parked outside Parkhead police station and walked up to the reception desk. The duty sergeant recognised him.

'I suppose you're here to see our high-profile prisoner, sir?'

Charlie nodded. 'I'd like a word with him.'

'Tommy!' he called out. 'Inspector Anderson's here. He wants to see McAteer.'

The uniformed officer opened up the cell and ushered Charlie inside, locking the door behind him. Billy McAteer was lying on his back on the low bed, hands clasped behind his head, staring at the ceiling.

Charlie stood in the doorway. 'You're going down for a long stretch this time, McAteer.' McAteer twisted his neck to see who it was, then swung his legs over the side of the bed and sat up straight. 'Laura Harrison's confessed to hiring you to bump off her old man,' Charlie said, 'and we can link the murder weapon to the gun used to kill your uncle, Harry Robertson, twenty years ago. We also have a police witness who saw you assaulting Mrs Harrison after she paid you off.'

McAteer stared unblinkingly. 'I suppose I might as well plead guilty then,' he said, stifling a yawn.

'Out of consideration for the taxpayer?'

McAteer snorted. 'I canny be arsed goin' through all that palaver in court – especially when the result's a done deal. Anyway, I want to be back in the Bar-L in time for the Hogmanay party. I haven't missed one of them in years.'

'You'll have plenty more to look forward to. Tell me something,' Charlie said, 'was Laura Harrison acting on her own?'

'Come again?'

'Was it her idea to have her husband bumped off, or was there someone else in it with her?'

McAteer showed his yellow teeth in a cold smile. 'Even if I happen to know the answer, what makes you think I'd tell you?'

'It might stand in your favour if you were to cooperate.'

'Pull the other one.'

'Don't you want to help Mrs Harrison?'

'Why should I give a monkey's about what happens to her?'

'Her uncle's the grand master of the Falkirk lodge. I thought you might want to help out one of your own?'

McAteer chortled. 'If you'd telt me he was the governor of Barlinnie I might've been interested.'

'The guy we suspect of putting Mrs Harrison up to it has the nasty habit of interfering with kids.'

McAteer studied Charlie suspiciously. 'An' you wouldny be sayin' that just to get me to cooperate?'

Charlie held McAteer's one-eyed stare and slowly shook his head. 'Not my style.'

McAteer sucked hard on his teeth and got to his feet, stretching his back. 'She did say something about a friend of hers bein' blackmailed.'

'Did she mention a name?'

'No.'

'Do you know if the friend was male or female?'

McAteer paused. 'It was a bloke who brought the briefcase to Kelvingrove Park.'

'Briefcase?'

'When we set Harrison up, a guy came to the park with a briefcase that was supposed to contain the pay-off money.'

'Can you describe him?'

'I didny see him. I was underneath the bridge.'

'How do you know it was a bloke?'

'I heard him wheezin' an' coughin' – sounded like he was a heavy smoker.'

'Thanks.' Charlie turned round and rapped twice on the cell door.

As Charlie was walking out, McAteer called out after him. 'If you do manage to nick this punter, be sure to send him to the Bar-L. I'll have a nice wee welcomin' committee waitin' for him.'

Charlie's mobile rang as he was hurrying back to his car. Pulling the phone from his coat pocket he cursed when he saw the call was from DS Hamilton. 'Yes?' he snapped.

'Where are you?' Hamilton demanded.

'Over in Parkhead. I've just been to see McAteer.'

'Get across to the City Chambers as quickly as you can.'

'What's the panic?'

'Santa Claus walked into the building half an hour ago and whipped a sawn-off shotgun out of his sack. He's taken a councillor and three admin staff hostage and he's holding them in a ground-floor office. A negotiating team have established phone contact with him. He wants a statement transmitted live on *Reporting Scotland* tonight. He asked for you by name and he insists that you're the only person with whom he'll discuss terms for releasing the hostages. We've nothing more than that to go on.'

'Tell them I'm on my way.' Charlie broke into a wheezing trot as he headed towards his car. 'What it is to be popular,' he sighed as he fumbled with his phone to call home.

'Hi, Tom!' Tony O'Sullivan exclaimed as he walked through the doors of Òran Mór. 'Fancy bumping into you here.'

'Good evening, sir,' Tom Freer said, half getting to his feet.

'Off duty, Tom – it's Tony.'

'Sure . . . Tony. This is Mel,' he said, indicating the attractive brunette sitting by his side. Tony took her hand in a firm grip.

'This wouldn't happen to be the Tony who sent Tom home rolling drunk on Sunday night, by any chance?' Mel said.

'Guilty as charged.' Tony grimaced and held up a hand by way of apology. 'I see you managed to find this place quickly enough, Tom.'

'Colin Renton told me it was one of the best pubs in the west end.'

'It is. And it's my local to boot. Mind if I join you?'

'Not at all.'

'What are you drinking?' Tony asked, pointing to the half-full glasses on the table in front of them.

'It must be my round,' Tom said.

'Plenty of time for that. What are you drinking?' he insisted.

'I'm on Stella,' Tom said.

'How about you, Mel?'

'A half of the same, please.'

Tony fought his way through to the crowded bar and returned with their drinks balanced on a tray. As he sat down on the available stool he felt in his jacket pocket and produced his mobile. 'I hereby declare Christmas to be officially started,' he announced, ostentatiously switching off his phone and dropping it back into his pocket.

'How long do you have off?' Mel asked.

'Just Christmas Day and Boxing Day – then back to the grind on Monday,' Tony said, raising his pint to eye level. 'Cheers!'

*

Keith Glancey arrived early at Ralston Golf Club for Jim Cuthbertson's sixty-fifth birthday dinner. Being in charge of organising the event, Glancey had booked the private function suite. A large round table had been installed in the centre of the room to accommodate ten couples and Glancey had arranged for a Michelin-starred chef and his team to take over the kitchen for the evening.

Jim Cuthbertson and his wife, Pamela, came into the room while Glancey was referring to his seating plan and putting out the place setting cards.

'Make sure you don't put Sheila next to Malcolm,' Cuthbertson called across. 'They're having an affair.'

'What!'

'Just kidding.'

Glancey shook his head and smiled as he walked round the table to take Cuthbertson's proffered hand in a firm Masonic shake. 'You had me going there, Jim.' Glancey hesitated. 'If you'd rather we postponed the dinner, Jim, everyone would understand. Given what's happening with Laura,' he muttered, fiddling with his bow tie.

Cuthbertson gazed at the immaculately set table. 'Not after all the trouble you've gone to, Keith. Anyway, it's not as if cancelling the dinner would do Laura any good. And I can just imagine the look on Malcolm's face if you told him he had to find somewhere else to eat on Christmas Eve at five minutes' notice.'

When Cuthbertson saw Nigel Hamilton and his wife arrive he went across to greet them. 'Glad you could make it, Nigel,' he said, taking his outstretched hand.

'Terrible business,' Hamilton said quietly.

Cuthbertson nodded. 'Not made any easier by the pig-headed attitude of your Inspector Anderson. He seems hell bent on letting Ramsay walk away from everything and leaving Laura to carry the can.'

Hamilton frowned and nodded. 'I'll have a word with him, Jim.'

Cuthbertson's mobile rang. Having checked who was calling, he made his excuses and went out into the hall.

'I've found Ramsay's car, boss. It's in the underground car park at the office.'

'Any sign of the cops snooping around?'

'Not as far as I can see.'

'If his car's there, he won't be far away. You know the pubs he hangs out in. Get the guys to check them out and as soon as he's spotted get Sam Davis down there straight away.'

'Will do.'

Simon Ramsay had driven to the lowest floor in the car park beneath his office block and had spent the night slumped in the driver's seat, the little sleep he'd been able to snatch being disrupted by nightmares. He'd stayed huddled in the car until early afternoon before getting out and wandering around the city centre, moving from pub to pub, never staying in the same place for more than an hour.

When he arrived at The Horseshoe just after six o'clock he found the place heaving with noisy office workers celebrating the start of the Christmas break. He elbowed his way through the crowd to order a Peroni, then threaded his way to the far end of the bar where it was quieter. Managing to find a bar stool, he perched on it as he sipped at his drink while staring round the room through unseeing eyes.

He was on his second beer when he felt a tug on his jacket sleeve. 'It *is* Simon Ramsay, isn't it?' Ramsay looked at him vacantly. 'Sam Davis. You must remember me? University.'

Ramsay gave a wan smile in recognition. Sam Davis, the science faculty's supplier of everything from Ecstasy to cocaine. Their paths hadn't crossed in years. 'How are you doing, Sam?'

'Fine. You're looking a bit rough. Are you okay?'

'Touch of flu, that's all.'

Leaning across, Davis whispered in Ramsay's ear. 'Fancy some of the old cough medicine?'

Ramsay's bloodshot eyes stared at him. 'Are you still dealing?'

'Now and then.'

'What have you got?'

Davis glanced in the direction of the toilets half-way down the bar. Ramsay followed his stare and gave a nod of comprehension. Taking a quick swallow of beer he put his glass down on the bar and followed Davis into the toilets.

'You have to be hell of a careful,' Davis said, checking the solitary cubicle to make sure it wasn't occupied. 'The cops are clamping down hard at this time of year. I reckon they must be on a Christmas bonus.'

'What have you got?'

'What do you fancy?'

'Do you have any smack?'

'I can do a lot better than that. How about a speedball?'

'I've never tried one.'

'You don't know what you're missing.' Davis wedged his heel against the toilet door to prevent it being pushed open from the outside. He slipped his hand into his jacket pocket and produced a handkerchief which he unfolded to reveal a sheathed syringe.

Holding it in the palm of his hand, he presented it to Ramsay. 'Believe me, there's nothing quite like this.'

Ramsay hesitated. 'How much?'

'Two hundred.'

'The going rate used to be a lot less than that.'

'You're talking years ago. Anyway, that was never for anything as good as this. Two hundred's the rock-bottom price.'

Ramsay fumbled for his wallet and counted out the contents. 'I've only got a hundred and sixty.'

Davis quickly withdrew his hand. 'I said two hundred.'

'Oh, come on, Sam,' Ramsay pleaded. 'It's all I've got.' He held out the banknotes. 'For old times' sake.'

Davis hesitated. 'I suppose – since it's Christmas.' He snatched the money and handed across the syringe. 'In there,' he said, indicating the cubicle. 'I'll stand guard.'

Having locked the door Ramsay took off his jacket and rolled up his shirt sleeve, slapping his forearm hard to get the circulation moving. He slipped the belt from the waistband of his trousers and looped it round his arm, just below the elbow. He took the end of the belt in his teeth and tugged on it hard until the veins on his forearm stood proud. Selecting a vein he breathed in deeply and, holding his breath, lanced it with the needle. He squeezed his eyes closed and slowly depressed the plunger. His head arched back and his breath hissed out from between clenched teeth. 'What a cracker!' he moaned as he felt the immediate rush. 'Right on the fucking button!' He let the belt fall loose as he sucked in air.

He heard a ringing in his ears and the sound of the piped music, filtering through from the bar, became distorted. He felt his tongue start to swell, filling his mouth, making it difficult to breathe. His vision was going in and out of focus. The cistern was receding rapidly, then accelerating towards him. His throat felt as if it had closed. He couldn't take in any oxygen, neither through his mouth nor his nose. He tugged at his shirt collar as he fumbled to sit down on the toilet seat, his body pitching forward and his head slamming into the closed toilet door.

When Davis heard the sound of laughter approaching the toilets he stood on a urinal and clambered from there over the top of the cubicle door, dropping to the floor beside Ramsay's slumped body. He pressed his back hard against the wall as he listened to the ribald banter of the two office workers discussing their respective chances of scoring with one of the secretaries. As soon as they'd left, Davis tugged on a pair of gloves and stuffed an envelope into Ramsay's jacket pocket. Unlocking the toilet door he weaved his way through the crowded bar and out into Drury Street.

'I'm really sorry about this, Sue. You know how it is.'

'It's not your fault, Mum – and it's not Dad's fault either.'

'Of course it's not,' Kay said. 'But it's a shame for Jamie's sake that we won't be together as a family at the panto.'

'Why don't you come anyway?'

'I don't think so. Thanks all the same. I wouldn't enjoy it. I'd just be sitting there all night worrying about what's happening at the City Chambers. I'd rather stay home and wait for news.'

'I understand.'

'You can pick the tickets up from the box office. They're in your dad's name – and they're paid for.'

'Thanks.'

'It would be a shame to waste our tickets. Can you think of anyone who might be able to use them at short notice?'

'Sue hesitated. 'There might be someone.'

'Enjoy yourself – and send Jamie our love.'

'I'll give you a call as soon as I get back home. And try not to worry, Mum.'

There being no reply from his home number, Sue tried Tony's mobile, tutting in frustration when she was switched to the messaging service. 'Hi, Tony,' she said. 'It's Sue. I realise this is very short notice but if you happen to pick this call up in time – and if you've nothing better to do this evening – how would you like to join me and Jamie at the panto? I'll put in a word with the Principal Boy on your behalf – and I'll even provide a spare seat for your coat. It's at the King's and it starts at eight. I'll wait for you at the box office until the last minute. I hope you can make it.'

When Jim Cuthbertson heard the ping of a text message arriving he surreptitiously flipped open his phone beneath the level of the dining table. He read: 'Mission accomplished successfully.' With a satisfied smile he deleted the text message and called across the waiter to order large brandies for everyone at the table.

The night air was crisp when Tony O'Sullivan emerged from Òran Mór. While waiting to cross at the Great Western Road traffic lights he switched on his phone to check for any messages. There was only one. He kicked hard at the base of the traffic lights in frustration.

CHAPTER 17

Monday 27 December

There was a stack of mail waiting for Charlie when he got to the office on Monday morning. On top of the pile was a brown envelope with a handwritten note from Pauline attached, explaining that it had been put into Pitt Street's letterbox sometime over the weekend – and that it had been through security clearance. Charlie studied the envelope. 'DCI Anderson' in bold type – no address, no stamp. Slitting it open with his paper knife he spilled out the contents: a Christmas card of a festive scene – no message, no signature – and an unlabelled DVD. Picking up the disc he walked along the corridor to the lecture theatre. He turned on the television set and slipped the disc into the reader. As he stared at the images, the bile rose in his throat.

'How was your Christmas, sir?' Tony O'Sullivan asked as he walked into Charlie's office.

'It got off on the wrong foot on Friday night but it got a whole lot better after that.'

'Was the panto that bad?'

'I ended up not going.'

'I guessed as much,' Tony said with a wry smile.

'Come again?'

'I thought you'd manage to find some excuse to avoid a theatre full of screaming kids.'

'Believe you me, screaming kids would've been vastly preferable to how I spent my Christmas Eve! Niggle called in a panic on Friday afternoon and sent me over to the City Chambers post-haste to resolve a hostage situation.'

'I read about that in the papers. I didn't realise you were involved.'

'It wouldn't surprise me in the least if Niggle took a perverse pleasure out of ruining my evening.' Charlie snorted. 'When I got to the City Chambers I was told that Santa Claus, wielding a sawn-off shotgun, had taken four people prisoner in a downstairs office and was threatening to shoot them unless his statement was read out on the television news. Santa had apparently insisted on talking to me because I was the only person with whom he was prepared to negotiate the hostages' release.'

'How come? Did you know him?'

'When I spoke to him over the phone line the negotiating team had set up, I'd no idea who he was. He told me he would pass the text of the message he wanted transmitted under the office door. When I read it, I twigged straight away. The statement was a warning to the Scottish people of the disaster that would befall the nation if all the nuclear power plants in the country weren't closed down forthwith. That, together with the fact that he'd asked for me by name, meant it had to be Ian Mulgrew, a nutter who's been running a one-man anti-nuclear campaign for the best part of twenty years – and I also knew there was no more chance of Mulgrew wielding a sawn-off shotgun than flying to the moon.'

'How did you handle it?'

'I went into the City Chambers and hammered on the office door. I told Mulgrew that if he didn't open up I'd have the door smashed down. He went quietly after that. His sawn-off shotgun turned out to be made of wood.'

'Weren't you taking a bit of a chance? He might have had a gun and been prepared to use it.'

'When you've been around as long as I have, you get to know your customers. Mulgrew knew there wasn't a snowball's chance in hell of his statement being transmitted to the nation. The hostage grab was just a publicity stunt to get his campaign reported in the papers.'

'Why did he ask for you?'

'He told me it was because he knew I'd figure out it was him – and I wouldn't send in the heavy squad to blast him out.'

'It takes all sorts,' O'Sullivan said. 'By the way, I got the information you were looking for about Ramsay's trip to Asia. He went on a cruise to Malaysia in June, stopping off in Singapore and Bangkok.'

'That figures,' Charlie said. 'There was a Christmas card and a DVD waiting for me when I got to the office this morning.' Charlie indicated the disc lying on his desk. 'Believe you me, you don't want to watch it.'

'Ramsay?'

Charlie nodded. 'Interfering with a wee Asian lassie. I reckon Mike Harrison must have somehow managed to get his hands on that DVD and used it to blackmail Ramsay. Are you up to speed with what happened in The Horseshoe on Friday night?' Charlie asked

'Only what I read in the papers. That Ramsay overdosed.'

'Not one of your run-of-the-mill overdoses – he injected himself with a mixture of cocaine and heroin that would have killed several horses. Did you know he left a suicide note?' Charlie added.

Tony raised an eyebrow. 'I didn't read about *that* in the papers.'

'You won't. It was found in his jacket pocket. In it, Ramsay accepts full responsibility for hiring McAteer to kill Mike Harrison and he says that Laura Harrison was little more than an innocent bystander.'

'How very convenient for Mrs H!'

'Great minds think alike.'

'Could the suicide note be genuine?'

'What we know is that there's a copy of it filed on Ramsay's computer at work, that it was printed out on the laser printer in his office, and the signature looks like his usual scrawl. The handwriting boys are examining it but the condition Ramsay was in on Friday will make it difficult for them to prove whether or not he actually signed it.'

'What's your gut feeling?' Tony asked.

'For a start, there are no fingerprints on the note or on the envelope. Why would anyone writing a suicide note go to great lengths to keep his prints off it? Besides, I don't reckon Ramsay's been in any fit state over the past few days to construct a coherent suicide note.'

'Which leads us to . . .?'

Charlie nodded. 'The one person who had ready access to Ramsay's office and his computer. A convenient suicide by Ramsay and a full confession plays right into Jim Cuthbertson's hands.'

'Do you reckon he was responsible for Ramsay overdosing?'

'I'm sure he was. But I'm equally sure we'll never be able to prove it. Talking of Cuthbertson, I got a call at home last night from Niggle to let me know in no uncertain terms that he didn't consider my attitude towards Cuthbertson to be, and I quote: "sufficiently respectful towards one of Glasgow's leading businessmen".'

'Ouch!' Tony suppressed a grin. 'Where do we go from here?'

'I've invited Cuthbertson across this morning to clear the air,' Charlie said, looking at his watch. 'He should be here any time. You're welcome to stay.'

'I'll get the coffees in.'

Jim Cuthbertson nodded curtly to O'Sullivan as he walked into the office and sat down facing Charlie. 'What is the situation now?' he demanded.

'Nothing has materially changed,' Charlie stated. 'I'll be asking the procurator fiscal to proceed with the charges against your daughter.'

'Surely Ramsay's suicide is a clear indication that he was the guilty party?'

'Suicide?' Charlie gave a puzzled look. 'What makes you think Ramsay's death was anything other than an accidental overdose?' Cuthbertson hesitated. 'Because of the size of the dose Ramsay injected, the press are speculating that it's more likely to have been suicide rather than an accident – and if that turns out to be the case, surely that has to be taken into account when considering what charges should be brought against Laura?'

'The procurator fiscal will examine the evidence and decide how to proceed.' Cuthbertson half-opened his mouth as if to protest. 'However, you might be interested to know,' Charlie added, 'that Ramsay left a suicide note.'

Cuthbertson moved forward onto the edge of his chair. 'Did he? What did it say?' he asked eagerly.

'Well, when I say he left a suicide note, what I should say is that a forged suicide note was planted on his body.' Cuthbertson furrowed his brow. 'No one writing a suicide note wipes it clean of prints,' Charlie said, 'which opens up the possibility, or should I say, the probability, that Ramsay didn't commit suicide. It's much more likely that he was murdered.' Charlie could see the sweat glistening on Cuthbertson's forehead.

'Who would want to murder him?'

'Perhaps someone who wanted to make sure he carried the can for Mike Harrison's murder?' Cuthbertson shifted uncomfortably on his chair. 'I will, of course, be making the note available to the prosecuting counsel and your daughter's defence lawyers,' Charlie said, 'but I doubt if any of them will see fit to produce it during Laura's trial. That would open up a completely new can of worms – and almost certainly initiate a full enquiry into the circumstances surrounding Ramsay's death.'

Cuthbertson glared long and hard, Charlie holding his stare without blinking. Getting slowly to his feet, Cuthbertson turned round and walked out of the office.

'Game, set and match, sir,' Tony said as Cuthbertson tramped down the staircase.

'Game and set, perhaps,' Charlie said. 'But there are still some loose ends – I don't like loose ends.'

'What's bothering you?'

'On the fifteenth of December Mike Harrison sent Ramsay an email with the paedophile picture attached. That's beyond any reasonable doubt. But the second ransom demand from Liam Black was sent on the twenty-third of December, by which time Harrison was dead. That means there's another "Liam Black" out there – someone who knew about the hold Harrison had over Ramsay.'

'The person who sent you the Christmas card?'

'Undoubtedly.'

'Any idea who that might be?'

'Someone close enough to Harrison to know he was trying to blackmail Ramsay. Someone who knew enough about computers to be able to use Harrison's "Liam Black" Hotmail account. Someone who was capable of routeing the second email half-way round the world so its origin couldn't be traced. Someone who showed Harrison how to delete not only – what did Porter call it? – the file something-or-other?'

'The file allocation table,' Tony said.

Charlie nodded. 'But also overwrite the data on the hard disk. Not many candidates spring to mind.' Tony started whistling the opening bars of 'Mama Mia'. Charlie nodded. 'Hard to see past him.'

'Should we pull him in?'

'All we've got by way of evidence is a deleted email from "Liam Black" on Ramsay's computer, with little or no prospect of identifying the source.' Charlie shook his head. 'Trying to pursue it would be a complete waste of our time, to say nothing of the taxpayers' money.' Getting stiffly to his feet, Charlie massaged the base of his spine with both hands. 'Some you win, Tony. Some you lose. Without Cuthbertson's diversionary tactic of a forged suicide note coming into play, at least Laura Harrison will get a fair trial. On the other hand, Cuthbertson will walk away from organising Ramsay's murder because there's no way we would ever be able to pin it on him. If you can't get the best possible result, sometimes you have to settle for the best result possible.'

'Pragmatism rules!'

'At least the chief constable will be pleased.' Tony raised an eyebrow. 'He'll take an accidental overdose on the stats rather than an unsolved murder every day of the week.'

Lying stretched out in his cell in Barlinnie, Billy McAteer read the newspaper report about Simon Ramsay overdosing in The Horseshoe, the speculation being that he had committed suicide because he was implicated in Mike Harrison's murder. It was with a tinge of disappointment that he got to his feet and weighed the Roman candle in his fist before tugging open the slit in his mattress and slipping it back inside.